LOVE
and
GARBAGE

Ivan Klíma

LOVE
and
GARBAGE

Translated from the Czech by
Ewald Osers

ALFRED A. KNOPF   NEW YORK
1991

THIS IS A BORZOI BOOK
PUBLISHED BY ALFRED A. KNOPF, INC.

Copyright © 1990 by Ewald Osers

Grateful acknowledgment is made to Edward Arnold Publishers for permission to reprint an excerpt from *The Bronze Horseman* by Alexander Pushkin, translated by Oliver Elton.

Library of Congress Cataloging-in-Publication Data
Klíma, Ivan.
[Láska a smetí. English]
Love and garbage / Ivan Klíma ; translated
from the Czech by Ewald Osers.
p. cm.
Translation of: Láska a smetí.
ISBN 0-394-58976-9
I. Title.
PG5039.21.L5L3713   1991
891.8'635—dc20   90-53573   CIP

Manufactured in the United States of America

First American Edition

LOVE
and
GARBAGE

I

◆

The woman in the office told me to go to the locker room: I was to
wait there. So I set out across the court to a door which bore the
notice LOCKERS. The office was grey and dismal, and so was the
courtyard, with a pile of broken bricks and rubble in one corner,
several two-wheeled handcarts, a lot of dustbins, and not a touch of
greenery anywhere. The locker room seemed to me even more
depressing. I sat down on a seat by the window which looked out on
that dismal yard, clutching a small leather case which contained
three small sweet buns, a book, and a notebook in which I was in the
habit of jotting down anything that occurred to me in connection
with what I was writing. Currently I was finishing an essay on
Kafka.

There were two other men sitting in the locker room already.
One, tall and greying, reminded me of the specialist who many years
before had removed my tonsils; the other, a short, stocky man of
uncertain age in very dishevelled and dirty trousers scarcely
reaching halfway down his calves and with enormous sewn-on
pockets rather like misshapen pistol holsters, wore on his head a
sea-captain's cap with a peak and a gleaming golden anchor above
it. From beneath the peak a pair of eyes the colour of shallow
coastal waters were watching me curiously. Those eyes, or rather
their glance, seemed somehow familiar. He obviously realised that I
was new here and advised me to put my identity card on the table. I
did as he said, and as he placed his next to mine I noticed that he did
not have a right hand; a black hook protruded from his sleeve.

3

By now my new workmates were beginning to arrive – the sweepers. A squat young idiot with a nervous facial tic sat down next to me, took out a pair of dirty shaft-boots from a locker, and turned them upside down. From one of them there ran out a quantity of liquid which might just have, but most probably did not, come from a tap. He immediately began to scream at us all in a language of which I was unable to make out a single word.

I am not sure myself what made me decide to try this unattractive occupation. Most probably I thought that I would gain from it an unexpected view of the world. Every so often you feel that unless you look at the world and at people from a new angle your mind will get blunted.

As I was waiting for what would happen next there suddenly came to my mind the scene, fifteen years ago, when I was about to return home from my stay in America and the dean there gave a dinner in my honour. The dean was a mathematician, and wealthy. He owned a stableful of horses and a house in the style of a hunting lodge. I had only met him once before and I didn't really want to go to the dinner: a crowd of strangers tends to depress me. But then, how could I have known anyone properly when I had been teaching at the university for a mere six months? In the event they all turned out to be pleasant to me and full of smiles as Americans are, and with varying degrees of urgency they asked me to explain what on earth possessed me to want to leave their free and wealthy country to return home, to a poor and unfree country, where they'd probably lock me up or send me to Siberia. I tried to be equally pleasant. I conjured up some kind of patriotism, some kind of mission, until I hit on a convincing explanation. I said that back home people knew me. Even if I had to sweep up garbage in the streets I would be for them what I was, what I wanted to be to the exclusion of anything else, a writer, whereas here, even if I could drive around in my little Ford, I would always be just one of those immigrants on whom a great country had taken pity. These were my boastful words. In reality I wanted to return home, to the place where there were people I was fond of, where I was able to speak fluently, to listen to my native language.

Now I knew that if I was a street-sweeper I would, for the majority of the people, be simply a person who swept the streets, a person hardly noticed.

At that moment a woman appeared in the cloakroom. She had a good figure, with slim hips in tight-fitting jeans. Her face was suntanned and wrinkled like that of the old Indian women I had seen in the market of Santa Fe. One of them, the oldest and most Indian-looking, had, to my great delight, a notice above her stall, revealing that her Christian name was Venus. This Mrs Venus here did not even sit down; from her handbag she produced a packet of Start cigarettes, and as she lit up I noticed that her hands were shaking. The match went out before the cigarette was alight, and Venus swore at it. Her voice was so drink-sodden, deep and hoarse, and her intonation so perfectly matched her appearance, that the leading ladies of the foremost theatres, who often have to play common women, could have taken lessons from her.

Then came a few nondescript elderly men. In the background a short plump man with shrewd features began to change into his working clothes. Like the little idiot next to me he had his own locker. From it he pulled out some khaki overalls.

On the dot of six the woman from the office entered and read out the names of those assigned to cleaning our district of the city that day. First she read out those who were to erect the traffic signs, then the team of three whose job it was to empty the public litter bins. Finally she gave the fat man in the overalls a sheet of paper and announced that the following were detailed for the work party: Zoulová, Pinz, Rada, Štych, and finally she read out my name. At the same time she handed me a sweeper's orange vest. I accepted it, quickly walked round the table and chose the locker nearest the corner. I opened the door, on which *Bui dinh Thi* was written in chalk, took my identity papers, buns, book and notebook from my case, stuffed everything into my pockets and closed the locker again.

We all walked out into the depressing yard, where some garbage trucks had arrived noisily and where two young men were flinging shovels, brooms, scrapers, wheelbarrows, traffic signs and battered dustbins onto a pick-up. It was only a quarter past six in the morning, and already I could feel the stifling expanse of the day stretching out before me.

The man in the overalls, who'd clearly been assigned to us as our foreman, strode over to the gate and four figures stepped out from the bunch of sweepers, including the only woman, then a youngster with a pale girlish face and a capacious postman's bag over his shoulder, and the man who reminded me of the ear-nose-and-throat specialist. Also the fellow with the captain's cap. These people seemed as alien to me as the work which I was about to perform; nevertheless I walked along, just as they did, at a pace which would have been more appropriate to a funeral cortège. With measured tread we strode through the streets of Nusle in our orange uniforms; all around us people were hurrying to work, but we were in no hurry, we were at work already.

This was not a state of mind in which I found myself often: most of my life I had been in a hurry, obsessed by the thought of what I had to accomplish if I wanted to be a good writer. I had wanted to become a writer ever since childhood, and authorship for a long time seemed to me an exalted profession. I believed that a writer should be as wise as a prophet, as pure and rare as a saint, as adroit and fearless as an acrobat on a flying trapeze. Even though I now know that there are no chosen professions, and that what appears to be wisdom, purity, exceptional character, fearlessness and adroitness in one person may seem eccentricity, madness, dullness and uselessness in another, that ancient idea has struck, against my will, in my conscious and subconscious mind, and that is probably why I am afraid to describe myself by the term 'writer'. When I am asked what I do I try to avoid an answer. Besides, who dare say of himself that he is a writer? At best he can say: I've written some books. Now and again I even think that I am unable to define clearly what the subject of my work is, or what distinguishes real literature from mere writing, the kind that anyone is capable of, even if he never went to school to learn his letters.

Now I was able to enjoy a leisurely walk and the reassuring

knowledge that I knew exactly what was expected of me. Slowly we passed the National Committee and the Supreme Court building and arrived at what used to be the Sokol gym hall, where our equipment was already waiting for us: brooms, shovels, scrapers and a handcart whose body was half a dustbin. To show my goodwill I took the biggest shovel.

As a child I had lived on the outskirts of Prague, not far from the Kbely airfield, in a villa which stood next door to a tavern patronised by hauliers. Every day, just before noon, the municipal sweeper would arrive. He'd draw up his cart in the open space where the hauliers had pulled up with their horses, take out his shovel and almost ceremonially sweep up the horse droppings, or any other rubbish, and drop it all into his cart. He would then push his cart up against the wall and make for the bar. I liked him: he wore a peaked cap, though not a sailor's cap, and an upturned moustache in memory of our last emperor. I also liked his occupation, which I thought must surely be one of the most important jobs a man could have, and I believed that street-sweepers therefore enjoyed everyone's respect. In reality this was not so. Those who cleansed the world of garbage or of rats were never shown any respect. A few days ago I read about a jilted stucco worker who, exactly two hundred years ago, in St George's church, had slashed the face, mouth and shoulders of his lover, for which he was gaoled, and taken to the place of execution, but was then reprieved and instead sentenced to clean the streets of Prague for three years. Respect as a rule was shown only to those who cleansed the world of human refuse, to bailiffs, judges and inquisitors.

When I wrote a short story twenty years ago about the slaughtering of horses I invented an apocalyptic scene about the incineration of their remains. I tried to get into the Prague incinerator, which as a boy I used to see burning in the distance, reducing everything to one gigantic pile of clinker, but the manager refused to let me inside. He was probably afraid I might wish to uncover some shortcomings in the operation of his crematorium.

Many years later, when I was working as a cleaner at the Krč hospital, I had to cart all the refuse to the big furnace every morning: blood-soaked bandages, gauze full of pus and hair, dirty rags smelling of human excrement, and of course masses of paper, empty tins, broken glass and plastic. I'd shovel everything into the furnace and watch with relief as the rubbish writhed as if in agony, as it melted in the fierce flames, and listen to the cracking and exploding sounds of the glass and to the victorious roar of the fire. On one occasion, I never discovered why, whether the fire was too fierce or, on the contrary, not hot enough, or whether it was the wind, the rubbish did not burn but the draught in the furnace sucked it up and spewed it out from the high chimney-stack, up towards the sky, and I watched with horror and amazement as all my refuse – rags, paper and tatters of bloody bandages – slowly descended to the ground, as it was caught in the branches of the trees, or sailed towards the open windows of the wards. And at that moment the idiots and imbeciles from the Social Welfare Institute, who were responsible for the upkeep of the hospital grounds, came rushing out howling with delight and pointing to a tall silver birch which was draped like a Christmas tree.

It occurred to me that what had just happened was no more than an instructive demonstration of an everyday occurrence. No matter ever vanishes. It can, at most, change its form. Rubbish is immortal, it pervades the air, swells up in water, dissolves, rots, disintegrates, changes into gas, into smoke, into soot, it travels across the world and gradually engulfs it.

We started in Lomnického Street. Our Venus, whose name was evidently Zoulová, was wielding a broom; she was helped, with a second broom, by the man with the captain's cap who most of the time chewed silently, now and again spitting out some frothy phlegm. They were sweeping the stuff onto my shovel and I would fling all the filthy mess into the dustbin on our handcart. When the dustbin was full we turned it upside down and tipped everything onto the pavement, all the rubbish in one heap; this would later be picked up and removed by the garbage truck. In this way we marked out our progress with those heaps and slowly advanced to

Vyšehrad. I looked at the tinted foliage of the trees, they were waving to me from the distance even though no one was waiting for me under them, even though she was no longer waiting for me. I think of her only as 'she'. In my mind I mostly do not give her a name. Names get fingered and worn just like tender words. Sometimes in my mind I called her a soothsayer, because she used to tell people's futures and she seemed knowing to me. Also she was surrounded by mystery, and made more beautiful by it. When she was christened she was named Daria.

I could not remember if we'd ever been here with each other. Our meetings over the years had blended together, and the years had piled up as in the folksong about the farm labourer. I'd met her as a result of visiting a friend who lived in a caravan; he was training to be a geologist's assistant. My attention was caught by a little sculpture whose fantastic character set it aside from the spartan interior of the caravan. My friend, who until a little while before had been writing art reviews, told me about the woman artist whose world was bounded by dreams, phantoms, passion and tenderness. He assured me that a visit to her studio was a profound experience, and I made a note of her address. One day when I was out looking for a birthday present for my wife I remembered that address.

Her workshop was in a modest-sized vaulted basement in Prague's Little City district. A third of the room was taken up by wooden shelves holding her work.

She received me courteously and we chatted for a while; she even told me about her little girl and asked me what I and my wife did. But I thought her interest was due to the fact that I had come to her as a customer.

She moved adroitly among her shelves. As she walked there was a movement of eyes and lips on her long skirt, a pattern of brown eyes and bright red lips. Her own eyes were blue and her lips rather pale. What would happen if I embraced her among her shelves? But I knew that I wouldn't.

I bought a bird with a slender neck on which sat a sharp-edged little head with small, impish, human eyes. She wrapped my purchase in tissue paper and saw me to the door. After that we didn't see one another for many months. But on the eve of my forty-seventh birthday she unexpectedly appeared at my front door: she wished to borrow her little sculpture for an exhibition that was to be held in Budapest. I asked her in and introduced her to my wife, who was delighted to make her acquaintance. The three of us sat in my study. Lída, who likes making people happy, said how much she liked her little figurine.

We were drinking wine, myself and my wife just to be polite. Daria spoke of her forthcoming exhibition and then about her travels. She told us about Kampuchea, which she had once visited. She talked of that country as like an Eden of happy and innocent people – this fascinated my wife, who is keen on liberating people of their sense of guilt – and we got on to our own culture, which is based on the knowledge of sin and therefore of metaphysical guilt. Daria maintained that the doctrine of sin was our curse, because it deprived us of freedom and interposed itself between one person and another, and between people and God. My wife made some objection. She believed that freedom should be limited by some kind of inner law, but then the conversation moved on to children and their upbringing. But I was concentrating less and less on what was being said and instead became aware of something different: the unspoken voice of the other woman. It seemed to me that it was addressing me in the expectation that I would hear it and understand it.

The evening shadows were creeping into the room and it seemed to me that the remaining light was focused on her high forehead, which, oddly enough, resembled my wife's. The strange thing was that the light did not die with the day. It seemed to be emanating from her, from a flame which undoubtedly was burning within her, and I thought that this flame was reaching over towards me and engulfing me with its hot breath.

After she had left I seemed to remain in its field of force. Lída said the sculptress was an interesting woman and suggested we might ask her to come again, perhaps with her husband, but I, either from fear or from a presentiment of a possible conspiracy, did not rise to the idea and turned the conversation to some other subject. My wife went to her room and I tried in vain to do some work. So I turned on the radio, which was broadcasting baroque organ music, but the music did not calm me, I was unable to take it in. Instead I could hear disjointed snippets of sentences: a litany in a strange voice pervaded me like the warmth of a hot bath. What had that voice really been like? I searched for an appropriate word to describe it. It was neither sonorous nor sweet and melodious, neither colourful nor obtrusive – I was unable to say what enthralled me about it.

When I embraced my wife that night, who was gentle and calm in lovemaking, slow as a lowland river in summer, I heard that voice again and suddenly realised the right word for it: it was passionate. I tried to dispel it – at such an inappropriate moment – but I failed.

We had turned a corner and were now moving away from Vyšehrad. I was still using my coalman's shovel to load scraps of paper, plastic cups and squashed matchboxes onto the cart, also the head of a doll, a torn tennis shoe, an empty tube, a smudged letter, as well as – the most numerous items all over the ground – cigarette butts. All that rubbish I shovelled into the dustbin on the cart, and when that was filled to the brim the captain and I got hold of it and together we tipped it out onto the pavement, where the wind, which was stiffening all the time, scattered the rubbish about again, but it didn't really matter: rubbish is indestructible anyway.

Rubbish is like death. What else is there that is so indestructible?

Our innkeeper neighbours had five children, the youngest boy had the same name as me and was about my age. We would play together, and his friendship enabled me to penetrate into the hidden parts of the tavern, such as the cellar where, even at the height of summer, huge shimmering blocks of ice were stored, as well as gigantic beer barrels – at least they seemed gigantic to me then – or into the·stables, whose walls, even though the horses had been replaced by a black Praga car, still reeked of horse urine and where a large number of cats of varied ages and colours had made their home.

The boy fell ill with diphtheria and within a week he died. At the age of five I did not understand the meaning of death. My parents did not take me along to his funeral. I only saw the innkeeper dressed in black and his weeping wife, and the funeral guests, and I heard the brass band playing incredibly slow march music.

When I asked when my namesake would come back, my mother, after a moment's hesitation, told me he would never come back, he had gone away. I wanted to know where he had gone but my mother did not reply. But the old serving woman at the tavern, once I had summoned up the courage to ask her, told me that of course he had gone to paradise. His innocent little soul was now dwelling in that delightful garden amidst the flowers, playing with the angels, and if I was a good boy I'd meet him there one day.

I grew up in an environment where no prayer was ever heard, and the only garden I knew was the one outside our windows, and that had no angels in it, although the trains would noisily roar past immediately beyond the fence.

I wanted to find out more about that garden of paradise and about the souls dwelling in it, but my mother dodged my questions and told me to ask Dad.

My sensible father, who I knew had thought up the engines for the fastest trains roaring past under our windows, as well as those of the planes thundering above our heads, and therefore was held in high esteem by people, was astonished at my question. He took me by the hand, led me outside, and there talked to me for a long time: about the origin of the world, about hot gases and cooling matter, about tiny and indeed invisible atoms which were ceaselessly revolving everywhere and in everything. They in fact made up the piles of earth, the stones on the path along which we were walking, and also our legs which were carrying us. We were walking along the railway line, through the sparse suburban wood, climbing up towards the airfield. The trains were now thundering along below us, while military biplanes were roaring overhead. My father also told me that people had always suffered from being tied to the ground, from not being able to detach themselves from it. But they had dreamed of leaving it, and so they had invented the garden of paradise, which had in it everything they yearned for but lacked in their lives, and they had dreamed up creatures similar to themselves but equipped with wings. But what in the past had only been dreamed of was now beginning to materialise, my father said, pointing to the sky. Angels did not exist, but people could now fly. There was no paradise for human souls to dwell in, but one day I would understand that it was more important for people to live well and happily here on earth.

Although I did not fully understand what my father was explaining to me, some inexplicable sadness in his words made me cry. To comfort me, my father promised that he would take me along to Open Day at the airfield the following Sunday, and let me fly in a plane over Prague.

And that Sunday he actually put me inside a roaring machine which bumpily rolled along the grass and then, to my amazement and horror, rose into the air, complete with me, and as it gained height the ground below me began to tilt and everything on it grew smaller and smaller until it had shrunk away to nothing. The first things to disappear were people, then the horse-drawn vehicles and the cars, and finally even the houses. I closed my eyes and found myself in a thunderous darkness which engulfed me. I was alarmed at the thought that I would never return to earth again, like my namesake who, as they said, had died.

Nothing happened at that time. Daria left and I went back to my work. I was writing some stories about my boyhood loves and I was flooded by memories of a long-past excitement. As I glanced at the darkest corner of my study, at the armchair she'd been sitting in, that ancient excitement seemed to take shape again.

I went out to a telephone box – the telephone in my flat had been disconnected – and dialled her number. I was still feeling an excitement that would be proper at my age only if one accepted that such a state was proper at any age. I enquired how the Budapest show had gone. For a while I listened to her account, which shifted between pictures and wine-cellars, then I said something about my own work and remarked that I had been thinking about her visit and that I should be pleased to see her again some time. But I did not propose anything definite, and she only smiled silently at my words. Even so the conversation had disturbed me, and instead of returning home I drifted through the little streets near where I lived and in my mind continued the conversation, which was becoming increasingly personal and brittle. I had lost the habit of such conversations, or of conversation generally. I had lost the habit of communicating with anyone.

I had been living in a strange kind of exile for the previous ten years, hemmed in by prohibitions and guarded sometimes by visible, sometimes by invisible, and sometimes only by imagined watchers. I was not allowed to enter into life except as a guest, as a visitor, or as a day-wage labourer in selected jobs. Over those years there grew within me a longing for something to happen, something that would change my life, while at the same time my timidity, which I had inherited from my mother, increased and made me shy away from any kind of change and from all strangers. Thus my home became for me both a refuge and a cage, I wanted to remain in it and yet also to flee from it; to have the certainty that I would not be driven out and also the hope that I'd escape one day. I clung to my children, or at least I needed them more than fathers normally need their children. I similarly needed my wife. The outside world came to me through those nearest and dearest to me, and through them I stepped into that world, from which I'd been excluded.

I don't think life was easier for any of them. The children, just as I did in my childhood, bore the brand of an inappropriate origin, and my wife spent years looking for a halfway decent job. Weary of queueing at departments charged with the protection of workplaces against the politically non-elect, she accepted the post of opinion researcher for some sociological survey. For a wage which was humiliating rather than an incentive she had to traipse around residential developments and persuade unwilling or even alarmed respondents to answer her questions. She did not complain, but she was sometimes depressed. Then she would shower the children and me with reproaches for some behaviour or action which normally she'd overlook. I didn't have to go to work. When they had all left in the morning I'd sit down at my desk, with stacks of white paper before me, as well as the boundless expanse of the day and the depth of silence. The telephone couldn't ring, and the occasional footsteps that echoed through the building usually alarmed me: I was more likely to have unwelcome than welcome visitors.

I wrote. For hours and days and weeks. Plays I would never see staged and novels which I assumed would never be published in the language in which they were written. I was working, but at the same time I was afraid that the silence which surrounded me would eventually invade me, paralyse my imagination and kill my plots. I would sit at my desk and be aware of the weight of the ceiling, the weight of the walls and of the things which might overwhelm me at any moment with their indifference.

Thus I would wait for my wife and my children to return. The moment their footfalls on the stairs shattered the silence I could feel tranquillity return to me – not the tranquillity of silence but the tranquillity of life.

I knew of course that the children would very soon grow up and leave home, that the ring of their footsteps was even more temporary than my own temporariness. I talked to them and shared their joys, but I felt them slipping away and I knew that I must not resist that movement if I was not to resist life.

I was also watching my wife seeking her own space to move in, trying to escape the deadening monotony of the work she had to do and to study in her spare time. She had decided that she'd try to understand what the human soul was, penetrate its secret in the hope of finding a way of alleviating its suffering. To me such an enterprise appeared almost too daring, and besides I was always seeing her as she was when I first met her, too childlike and with too little experience of life to master such an undertaking, but I encouraged her: everybody sets out in the direction from which he hears at least the hint of a calling.

I too followed my own direction. I was less keen now on what used to attract me, things had ceased to excite me. Until not so long before I had collected old maps and books, and now dust was settling on them. I no longer tried to find out what was happening anywhere, or to discover when the conditions, which could be described as not favouring me, might at last begin to improve. I wanted to know if there was anything beyond those conditions, if there was anything that might raise our lives above pointlessness and oblivion, but I wanted to discover it for myself, not accept anything revealed and given shape by others. I wanted to achieve this not out of some kind of pride but because I realise that the most important things in life are non-communicable, not compressible into words, even though the people who believe they have discovered them always to try to communicate them, even though I myself try to do so. But anyone who believes that he has found what is truly enduring and that he can communicate to others the essence of God, that he has discovered the right faith for them, that he has finally glimpsed the mystery of existence, is a fool or a fantasist and, more often than not, dangerous.

I got home late, and as soon as I'd walked in I could sense the tension in the air. My daughter was sitting at the table, rebelliously staring at the window, my wife was washing the dishes rather too noisily, and my son's cassette player boomed out protest songs. I didn't feel like asking the reason, but Lída at once flooded me with complaints about the children, who she said were untidy and lazy, and demanded that I do something about it.

It was clear to me that whatever I might say she had already said to them and I was in no mood to engage in peacemaking. I went to my room and tried to work, but the flat (or I myself) was too full of disturbing noises.

It occurred to me that for a long time now I had only moved from one day to the next, from getting up to going to bed, and that, while I composed plots, my own plot had ground to a halt, was not developing, and was beginning to come apart. I should have liked to talk to somebody about it, but when we were at last on our own I sensed her irritation, which instantly separated me from her. I asked if I had done anything to hurt her. She replied that I was hurting the children by refusing to bring them up properly, that I was weak and indulgent towards them, that I didn't correct their faults, that I tried to curry favour with them. I protested that she was being unfair, but she embarked on one of her monologues composed of criticism, well-intentioned advice and instruction. From time to time she would heap these upon me and the children, and whether justified or not she came up with them invariably at a moment when those to whom they were addressed refused to listen to them or themselves had a need to speak and be listened to.

It was getting on for nine o'clock and our orange procession was moving down Sinkulova Street towards the water tower. The street is cobbled and in the cracks along the kerb clumps of dandelions, plantains and all kinds of weeds had taken root. The youngster with the girlish face was either pulling them out by hand or digging them out with his scraper. Even when he was bending down to the ground his face remained sickly pale.

Under the trees on the pavement some cars were parked. By the wreck of an ancient Volga our party halted. The foreman lifted the bonnet and established with satisfaction that someone had removed the radiator during the week.

A car is also rubbish, a large conglomeration of refuse, and one of them gets in our way at almost every step.

When fifteen years ago I went to see the première of a play of mine in a town not far from Detroit, the president of the Ford company invited me to lunch. As we were sitting on his terrace on the top floor, or more accurately on the roof of the Ford skyscraper, from which there was a view of that hideous huge city through whose streets countless cars were moving, instead of asking about his latest model – a question which would have delighted my father – I wanted to know how he removed all those cars from the world once they'd reached the end of their service. He replied that this was no problem. Anything that was manufactured could vanish without trace, it was merely a technical problem. And he smiled at the thought of a totally empty, cleansed world. After lunch the president lent me his car and his driver. I was taken to the edge of the city, where an incalculable mass of battered and rusty sedans were parked on a vast area. Negroes in brightly-coloured overalls first of all ripped the guts out of the cars with enormous pliers, stripped them of their tyres, windows and seats, and then pushed them into gigantic presses which turned the cars into metal parcels of manageable dimensions. But those metal boxes do not vanish from the world, any more than did the glass, the tyres or the spent oil, even if they were all burned in incinerators, nor did the rivers of petrol that were used on all those necessary and unnecessary journeys disappear. They probably melt down the crushed metal to make iron and new steel for new cars, and thus rubbish is transformed into new rubbish, only slightly increased in quantity. If ever I were to meet that self-assured president again I'd say to him: No, this isn't a mere technical problem. Because the spirit of dead things rises over the earth and over the waters, and its breath forebodes evil.

During the war filth descended upon us: literally and figuratively it engulfed us just like death, and sometimes it was difficult to separate the two. They certainly merged in my mother's mind, death and garbage; she believed that life was tied to cleanliness – literally and figuratively.

The war was over, we were looking forward to living in love and peace, but she was struggling for cleanliness. She wanted to know our thoughts and she was horrified by our boots, our hands and our words. She inspected our library and stripped it of the books which might make our minds unclean, and she bought a large pot in which she boiled our underwear every day. But even so she felt revolted by us and forever sent us back to wash our hands; she would touch other people's possessions and doorknobs only when wearing gloves.

Sometimes at night I'd hear her sighing and lamenting. She was mourning the relatives she'd lost in the war, but she was surely also lamenting the dirtiness of the world she had to live in. In our home, therefore, cleanliness and loneliness reigned. Dad hardly ever came home, he'd found a job in Plzeň so he could breathe more freely.

When he turned up on Sundays, he'd walk barefoot to his study over a path of newspapers, but even that moment of crossing the hall was enough for it to be filled with a smell in which mother recognised the stench of some unknown trollop. In vain did Dad try to wash it off, in vain did he help to cover the carpet with fresh newspapers.

I was quite prepared for father not to come back one day, for him to remain with that strange malodorous woman of his, and I wouldn't have blamed him for it. But he turned up afresh every weekend, and sometimes he even urged me not to judge Mother: she was a good woman, only sick, and not everyone had the strength to come unmarked through what we'd had to endure.

Then they locked Dad up again. The pain inflicted on my mother by others at least partly diverted her from the pain she inflicted upon herself.

A sewage service truck overtook our gang and pulled up a little way in front of us. Its crew exchanged greetings with our foreman and began to examine the nearest drain grating.

'What can they be looking for?' I asked Mrs Venus.

'They're just making sure their sewer isn't all blocked up,' she explained. 'We're not allowed to tip anything into the sewer. One day young Jarda here,' she pointed to the youngster with the girlish face, 'threw some flowers down and just then their inspector came driving past and wanted to fine him fifty crowns on the spot. And all the time they're rolling in it, just like the rat-catchers!'

'Don't talk to me about rat-catchers,' the foreman joined in. 'In Plzeň underneath the slaughterhouse the rats went mad and came up through the sewer gratings at night and ran about the streets like squirrels, squealing. They were desperately looking for a rat-catcher, they were actually ready to give him twenty grand a month, but there were no takers because it was obvious that if a rabid rat bit you, you'd be finished! I've a mate in Plzeň, from back in the para corps, and he got annoyed and said: "I'm not going to shit myself over a few mice!" So he got a diving suit and a sheet of asbestos rubber to throw over himself if the rats attacked him.'

'They'd do that?' I expressed surprise.

'Sure they would. I told you they were rabid. You chase after them, but when they've nowhere to escape to they'll turn and go for you. If that happens you lie down, throw the sheet over you, and they'll run straight over you. So that's what my mate did. Once he was under that sheet nothing could happen to him, but as those rats trampled over him he shat himself from fear.'

A few days later she sent me a card to say she would come round to see me, giving the day and the hour, and hoping she'd find me in.

She turned up as promised. Outside the window the autumnal clouds were driving and the room was once again in twilight. I don't know whether a similar glow issued from me too. A person never sees his own light in another person's eyes, or only at moments of special grace. But maybe she'd seen something after all, because otherwise she wouldn't have wished to meet me again, she wouldn't have voluntarily set out on a pilgrimage which, in moments of anger, she was to proclaim had led her only to pain. I have myself sometimes been amazed that she had come so close to me.

For the first few weeks we'd walked in the countryside, through forests and parks. She knew the names of plants, even the most exotic ones, as well as where they came from. And she led me through those places, as if through the land of the Khmers, and along the majestic river Ganges, through the crowds in stifling streets, she even led me through the jungle and into the ashram so I could listen to what a wise guru had to say about the right way to live. She told me about her family, which included industrialists as well as National Revival schoolmasters, a wanderer who settled on the western slopes of the Andes, and a romantic aunt who, when she failed to keep the lover she longed for, decided to starve herself to death. There was also a highly gifted law student who could reel off the whole statute book by heart but who tired of the law and turned to philosophy and who, when he had irrefutably established the vanity of human endeavour, sat down and wrote his philosophical testament, whose conclusion was that happiness was just a dream and life a chain of suffering, and directly over that philosophical testament he shot himself through the head, so that the blood pouring from his wound put several final stops under his writings.

Everyone on her father's side of the family, she explained, had a touch of genius, an inflexible will, and clear-sightedness – her father most of all. She often spoke of him to me and, even though I had never seen him, I was reminded of my own father, not only because he was also a graduate engineer but because he too knew no greater happiness than his work, than the calculations in which no one was allowed to disturb him, and because he was strong, healthy and capable of cheerfulness once he decided to set aside that work.

I would have liked to tell her something similar about my ancestors, but I didn't know their stories. I knew that some of them had come from far away, but I don't know whether that was two hundred or a thousand years ago. I assume that even then they knew how to read, though it was a different script from the one I can read now, and that they prayed in a language of which I no longer understand a single word. I don't know what they did for a living. Both my grandmothers had come to Prague and tried to trade there but failed. My grandfathers too came from the country. My father's father had studied chemistry and worked as an engineer in a sugar refinery down in the Hungarian part of the monarchy. There, when my father was only eleven, he fell under a plough drawn by a rope and was fatally injured. My mother's father, on the other hand, lived to a ripe old age: he'd been a clerk at the law courts and at the age of eighty he lived to experience the second great war as well as having a yellow star put on him and being forcibly deported to a ghetto. Even of this stocky old man with his grey, slightly tobacco-stained moustache I was unable to report anything remarkable, except possibly that, like his ancestors, he stubbornly believed in the coming of the Messiah, but for him that meant the mirage of the socialist revolution. That mirage helped him survive the blows of fate, the death of his wife, the loss of his home, his humiliation, hunger and the hardships of imprisonment. More and more often in that unhappy place he would preach to anyone who would listen to him, and more and more often I would be the only listener to remain. He too urged me not to believe in a god whom people had invented, whom the masters had fobbed off onto the poor so they should more readily bear their fate. As he grew older his litanies became an unchanging prayer which I knew by heart and to which I no longer had to listen. And then one night I awoke. Everyone else was sleeping, and from the corner of the room where Grandfather slept I could hear a strange muttering. I recognised the old man's voice and the plaintive intonation of a prayer spoken in the language he still knew but of which I no longer understood anything, a prayer addressed to God. I did not stir and listened with amazement to the voice which seemed to come from a great distance, from some long-past time. That was the first time I realised that the depth of the human soul is unfathomable.

Her father would desert his drawing board from time to time to wander about the mountains and climb rockfaces. He would take her with him, and taught her not to be afraid of heights. My father would only wander through the landscape of numbers into which the visions of his machines turned for him. He even took his calculations with him on holiday, and when he was seized by a new idea, which would happen almost continuously, he would forget about the rest of us. When he then found us at the dinner table or outside his window he'd wonder where we'd sprung from. But they forcibly expelled him from his landscape, put him into convict's clothes and locked him up behind electric wires whose windings were all too easily calculable. He concentrated all his willpower and strength on surviving, on surviving with dignity, so that he might once more return to his beloved landscape. Apart from numbers and machines, Father, as I understood later, also loved pretty women and socialist visions of a better world. Like every man in love he invested the object of his adoration with excessive and deceptive hopes.

Do you think every love indulges in false hopes? she asked.

I realised that she was asking about us, and I dared not say yes, even though I could see no reason why we should be exceptions.

'Like it was with them cemeteries on the motorway,' said Mrs Venus. 'When they destroyed them they had to dig up the corpses and they offered a hundred an hour, plus a bottle of rum a day, and even so everybody told them where they could stick it. They had to send in convicts to do the job and of course they paid them bugger-all!' She stopped, stretched, leaned her shovel against a wall and lit a cigarette. 'Corpses ain't no joke, there's poison in them that goes right through your rubber gloves, and once it gets in your blood you've had it.' She was smoking and seemed to be gazing into the distance, somewhere only she could see. If I had met her years ago I would certainly have repeated her words to myself, I would have been in a hurry to write them down in order to preserve her speech as faithfully as possible. At that time I believed that anything I saw or heard would come in useful for some story. But I have known for a long time now that I am most unlikely ever to find any events other than those I experience myself. A man cannot gain control over someone else's life, and even if he could he would not invent a new story. There are nearly five thousand million people living in the world and every one of them believes that his life is good for at least one story. This thought is enough to make your head spin. If a writer emerged, or better still, was produced, who was obsessed enough to record five thousand million stories, and to then cross out all they had in common, how much do you suppose would be left? Scarcely a sentence from each story, from each human fate, a moment like a drop in the ocean, an unrepeatable experience of apprehension or of a meeting, an instant of insight or pain – but who could identify that drop, who could separate it from the flood of the ocean? And why should new stories have to be invented?

Daria, in tears, once accused me of regarding her as some beetle I had impaled on a pin in order to describe it better. But she was mistaken: in her presence I usually forgot that I sometimes tried to invent stories, and I would watch her so closely only because I wished to understand the language in which she spoke to me when she was with me in silence.

'But I had a great time with those corpses. Got myself a job down there,' Mrs Venus gestured towards the Vyšehrad ramparts, 'on the path lab. That's where they carted all the stiffs that had had their throats cut or been knifed. Got it through a girlfriend, a dicey job, she said, but with bonus payments, and in the end they gave me bugger-all. Anyway I only did it because of the old boy that gutted the bodies, he was a mad one and crazy about stiffs. "Zoulová," he'd say to me, "you've got some arms. I'd love to have a good look at your humerus one day."' And Mrs Venus spread her arms – they really were long and slim.

The sickly smell of decay seemed to engulf me. When I took on the job of a hospital cleaner my colleague could not deny himself the pleasure of taking me to the morgue the very first day in order to show me the corpses on the tables, on the floor and in the refrigerator, and while doing so he was watching me out of the corner of his eye to see if I was turning pale or making for the door. But I was used to dead bodies from childhood, to such quantities of dead bodies that the few solemnly-dressed recent deceased neither frightened me nor turned my insides.

Now I recalled not only that tiled room but principally the wide table, which I saw as clearly as in a dream, and on it lay my father.

My father was gravely ill, the disease was gradually destroying him from within, so that he, who had always been so strong and irrepressibly healthy, was now scarcely able to hold a pen in his hand. When I looked at his notes, which were still swarming with numbers and formulae I didn't understand, the figures were so shaky I could hardly read them. Whenever I regarded these figures and formulae, I was gripped by sadness. I knew that he had not published his calculations for years, although he was being asked to do so, and I also knew that these numbers were a road to some new knowledge and that knowledge to him meant his life, but from them I could see that Father's life was by now shaky, that these figures were getting ready to accompany him on the road to where there are no numbers.

I would have liked to dispel that unhappy vision, but no matter how intently I fixed my eyes on my cart, my father's motionless features remained before me. What is the purpose of a life of suffering? It may teach a man to humbly bow to the inevitable, but he will still be crushed by the approaching death of someone dear to him.

But I still tried to reassure myself that my father, who had come through so many trials in his life, would not succumb this time either.

On that day long ago my father had to carry me out of the aircraft when it landed. I was shaking and sobbing and refusing to look up at the sky, where bold aerial acrobats were turning somersaults in their machines, winding their way up into the clouds and diving steeply towards the roofs of the hangars. My father lifted me up on his shoulders. He didn't even say: Poor little boy, he didn't reprimand me, he just carried me and on the way showed me the trains which flashed by below us, giving them their names, just as if they were relations or children. He carried me as far as the wooden footbridge over the railway line and said I could spit down into the funnel of a locomotive if one came along. When at last one came, spewing sparks and smoke, he himself leant over the railing to set an example for me, and the powerful rush of smoke and steam emitted by the funnel lifted his hat off his head and all we could do was to watch it sail down to settle on a pile of coal on one of the wagons and disappear with it in the distance. Dad laughed and said his hat was an acrobat too, and I, gazing delightedly after the vanishing hat, forgot the terrors of my flight.

That same evening Dad brought his hat back from somewhere, all black with soot and grime, and to my delight converted it into a bowler, put it on his head, and for a while clowned about with it like Charlie Chaplin. He liked entertaining people, and when he laughed he laughed unrestrainedly and with his whole being. He could laugh at what people normally laugh at, but also at what they are angry about or what they despair over. I have often wished I knew how to be as joyful and relaxed, but I lacked my father's strength, lightness and concentration.

Mrs Venus tossed some rubbish into my cart. 'D'you know how many people he'd had on his table?'

I didn't know, and she said triumphantly: 'Fifty thousand!'

'Nonsense,' came the youngster's voice from behind me. 'You're making it up. That would be several regiments!'

'But that's what it was, Jarda dear. And all of them had come to a sticky end!' Mrs Venus laughed as if she had just said something very funny.

Then one day before Christmas we first made love in a tiny attic room with small windows and thick walls under the roof of a baroque building. Facing it was a noble town house with enormous windows on the sills of which sat some freezing pigeons. There was a smell of oil in the room, as well as the faint odour of gas, and though it was midday the room was quite dark. The small windows were moreover partly obstructed by a statue of Saint Stephen the Martyr. The restoration of the statue was nearly complete, but my lover had stopped working on it, she didn't like having her hand controlled by someone else's instructions.

I wanted her to enjoy our love-making. I was thinking of it so much I was trembling with excitement, and she was trembling too. After all, she had a husband at home, and a little girl, but now she curled up in my embrace and let herself be carried to a place from which there would be no return. So I carried her, and at each step I felt her getting heavier until I could scarcely drag her. I was afraid, we were frightened of one another we wanted each other so much. The big surprised bed creaked at every movement and we tried to drown the sound by whispering tender words. We looked each other in the face and I was amazed by the way she was being transformed, she was softening and taking on some ancient, the most ancient, shape. Perhaps it was the forgotten shape of my mother or a recollection of my first visions and dreams of the woman I would love one day.

I got back home late at night and went to bed by my wife's side. She suspected nothing and snuggled up to me. She was still as trusting as a child. When I closed my eyes I realised that sleep wouldn't come to me. In the garden a bird was piping, trains were rushing along in the distance, and out of the darkness before me, like a full moon, there rose the face of the other woman: calm, beautiful, as if it had always been concealed within me, and yet motionless like the faces of her statues. Thus she gazed down on me, suspended in space beyond all things and beyond all time, and I felt something like nostalgia, unease, longing and sadness.

There was a lot of snow that winter. She'd take her little girl to her piano lessons. I'd walk behind them, without the child being aware of me. I'd sink into the freshly fallen snow because I wasn't looking where I was going, I was watching her walking: there was in her walk something of an ill-concealed hurry, or maybe of an eagerness for life. She was holding her little girl's hand and only occasionally did she glance behind. Even at that distance I could feel her love.

At other times we'd set out across the snow-covered fields not far from the city. Below us was an abandoned farmstead and a forest, above us the sky was frosty under a cover of mist. We stopped, she leaned her back against me, I embraced her – a little plump in her winter coat – and at once we were amidst eternity, lifted out of time, lifted from horrors and joys, from the cold and the blowing wind, and she said softly: Is it possible we love each other so much?

On the pond, just as in a Brueghel painting, children were skating. The inn was almost deserted, a fire was crackling in the huge fireplace, and a picture showed a farmhouse on fire, with gallant firemen fighting it. The innkeeper's wife brought us some hot whisky, turned a knob, and the fire in the picture was lit from behind by the red flames.

Daria was as pleased as a child: So many fires, not counting the two of us.

I really feel the warmth enveloping me, I feel it inside me, I feel like a seed in the spring soil, bursting and struggling towards the light.

She reads my thoughts and says: You see, now at last you'll achieve something!

What makes you think so?

Because you're only now beginning to live.

She believes that I have not lived until now. That I'd been fettered, shaken by frost, that the springs within me produced only a few cold drops. She adds: You've only lived with your head, but what you are doing you can't do with your head alone. Maybe you can control an engine with just your head. She promises to teach me to listen to the hidden voices.

I want to know what I shall teach her.

Surely she'd be listening to those voices with me. Then she says: I'll be listening to you, I don't need to learn anything now, I need to be with you!

The innkeeper's wife switches the lit picture off again and we walk out into the cold dusk. Before parting we kiss; we kiss as if we had nothing ahead of us and nothing behind us, as if we wanted to squeeze our whole lives into those kisses. Then she asks: Have you ever loved anyone truly?

Of course she doesn't wish to hear about my wife or about my children, or about my father, she doesn't wish to hear about anyone living, she wants to hear that she alone is the one I have truly loved. But perhaps I am mistaken, perhaps she is asking out of anguish, she is surprised that I am leaving her already, why don't I take her away with me somewhere, she fears betrayal, she suspects in me spaces which frighten her.

✗   My wife also used to suspect them. During attacks of sudden self-pity she used to maintain that I was unable to get close to her, that in my childhood, when death was ceaselessly hovering all round me, I had suffered an injury to my soul and that I have never recovered from it.

✗   What feelings does a person experience in a place where death spreads his wings more often than birds?

There were a lot of girls in the fortress ghetto, I talked to them, I walked past them, I was scarcely twelve. Amidst all that horror, how could it occur to me that something might happen to alarm her, even though armed guards, hunger and deportations were all around us?

They had only brought her in at the beginning of 1943. I met her, all terrified, in one of the corridors of our barracks: she was lost. She asked me the way, and I – an old inhabitant – effortlessly conducted her to the door of the room she'd been assigned to.

On the way she just managed to tell me where she came from, that she had no father, and that she was afraid there.

I reassured her that there was no need to be afraid, that it was possible to live there – and besides, if she wished, I would protect her.

She said she would never forget my kindness.

The next day I collected her and took her to meet my friends; none of them would have hurt her and there was no need for me to protect her against them – but I realised that she saw things differently, that she needed my presence, that with me she felt safer.

She was the same age as myself, and she differed from all the other girls in that she had fair hair, the colour of rye or wheat. We were never alone together, away from the company of our playmates, but I always tried to get as close to her as possible. We also lent each other the few books we owned, but we dared not go any further, I dared not go any further; and yet everything was suddenly changed, life was moving between different milestones, no longer from morning to evening or from meal to meal, but from meeting to meeting. The fortress ran out of salt, the potatoes were black and rotten and the bread was mouldy, but I didn't care; they took grandfather to the camp hospital and we guessed that he'd never come back, but I scarcely took it in. The fortress corridors, always so overcrowded, seemed empty when she walked alongside me, and the tiny space allotted to us grew wide, or rather it was enclosed in itself and thus became infinite.

I owned a few coloured crayons and blank sheets of paper, and I tried in the evening to draw her face from memory. But I didn't succeed. Then it occurred to me that I might compose a poem for her, and I did in fact put together a few verses which, admittedly, dealt more with meteorological phenomena than my feelings, and I took them to her. She said she liked the poem and carved me a little puppet with a smiling face out of conkers. I hung it up on the post of my bunk, right by my head so I could look at it before going to sleep. That was the time of day when I was with her most, because then I was rescuing her from danger. I'd carry her in my arms from the cell into which she'd been thrown naked to be tortured, and which I'd penetrated in disguise to save her. Night after night I thus performed my loyal, heroic deeds until I fell asleep.

She had brought a small porcelain mug with her from home, the porcelain was almost translucent and decorated with Chinese dragons and flowers. Several times she had given me some herb tea from it, we drank from the same mug and she acted solemnly. One day somebody, as was scarcely avoidable in that constant rush and confusion, knocked the little mug to the floor. When she cried over it I asked her for the fragments, cautiously threw them into the hot stove and watched what was happening to them. It looked to me as if the fire was really digesting them, that the fragments glowed in their own particular way, but later, when I cleared out the ashes, I found the fragments unchanged, perhaps a little sooty but otherwise intact. I fished them out of the ashes, carefully wiped them clean, and kept one of them. The rest I returned to her. I felt some attachment to them or admiration that they should have survived their fall into the fire and its heat. Maybe they will help us; maybe we shall one day be dug out of the ashes equally intact.

In my fantasies I defended her against all evil, but in real life I could not save her. She was assigned to a transport, as were nearly all the occupants of our barracks.

She ran out from the room, which was filled with confusion and tears, where the pitiful remains of the inmates' belongings were being sorted out and packed in a hopeless hurry; she only had a moment, she wanted to be with her mother who was in despair. We knew of a spot in the recess of the ramparts, the slope there was overgrown with grass and shaded by ancient lime trees. It was quieter there than anywhere else in the fortress. That was where we'd most frequently been with the others, but now there was no one else there. We told each other which of our friends had also been listed for deportation and we reassured each other that the war would be over quite soon, that liberation was so near we need not be too much afraid of anything, and then we'd meet again, we'd all of us meet again, we didn't quite know where we'd meet but that didn't seem important. Then we were silent. What was there to talk about at such a moment? We walked round the spot and then she said she had to go back. She stopped for a moment, then suddenly she came close up to me and I felt the touch of her lips on mine. Her breath was on my face and I froze. Then she turned and fled. When I caught up with her she asked me not to come with her any further, we'd said goodbye already.

That afternoon she left. I stood by my window, I was not allowed out. I tried to spot her in the crowd which moved down the street, but I didn't see her. It suddenly occurred to me that she hadn't left, that it wasn't possible that she had vanished, that she was no longer there.

I tore myself away from the window and knocked at the door of the next room, and when there was no answer I opened it. The room which a little while ago had been full of people and voices and things now yawned with emptiness. It seemed to me that I was standing on a rock, on a cliff so high and so steep that the land below me was out of sight. And I was seized by vertigo, I realised that I too was falling, that there was no way out, that it was only a question of time. What seemed solid collapsed in a single instant, and what seemed indissolubly linked to the ground was dissolved.

I escaped from that empty room, lay down on my mattress and closed my eyes. At that moment her face rose above me like the moon and looked down on me from the night sky, serene, remote and inaccessible, and I was engulfed by happiness together with pain and despair.

At nine o'clock precisely we sat down in the Boženka Tavern. It was a run-of-the-mill place. Nothing enlivened the blackened walls except some slogans and prohibitions. The table-cloths bore the stains of yesterday's food. In the corner stood an abandoned and battered pool table, its green cloth long faded and become grey from cigarette ash and smoke.

The hauliers' tavern of my childhood was full of colour. After my friend's death I did not go in all that often, only when Dad sent me out for some beer, and he only drank about once in a month. Right behind the door a purple pheasant spread its colourful wings, and on the walls were bright pictures of horses and hauliers' carts, the work of some local painter of shop signs and fairground rifle targets. And the landlord wore a neat clean check apron. When he'd drawn the beer for me he'd come round from behind the bar to place the jug securely in my hands. In the tavern of my childhood there was still a spirit of freedom.

Dad never tried to bring me up, he never ordered me to do anything or forbade me to do anything. Instead he would now and again set out on a walk, along with Mother and me, mostly in the direction of the airfield, because Dad, though he loved woods, parks and any kind of water, was primarily interested in machines, and among these chiefly in machines which could fly. When we got to the airfield he would look at the taxiing aircraft, at the massive biplanes and the lightly-built gliders, and at that moment he certainly forgot that we were there with him, he would even chase after men in overalls and talk to them while we were hanging about the windy field.

Dad was interested in anything that flew. He taught me to make missiles from folded paper, not those ordinary ones that are launched in class as soon as the teacher turns his back, but aerial craft which beautifully and smoothly sailed into the air, some of them even rising before circling down to the ground.

We also made kites, and just before all our playing together came to an end we constructed a large model aeroplane from skewers, balsa wood and soft firm paper. We threaded a rubber band through the fuselage; once wound up this would drive the propeller. Dad promised that it would rise high enough to fly over the tower of the church in Prosek.

And when in fact we had carried it to the end of the airfield one Sunday morning and wound it up by the propeller, the little plane made a leap, hurtled forward and a moment later rose up to the sky, where it began to describe a large circle. But it did not complete it, something must have happened, the plane wobbled and suddenly broke up, spun to the ground and crashed.

When we rushed over all we found was a heap of skewers, balsa wood and pieces of carefully stretched paper.

I lamented and mourned our loss, and it was then that Dad said to me: Remember that a man never cries! It was one of the few lessons I ever received from him. He laughed at the heap of rubbish as he picked it up, adding that that was the fate of things, and anyone worrying about it merely harmed himself.

I ordered tea for myself while the others, without having to ask, were each served a large beer. The youngster drank mineral water. Venus produced her cigarettes, extended the packet to her neighbour on the other side and then to me. I thanked her and said I didn't smoke.

'Quite a paragon, ain't you?' she said. 'Your wife must be pleased with you.'

'If I hadn't got drunk,' the foreman said, 'I most likely wouldn't have got married at all. Because I had a fair idea that marriage is the end of life.'

I didn't meet Lída until after I'd finished university. There was nothing exceptional about our meeting, it was unaccompanied by any special events or auguries. We just met and found we liked each other. She was only six years younger than me but I felt as if a lifetime lay between us.

What depressed me were certainly not doubts about the rightness 𝒦 of my choice, but the knowledge that I'd made a decision once and for all. I suspected that for me the most blissful prospect was not so much having the person I loved permanently by my side as a need, from time to time, to reach out to emptiness, to let longing intensify within me to the point of agony, to alternate the pain of separation with the relief of renewed coming together, the chance of escape and return, of glimpsing before me a will-o'-the-wisp, the hope that the real encounter was still awaiting me.

Man is reluctant to accept that his life has come to a conclusion in 𝒦 that most important respect, that his hopes have been fulfilled. He hesitates to look death in the face, and there is little that comes so close to death as fulfilled love.

For our honeymoon we flew out to the Tatra mountains.

It was the beginning of windy autumnal weather, the larches were turning golden and the meadows were fragrant with ripe grass. We climbed up to the treeline, to where the forests ended, and above us towered the sharp ridges of bare rock. I lay down in the grass, Lída sang to herself and I felt as if her singing was filling the entire space from the sky down to the base of the rocks, marking out the space in which I would now forever move.

'You must have been a one, Mr Marek,' Venus said. 'When my old man came home pissed I made him sleep with the horses or in the garage.'

'So when did you have your own wheels?' the foreman asked curiously.

'When we were in Slovakia, of course. Míla got hold of an old Wartburg. When we went off with the kids on our first outing, just past Topolčianky its exhaust snapped and the thing made a row like a bloody tank. He had to knock back a couple of doubles, he was so worked up about it, then he got down under the car so he could at least hold it up with wire, and when he'd finished we drove downhill again, and he'd cut out the engine so it wouldn't make such a row, and we were going faster and faster, the kids loved it each time he skidded round the bends, but I was screaming at him: "Míla, d'you want us to end up as mincemeat? Have you lost your marbles?" And he said: "Not my marbles, my brakes!"'

I realised that Mrs Venus was relating this story mainly for my benefit, because I was the new boy, so I asked: 'And how did the trip end?'

'He used the engine to brake. He's always managed to tame any mare yet.'

'Except you,' said the foreman. He chuckled and thereby gave the signal for general merriment. The one who enjoyed himself most was the captain, whose vaguely familiar face was still niggling at me. It suggested something, it pointed back to something, only I didn't know what. The youngster with the girlish face scarcely smiled: it suddenly occurred to me that death was hovering over him. I had that sensation from time to time, more often in my childhood. I'd look at somebody and suddenly I'd be scared that the person would soon be gone. I'm not trying to suggest that I have second sight. I've been wrong on numerous occasions. And some people exude the breath of death for years while being alive and well.

During the war my father was living in the same fortress ghetto, within the same ramparts, but I couldn't see him, a lot of walls and prohibitions divided us. Until one day the door opened and there, unexpectedly, he stood. Grown thin, his hair recently shaved off, wearing a boilersuit, he appeared in that door and his eyes swept the far corners of the dormitory. I cried out and suddenly he saw me and said: Quiet, quiet, I'm only here to repair the wiring. And he laughed at me. Then he took me in his arms, although I was a big boy, hugged me to himself and said: My little boy! And all the time he was smiling, but somehow oddly, his eyes were moist, and as I looked up at him I saw with amazement that my big, strong and powerful father was crying.

When I learned after the war that all those I had been fond of, all those I had known, were dead, gassed like insects and incinerated like refuse, I was gripped by despair. Almost every night I would walk by their sides, entering with them into enclosed spaces. We were all naked, and suddenly we were beginning to choke. I tried to scream but was unable to, and I heard the rattle in the others' throats and I could see their faces turning into grimaces and losing their shape. I awoke in terror, afraid to go to sleep again, and my eyes roamed feverishly through the empty darkness. At that time I slept in the kitchen, near the gas cooker. I'd get up time and again to make sure no gas was escaping. It was clear to me that I had only been spared through some oversight, some omission that might be put right at any moment. In the end I was so crushed by horror and fear that I fell sick. The doctors shook their heads over my disease, unable to understand how a microbe could have got into my heart, but they never thought of the real gateway.

They prescribed bed and absolute quiet. But in that quiet I was able to surround myself with my friends, who had turned into spectres, and spend with them all that slowly passing time, and be drawn into their world, in which time no longer passed at all. I told no one about them but I was with them and they invited me to them, they repeated their invitations so persistently that I understood that I too was to die.

But I was still afraid of death, so much afraid of it I didn't dare to look in the mirror. Thus I spent weeks in immobility, until one day my mother brought me *War and Peace* in three volumes, put them on my bedside table and told me not to pick them up myself, they were too heavy. I really was weak, I could hardly lift one of the volumes although they were just ordinary books. But when my mother handed me a volume I propped it up against my knees and read lying down. And as I read I was gradually transported into a different society. At times it occurred to me that the people I was reading about were also dead by now, that they had to die even if death did not overtake them on the pages of the book. Yet at the same time, though they were dead, they were living. It was then I realised the amazing power of literature and of the human imagination generally: to make the dead live and to stop the living from dying. I was seized by wonder at this miracle, at the strange power of the author, and there began to spring up within me a longing to achieve something similar.

I asked my mother to buy me some exercise books, and when I was on my own I began to put together my own experiences and to give back their lives to those who were no longer alive. At that moment, as though miraculously, their rigidified, cold and dismal features increasingly began to fade. When the doctor allowed me to get up six months later all the dead faces had dissolved, as though clearing out of my way. I was no longer able to command them, and if anyone had shown me a picture of any of my dead friends I'd have said: I don't know him. But it was not the oblivion of death, nor the oblivion so common in our day when the dead and even some of the living are concealed forever by a blanket of silence, one which even swallows up speech. Instead it was a different kind of remembrance, one which lifted the incinerated from the ashes and tried to raise them up to new life.

So I lived again, and the doctor was pleased at the miracle

wrought by some new tablets he'd prescribed for me. But I knew why I was alive. So long as I was able to write I'd be able to live, I'd be free from my spectres. I know that to this day, and I also know that nothing on earth can disappear, that even the picture of a young girl murdered long ago would remain latently somewhere, maybe in my mind, that it would rise from its depths just as her soul rose above the earth and the waters. And it seemed to me, as I was gazing at the face of the woman whom I had now, nearer the end of my life, met, who seemed familiar to me from the depth of my being, that by some miracle the one who had stood at the very beginning had returned, and as after so many years I again saw that motionless, dreamlike, loving face before me at night I was engulfed by a wave of joy mingled with sadness, even though I worked out with some relief that Daria had already been alive for three years when they gassed the other.

· 'Well, you were shooting downhill,' the foreman turned to Mrs Venus. 'But what would you say if you were whizzing straight up into the air at the same lick?' And he pointed to the ceiling with such a commanding gesture that everybody looked up towards it.

Thirty-five years ago the following had happened to him. He'd been stationed at an airfield near Stříbro in Western Bohemia, and there, as well as the splendid S-199s, they'd inherited a training balloon from the Germans. Anyway, his sergeant had ordered him to get the balloon ready, which meant loading a parachute and ballast bags. The sergeant was giving him a hand himself. But just as they were getting the first sand-filled bag on board the anchor cable got loose and they shot up at such a pace that within a few seconds they were above the clouds. 'I can tell you it was faster than a rocket. We were in shirt-sleeves' – the foreman was getting carried away by his experience – 'because down there it was mid-summer, and suddenly we were at the bloody North Pole. "Comrade sergeant," I said, "Private Marek reporting we're flying, destination unknown, but most probably we'll find ourselves in the shit." He was a fair sort of bloke so he said: "Marek, that was a damn silly order I gave you, to get inside without a parachute. See if you can get out of it alive. I'll manage somehow." And he held out his parachute to me, the only one on board. So I said: "Sergeant, you've got a wife and kids, if we're in the shit you'll jump." And he said: "You're a good bloke, Marek, we'll either be in the shit together or we'll both be bloody heroes." By then he had frost on his face!'

'But why didn't you try to let out the gas?' the youngster wondered.

'Imagine we didn't think of that? The bloody valve was frozen up, so we couldn't do nothing.' The foreman went on for a while to describe the terrible conditions at those freezing altitudes before, three hours later, they came down at Lysá.

'Thirty-five years ago,' the man who reminded me of my ear-nose-and-throat specialist joined in, 'I was in a penal camp near Marianská, a short way from the frontier. At that time the Americans were beginning to send over little balloons with leaflets. Some of them came down near us, but anyone picking them up risked being put inside.'

'What did they say?' the youngster wanted to know.

'Nothing worth a stretch inside. Anyway, what do you expect from a piece of paper?'

'Balloons and ships may both have a future, but I wouldn't get into one of your balloons.' The captain brought the conversation back to appropriate bounds. 'Or into a plane. If a ship goes down you've got a chance, but when a plane comes down . . .'

'You don't have to tell me!' the foreman said, offended. 'They were goners all right, there wasn't as much as this left of them.' He flicked a cigarette stub with his finger. 'And if by some miracle one of them got out – well, obviously he was no use for anything, ever again.'

With Daria I was moving above the ground and above the waters; day after day, month after month. Even at night, when distance intervened between us, our dreams or visions were often similar to each other's.

That, she explained to me, was because at night our souls would meet.

You think that the soul can leave a body while it is alive?

She then told me the story of the hundred-year-old sorcerer who disguised his real appearance by means of charms. He lived in a stone house in the middle of the forests which extended all the way to the northern ocean, and he spent his time in solitude. When he got tired of living alone he bewitched a beautiful young girl with his magic charms and tried to make her his wife. But she saw through him and realised his real nature. She was frightened and begged him to let her go: he was an old man, near the end of his days, while she had her whole life before her. The sorcerer replied: I may look old but I shan't die because my soul does not reside in my body. When she wanted to know where his soul resided he explained to her that it was a long way away. Over the mountains, beyond the rivers, there was a lake, and in the middle of it an island, and on the island a temple, a temple without windows and with just one door, and that door could not be opened. Inside a bird was flying around, and unless someone killed it, it would never die, and in it was the sorcerer's soul. While the bird was alive he too would live.

The girl had a lover, to whom she sent word of her fate. The young man set out to find the island and the temple. With the help of good spirits he opened the door which couldn't be opened, and caught the bird which could not, of its own, die, and with it he returned to his beloved. She hid them both under the sorcerer's bed and told the young man to squeeze the bird hard. The young man obeyed and the sorcerer immediately felt sick, and as the young man squeezed harder the old man got worse. That was when he began to suspect something, and looked around the room. 'Kill it, kill it!' called the girl. Her lover crushed the bird in his hand and at that moment the sorcerer breathed his last.

I understood that she was telling me this story so I should never forget that her soul was a bird which I held in my fist.

The soul leaves the body after death and enters a different body, an animal or even a tree. That was why she preferred to work with stone or with clay rather than with wood. She could hear a tree groaning when it was cut down. On its journey to a new body the soul could overcome any distance whatever. So why shouldn't it be able to do so during life? After all, it was not corporeal, so there was no force on earth that could fetter or imprison it when a soul wished to escape, rise up or join someone else.

Another time she told me that once in plain daylight she saw a golden ball moving among rosebeds, the blooms were mirrored in the ball and everything was in motion, free and exalted. A little while later, as she was returning home in the evening, or rather at night, she caught sight of me on the other side of the street, leaning against a lamp post; she'd run over to me but I had dissolved before her eyes. Was that a delusion sent her by some evil power or a sign of love?

Everything that happened had to have some superior cause, and she therefore sought for an explanation in the position of the planets. She established that my strongest and lucky star was the sun, which I had in Virgo and in the tenth house, and it was thanks to my sun that I had survived what I had, and thanks to it I would lead my life happily to the point when I had to leave it. I would not step out of my body until I had accomplished my task and performed the work I had to perform. What fate could be happier?

On Twelfth Night we poured melted lead together, and my figure was a woman covering her face and a beast of prey or perhaps a winged Hermes. In the woman she recognised herself, and in the winged creature, me. I was descending to her to carry her off or to bring her a message from heaven.

And why is the woman covering her face?

Probably because she is afraid of me.

She had a pack of fortune-telling cards of the famous Mademoiselle Lenormand and several times told her own and my past, present and future, the immediate as well as the distant future, and surprisingly the cards foretold an encouraging or even a splendid future for me.

I regarded this fortune-telling as a kind of lovers' game, but I said to her that everything was bound to turn out right because I had a charmed life like that man who alone survived the crash of the aircraft which some years ago hit a church tower in Munich, or like that girl who survived an air crash in the Andes and then alone, for several days and nights, tore her way through the jungle until with her last strength she reached some human habitation. It so happens that I met that man not long ago and we got on well together; and although I've never seen that girl we would surely also agree that what crushes others is for us no more than an unimportant trifle, and the other way about.

In reality nothing was a game to her, to her everything was life, every second we spent together was to be filled with love, when we were not together spectres were creeping out on all sides as in the Apocalypse and many-headed serpents were coiling round her legs. She fought back and asked me for help, asked me not to leave her, to remain with her if I loved her, at least for a while. But I was already escaping, in my mind I was hurrying home, chasing the tram that was just leaving to make sure I got home before my wife, who suspected nothing, who smiled or frowned according to her mood and not according to what I did. So we parted, kissed once more at the corner of the street, turned back once more, waved to each other, and I could just see her smile freezing on her loving lips and tears flushing the tenderness out of her eyes.

I'd always been devoted to my work, I'd always fought for every extra minute for my writing. Now I was trimming my work minute by minute, and these minutes were adding up to hours and days. I was still determined to rebel, to ask for at least one moment's respite. Writing, after all, meant life to me.

She said: How can you talk like that? What is art compared to life?

When I can't write any more I'll die. But I'll die loving.

Even though my wartime memories were getting dimmer, I kept returning to them. It was as if I had a duty to those whom I'd survived, and had to repay the benevolent forces which had snatched me from the common fate and allowed me to live.

With that burden I entered life. I was barely eighteen when I began to write a play about a revolt in a women's concentration camp, about a desperate decision either to live in freedom or to die. Suffering resulting from a life deprived of freedom seemed to me the most important of all themes to think about and to write about. As then in the fortress town, so now, after the war, I felt that my whole being was clinging to freedom. I was able to quote by heart the thoughts of the captured Pierre Bezukhov on the subject of freedom and suffering, which are so close to each other that even a man in the midst of suffering may find freedom.

I didn't understand Tolstoy, just as I failed to notice that a short distance from my home new camps were being set up, where people again had that final opportunity of seeking freedom in the midst of suffering. I only knew the camps of my childhood.

We walked down the street called V dolinách, which was perfectly clean; we had been preceded by the automatic cleaning machine driven today by Mr Kromholz. It had evidently worked so painstakingly that it hardly seemed to belong to our age at all, and so we approached the monstrous building they'd set up on the Pankrác plateau. Originally they'd wanted to call it the Palace of Congresses, for that was its proper purpose: to create an appropriately grandiose setting for congresses of all kinds of useful and useless organisations, especially the one which ruled over everything and over everybody, but then they called it, rather absurdly, the Palace of Culture.

'Yeah, they have a different kind of mechanisation here,' said the foreman, having noticed what I was looking at. 'They have tiny little automatic refuse machines running along the corridors, parquet cleaners and floor-polishers – all imported stuff. Only for their use. D'you know how many people they have in there?'

'It's a monstrosity!' the captain spoke up. 'Eats us all out of house and home!'

'Last week,' Mrs Venus cut in, 'some little kid got inside. They thought he'd got lost on Vyšehrad but all the time he was inside there, he'd walked into one of their smaller reception rooms and fallen asleep. And when he woke up he kept running round and round the corridors and in the end he got into the boiler-house and by then he was completely lost, wandering around between those coloured pipes and turbines. When they found him in the morning he'd gone completely round the bend.'

Coming up to meet us, in a manner combining clodlike indifference and self-importance, were two policemen. One of them was well-built with a foppish little moustache adorning his pleasant face, while the other seemed to me like a rather tall but sickly fair-haired child with sky-blue eyes. At the sight of them something in me stiffened. Although I hadn't done anything, my experience as an innocent person with members of the police, whether in uniform or not, had not been happy. It didn't occur to me that thanks to my orange vest I was now myself on the borderline of being in uniform.

'Well then, you sweepers,' the more foppish of the two addressed us, 'a bloody mess?'

'Not too bad,' replied the foreman. 'We didn't do the housing estate today – that's where they live like pigs.'

'Ah, but we had some fun and games around here, believe me.' The foppish one put a friendly hand on his shoulder. 'Right next door.' He pointed towards Vyšehrad. 'What with that pervert about, the one who strangles women, some old hag thought he was after her and yelled for help. Some fuss, I can tell you! We combed the whole park, we had five flying squad cars there, all the way from Vršovice HQ, and all we got was one bloke. I could see at once that it wasn't him, because that pervert is no more than twenty and stands 6 foot 3, and this fellow was getting on for fifty and the size of a garden gnome, but he didn't have as much as a tram ticket on him, so why did we bother?'

'He was some sort of editor,' his colleague added, 'kind of taking exercise after a heart attack.'

'Is it true he's strangled seven women already?' asked Mrs Venus.

'And who told you such rubbish, Missus?' the foppish one said angrily. 'We have two murders reported and four attempted rapes, and that's the lot!'

'And when are you going to catch him?' asked Mrs Venus.

'Don't you worry.' The foppish one stroked his pistol holster. 'We know what to do. We've already established that he's fair and over six feet tall, thin, and with blue eyes. So there!' And he looked at his colleague, whom the description fitted surprisingly well. 'If you see a bloke like that . . . Get me?'

'Sure,' the foreman promised.

The foppish one then turned to the captain. 'And what about your trousers,' he joked. 'When will you grow into long ones?'

'In my coffin,' the captain replied. 'I've got them all ready at home.'

The foppish policeman gave a short chuckle, then raised his right hand in the direction of the peak of his service cap. 'All clear then. More eyes we've got, the more we see.'

'We'll just have to watch out we don't sweep up your clues,' Mrs Venus said when he'd turned away. 'And for that they get more than a miner!'

By twenty past eleven we had finished cleaning up around the Palace of Culture. This completed our assignment for the day. We took our equipment back to the former Sokol gym hall, and we now had only one task left: to wait three hours for the end of the working day and then collect our wages. My companions of course had already marked out the tavern they'd go to. I could have gone with them but I didn't feel like it. Going to a tavern once in a while is enough for me.

The first story of Franz Kafka I ever read was one of the few longer prose pieces he'd finished. It told the story of a traveller to whom an officer on some island wants to demonstrate, with love and dedication, his own bizarre execution machine. During the demonstration, however, the machine breaks down and the officer feels so disgraced by this that he places himself on the execution block. The author coolly and matter-of-factly describes the details of that dreadful machine, as though by doing so he can shroud the mystery and the incomprehensible paradox of the recorded event.

I was thunderstruck and fascinated by the seemingly impenetrable mystery of an event which, at the same time, depressed me.

But I was able only to comprehend it at its most superficial level. The officer – cruel, pedantic, enthusiastic about his executioner's task – seemed to me like a prophetic vision of the officers I had encountered, a pre-image of Hoess at Auschwitz, and I was amazed that literature could not only bring back to life those who had died but also predict the features of those who were not yet born.

Suddenly I found myself back on Vyšehrad hill. I walked through the park to the cemetery and to the ancient round church, which was surrounded by scaffolding. I'd never been inside the church although I can see it in the distance from the bluff behind our block and I actually own an old engraving of it: *Sacro-Sancta, Regia, et exempta Ecclesia Wissehradensis SS Apostolorum Petri et Pauli ad modum Vaticanae Romanae a Wratislao 1. Bohemiae Rege A.° 1068. aedificata, et prout ante disturbja Hussitica stetit, vere et genujne delineata, et effigiata. A.° 1420. 2. Novembris ab Hussitis destructa, ruinata et devastata.*

The building on the print looked different from the one now before me, and not only because it had been *destructa, ruinata et devastata* by the Hussites, but because the church had been rebuilt several times since the days when my engraving was made, and each time a little for the worse. In our country everything is being forever remade: beliefs, buildings and street names. Sometimes the progress of time is concealed and at others feigned, so long as nothing remains as real and truthful testimony.

As I walked around the little church I noticed that the door was half open. I glanced inside – there was an untidy heap of builders' requisites, scaffolding and buckets, and some of the pews were covered with a tarpaulin. On one side of the altar I caught sight of my companion of the morning, the one who reminded me of the specialist who took out my tonsils. Now without his orange vest he was evidently engaged in meditation.

I preferred not to enter. I didn't want to disturb him, nor to start a conversation with him.

He caught up with me in the park. 'Such nonsense,' he complained, 'the time you mess around waiting for your pay.'

I nodded. He told me his name was Rada. He'd taken note of my name first thing in the morning. He'd shared a room at the Litoměřice seminary with a man of that name forty years ago.

I said that all my relatives had lost their lives during the war, that the only surviving one was my brother who was a good deal younger than me.

He had two younger brothers. The middle one lived in Toronto and the youngest one was a doctor, a radiologist, apparently a good one, but he would have liked to be a traveller, he really came to life only when he saw some foreign scenery. As a matter of fact he was nearly always somewhere abroad, most recently in Kampuchea. 'Would you believe it, he actually learned to speak Khmer. To him it's just a bit of fun, he can learn a language in a few weeks!'

We passed through a brick gateway and approached the areas we'd cleaned that morning. I was glad that my shift was behind me and that I could now walk through the quiet little street onto which, by then, more yellowing leaves had dropped from the adjoining gardens, past the dark eyes of the houses which gazed on me wearily but also contentedly.

Suddenly I froze. In one of the windows I caught sight of a hanged man, his face pressed to the window-pane and his long tongue hanging from his open mouth. From below he was flooded by a blood-red glow.

Mr Rada noticed what I was staring at and said: 'Let's see what our artist has put on show for us today.'

I realised that the figure in the window was only a skilfully got-up dummy. As I looked more closely I saw another head, half female and half dog, its teeth dug into the hanged man's thigh.

'Oh dear.' My companion was not happy. 'He must have got out of bed the wrong side. He usually puts something more entertaining in his window. A little while ago he had some colourful acrobats turning somersaults. I sometimes come here specially to see what he's thought up. My brother, who came along with me once, declared that they're the work of a lunatic.' Mr Rada again returned to the subject of his brother, who seemed to play an important part in his life. 'To him everybody he can't fit into a pattern is a lunatic. He actually believes that the whole world is crazy, he says the world needs some terrible shaking-up, some great revolution to equalise the differences between the sated and the hungry. We argue a lot. At least until quite recently, when he came back home and told me about such a revolution that even I wouldn't credit it. Right next to a hospital a well full to the rim with murdered people. Corpses everywhere, he just couldn't have imagined it. Maybe he simply saw what any revolution always brings to the people.' Mr Rada stopped and looked about him, but we were alone in the swept street. 'The Apocalypse! That was the word he used, even though he never decided to believe in the Last Judgement and regarded Revelations as, at most, a poetic vision.'

My wife's consulting room was not far from where we were.

Luckily her waiting room was empty. I knocked. After a moment a young nurse put her head round the door, choked back the reproof on the tip of her tongue and asked me to come in.

I saw Lída sitting behind a desk half taken up by a bunch of gerberas. She was examining some sheets of Rorschach blotches.

'You've stopped by to see me? That's nice of you.'

'I was walking past.'

'Are you going straight home?'

'I thought I might look in on Dad first.'

'It's nice of you to have dropped in. Would you like some coffee?'

'No, thank you.' My wife had been offering me coffee for the past twenty-five years; I would have been interested to know if she'd noticed that I don't drink coffee.

The young nurse had disappeared somewhere, I could hear a door shutting quietly. I sat down in the armchair in which normally people would sit with depressions, anxieties, suppressed passions, Oedipus complexes, or even suicidal tendencies. My feet ached.

'Have you noticed the flowers I got?' she pointed to them.

I said they were beautiful and asked who'd given them to her. Her patients liked her. She was pleasant to them and gave them more time than she was obliged to, and in gratitude they brought her flowers. When was the last time I'd brought her flowers?

I used to give the other woman flowers and repeat to her ad nauseam how much I loved her; she aroused a sense of tenderness in me time and again.

I also felt some tenderness towards my wife, but I was afraid to show it, probably because she might begin to talk about such an emotion and even commend me for it.

She'd got her flowers from a woman patient about whom, as a matter of fact, she was worried. A girl of nearly nineteen, but still unable to come to terms with the fact that her parents had separated. She'd stopped studying, she'd stopped caring for herself, I wouldn't believe how much she'd gone down over the past few weeks.

For a while my wife continued to tell me about the girl whose future was worrying her. My wife always took on the burdens of her patients. She'd try to help them, and she'd torment herself if she failed. Perhaps she was telling me about that girl to make me realise the devastating effect that the break-up of a marriage might have. Certainly situations like this one touched her most closely.

Today the girl had told her about a dream she'd had: at dusk she was walking along a field path when suddenly, ahead of her, she caught sight of a glow. The glow was coming towards her, and she realised that the ground before her was opening and flames were licking up from the depths. She knew she couldn't escape them, but she wasn't afraid, she didn't try to run away, she simply watched the earth opening up before her eyes.

I am looking at my wife, at her vivid features. She is still pretty, there are no lines as yet on her face, or else I don't see them. Whether I like it or not, in my eyes her present appearance blends with that of long ago.

'I'm worried she might do something to herself!'

I stood up and stroked her hair.

'You want to leave already?' She half-opened the door and looked into the waiting room. 'There's no one there, you don't have to go yet. You haven't even told me,' she suddenly realised, 'what it was like there . . . doing that . . .' She was vainly looking for a word for my street-sweeping.

'Tell you about it in the evening.'

'All right, let's have a cosy evening.' She saw me to the door. She said I'd given her pleasure. She's always pleased when she sees me unexpectedly.

I would have liked to say something similar to her, such as that I always revive in her presence, that I feel warm when I'm with her, but I couldn't bring myself to say it.

She went back once more, pulled the biggest flower out of her vase and gave it to me, to take to Dad. It was a full bloom, dark yellow with a touch of amber at the tips of the petals.

She didn't know, she had evidently never noticed, that my father didn't like unnecessary and useless things such as flowers.

I kissed her quickly and we parted.

'And the fourth angel sounded,' I read at home in the Apocalypse, 'and the third part of the sun was smitten, and the third part of the moon and the third part of the stars; so as the third part of them was darkened, and the day shone not for a third part of it, and the night likewise . . . And the fifth angel sounded, and I saw a star fall from heaven unto the earth: and to him was given the key of the bottomless pit. And he opened the bottomless pit; and there arose a smoke out of the pit, as the smoke of a great furnace; and the sun and the air were darkened by reason of the smoke of the pit.' And somewhere else I read: 'And when the thousand years are expired, Satan shall be loosed out of his prison, and shall go out to deceive the nations which are in the four quarters of the earth . . . to gather them together to battle: the number of whom is as the sand of the sea . . . And fire came down from God out of heaven and devoured them. And the devil that deceived them was cast into the lake of fire and brimstone . . . And I saw a great white throne, and him that sat on it, from whose eyes the earth and the heaven fled away; and there was found no place for them.'

Throughout the ages, probably ever since they began to reflect on time, and hence on their own past, men have assumed that at the beginning of everything there had been paradise, where humans had lived happily on earth, where

> *non galeae, non enses erant: sine militis usu*
> *mollia securae peragebant otia gentes . . .*

Yet simultaneously they had prophesied the advent of ruin. It was inescapable, because it would happen by the decision of heaven.

In the evening a French woman journalist unexpectedly turned up at our place. She was young, and she radiated French perfume and self-assurance. She smiled at me with a wide sensuous mouth as if we were old friends. She wanted to know how the struggle for human rights would develop in my country, what was the attitude of my fellow-countrymen to her fellow-countrymen, whether they would welcome them if they arrived as liberators. She was also interested to know whether I regarded war as probable, the peace movement as useful, and socialism as practicable.

Perhaps she really believed that any one of her questions could be answered in a form that would fit into a newspaper column. She questioned me as though I was the representative of some movement, or at least of some common fate. She didn't realise that if I were the representative of anything whatsoever I'd cease to be a writer, I'd only be a spokesman. But then this didn't bother her, she didn't need me as a writer, she wasn't going to read any book of mine anyway.

✗ I recently read an article in an American weekly about how fourteen complete idiots incapable of speech had learned 'jerkish'. That was the name of a language of 225 words, developed in Atlanta for mutual communications between humans and chimpanzees – and there was no doubt, the author of the article believed, that more and more unfortunate creatures would be able to talk to each other in jerkish. It occurred to me immediately that at last a language had been found in which the spirit of our age could speak, and because that language would spread rapidly from pole to pole, to the east and to the west, it would be the language of the future.

I do not understand or make myself understood by those who recognise only the literature they control themselves and which, because of them, is written in jerkish, and I am afraid that I cannot communicate either with the pretty journalist, even though she assures me that she wishes absolute freedom for me and for my nation just as she wishes it for herself and her nation. I am afraid that we speak in languages which have moved too far apart.

As she was leaving she asked, more out of politeness than anything else, what I was working on at the moment. She was surprised to hear that I wanted to write about Kafka. Clearly she believed that people in my position should be writing about something more weighty – about oppression, about prisons, about the lawlessness practised by the state. Anyway, she asked if I was interested in Kafka's work because it was forbidden.

But I am writing about him because I like him. I feel that he is speaking to me directly and personally from a distant past. For the sake of accuracy I added that his work was not forbidden; they were merely trying to remove it, from public libraries and from people's minds.

She wanted to know why they did this to his work in particular. Was it politically so subversive? Or was it because Kafka was a Jew?

I think it would be difficult to find, in our century, many writers who were less interested in politics or public affairs than Kafka. There is no mention in his work of war or revolution, or of the ideas which may have helped to bring them about, just as there is nothing in his work which directly points to his Jewishness. The reasons why Kafka's work was suppressed in our country were different. I don't know if they can be simply defined, but I'd say that what was being most objected to in Kafka's personality was his honesty.

The journalist laughed. Who wouldn't laugh at such a reason?

She left before midnight. I hurried to get to bed. I was tired after a day which had started for me at five in the morning.

My wife curled up against me in her sleep, but I was unable to put my thoughts to rest. A heavy paw lay chokingly on my chest.

Long ago, after I'd got well again, I was impatient every evening for the next morning. Night was like an angry dog lying in my way. Almost as soon as I was awake in the morning I'd walk past all the windows of our flat, which looked out to three points of the compass, to enjoy the distant view clothed in fresh green or white with snow. I enjoyed my work and the people at the newspaper office, I looked forward to seeing them and to those unexpected encounters which might occur. I also always opened my letters full of hope: I was forever expecting some good news, some exciting revelation or some declaration of love. And I looked forward to the books I'd read. I would read at every spare moment: in the tram, in the doctor's waiting room, in the train, and even at mealtimes. I soaked up such a vast number of events and plots that they began to intertwine in my mind and I no longer knew which belonged where. I was enjoying life, and so I rushed from one experience to another, until I became like some obsessive eater who, out of sheer greed for the next course, is unable to savour the one he is eating. I didn't drink or smoke – not from any puritanism but through fear that I might blunt the edge of my perception and thus be deprived of an exciting experience or a possible encounter. I had known ever since my wartime childhood that we are all living on the edge of an abyss, above a black pit into which we must fall one day, but I felt that its jaws were now receding from me and that I was tied to life by a countless number of threads which together formed a firm net on which I was, for the time being, swinging at life's vertiginous height.

But the threads were quietly breaking, some gone rotten with age, some snapped by my own clumsiness, and others severed by other people. Or I might say: by the time we live in.

And so, every now and again when I lie down, I feel that heavy paw on my chest. In the morning, when I wake up, I want to shut my eyes again and sleep on.

Some time ago a classmate of my daughter's came to see me, a youngster who'd already cut his wrists once, and who asked me: Why should a person live?

What could I say to him? We live because that is the law of existence, we live so that we should pass on a message whose significance we cannot quite fathom because it is mysterious and unrevealable. My father, for instance, lived for his work: whenever he'd managed to set some inert matter in motion he'd be so pleased he'd think of virtually nothing else, and for that goal he would give up all other pleasures and even his sleep. But maybe just because of that he was able to be startled when he saw the sun rise or when he heard a Schubert quintet. It also occurs to me that we live because there are a number of encounters ahead of us for the sake of which living is worthwhile. Encounters with people who will emerge when we least expect them. Or else encounters with other creatures whose lives will touch on ours with a single shy glance. What more could I say to him?

Anyway he cut his wrists again one evening, and with his hands bleeding even managed to hang himself on a tree at the northern tip of the Žofín island in the Vltava while his young friends were having a good time in the old dance hall there. My daughter cried bitterly as she told me about it, and in conclusion she said of her dead classmate: 'But otherwise he was quite normal!'

While I was visiting my father in the afternoon his temperature suddenly began to rise steeply. His teeth were chattering and his eyes grew dim. I soaked a sheet and tried to wrap his emaciated body in the wet cloth, but he resisted, snatched the sheet from my hands and several times shouted: Take it and burn it!

Yes, I replied, I'll take it and burn it.

Father had been imprisoned twice in his life, two different secret police forces had searched our flat – he was probably talking about some letters or papers. But then I asked after all: What is it that I should take and burn?

He looked at me with a lifeless gaze from his greyish blue eyes, which, when I was a child, were still the colour of blue lichen, and said: This fever, of course!

So I took his fever and made a little fire on the parquet floor from newspapers and some old manuscripts of mine which had been lying in a cupboard here uselessly for some thirty years. And as I was burning that fever I could see its face in the flames, it looked like the face of a pale china doll and I was waiting for it to melt or at least to crack up, but it stood up to the fire, only writhing in agony, and I noticed that the doll was crying, amidst the flames tears were glistening on her pale cheeks.

The flames had died down. I walked up to my father and touched his forehead. It was cool and moist with sweat. Dad opened his ever-seeing eyes and attempted a smile which was almost guilty. He could smile so tenderly and genuinely that even someone seeing him for the first time could not but realise that here was someone special.

I looked about me. The fever lay in ashes, its china-doll face was dry again, parched and greedy.

I wanted to fall asleep but I could feel the night creeping around me softly, like a cat out hunting, nothing mattering to it except its intended prey. I examined the threads by which life was still tying me to itself, still holding me above the black pit, its jaw so close that sometimes I could make out its smooth edge.

What tied me most firmly to life was my writing: anything I experienced would become images for me. At times they would surround me so completely that I felt I was in a different world, and my stay there filled me with happiness or at least with a sense of relief. Years ago, I persuaded myself that I would be able to communicate these images to someone, that there were even people about who were waiting for them in order to share my joys and sorrows. I did all I could to meet their supposed expectations: I was doing this not from pride or any sense of superiority but because I wanted someone to share my world with me.

Later I realised that in an age when so many were obediently and devotedly embracing the jerkish spirit, if only to avoid having to face the horsemen of the Apocalypse, very few people were interested in someone else's images or someone else's words.

I am still writing, putting words and sentences together to make incidents and visions. Often I labour for days over a single paragraph, I cover pages with writing, then throw them away, I keep trying to lend the most complete and the most precise expression to what I have on my mind, to avoid any misunderstanding, to make sure none of those I am addressing should feel cheated.

Whenever I finish a book or a play my body rebels and punishes me with pains, and all the time I know that when I send my manuscript to the publishers I'll get a one-sentence reply: We are returning your manuscript because it does not fit into our editorial plans. I then lend it to a few friends, and some who still refuse to submit to the jerkish spirit will probably copy it and lend it to some of their friends. I also send it abroad and, provided it doesn't get lost on the way, it will be published there. So maybe after all – this is the thread I cling to – there may be a handful of people in the world with whom, despite all my irritations, I make contact.

I kept writing through all those years when not a single line bearing my name was allowed to be published in our country, when some of my recent friends would avoid me because they couldn't be sure that meeting me might not cast a shadow on their respectability. I wrote stubbornly, although sometimes the weight of my loneliness lay heavily on me. I'd sit at my table and listen to the silence which was swallowing me up. I could hear nothing but a barely perceptible snapping sound as some of the individual threads broke, and I longed to discover some hope I could attach myself to. That was when she appeared. If we had met at some other time we'd probably have passed each other by, but at just that moment I raced after her like a man drugged, and it took years for me to come to again. At the same time I never stopped conducting a silent argument with her. Even when I longed for her most my words died in my throat the moment she looked at me, whenever the night separated me from her embracing and comforting glance I would compose answers to questions, reproaches, wishes and yearnings which until then I had left unanswered.

And now, as the night lazily stretched its back over me, I was continuing, by force of habit, with the silent letter in which I defended myself and tried to prove that I didn't want to hurt her. Before throwing it into the big box full of unsent letters and wishes, full of promises, requests and half-whispered hopes, I tried once more to visualise what she was doing just then, at least to visualise her room. Who knows if she was even there. I no longer knew how she spent her nights. Maybe she was just returning home, her swift footsteps were closing the circle. If I got up now and ran after her, maybe I could cut the circle open, clutch her to myself, within the confines of that circle forget everything outside it, everything that was, that is, and that would inevitably be. But I knew I wouldn't do it. I'd only get up in the morning to set off for the streets I'd decided to sweep clean. It suddenly occurred to me that this was the reason why I'd found myself in the street with a handcart yesterday morning. I needed to go somewhere in the morning, at least I'd now have a natural objective for a while: set out somewhere, perform whatever kind of activity and listen to whatever kind of talk, just so I don't have to sit amidst the silence listening to the snapping of the threads.

Perhaps, it occurred to me, I was in some new space. I'd entered the place where oblivion was born. Or despair. And also understanding. Or perhaps even love – not as a mirage but as a space for the soul to move in.

II

◆

Four weeks later, again at nine in the morning, we were once more, the same team, sitting in the same tavern as on my first day.

When I'd put on my orange vest then I wasn't sure how often I'd decide to repeat the experience, but to begin with I would come to work at least every other day. I was curious about what parts of Prague my work would take me to, what narrow little streets that otherwise I'd never venture into.

I am fond of my native city, not only of the part through which the tourist crowds stroll, but also of the outskirts, where, among blocks of flats from the Secession period, a few little rural houses have remained standing, either forgotten or, more probably, already sentenced to death in some development plans, where unexpectedly an avenue of ancient poplars has survived or a little wooded hill, or fences bearing appeals and announcements whose bright colours I was aware of but whose texts as a rule I didn't read. More than once, as I pushed my cart with the dustbin I discovered a faded plaque on some familiar and usually dingy wall, a bust, or even a memorial huddling in some recess. These were meant to remind us that here, years ago, was born, lived or died some artist, thinker, scientist or national figure, in other words a spirit of whom it might be presumed that he rose above the rest of us. But more often, in one of those little streets or among the fading gardens, I remembered that here lived someone I knew, an artist, a thinker, a scientist or a national figure, someone who was here no more, someone beyond the hills and beyond the rivers, though mostly not over the river Styx, which would be sad but the common human lot, but someone now a refugee, someone driven out to our common shame. The walls of these houses, needless to say, did not bear plaques or a bust or even a visiting card to remind us that here lived a human spirit that had endeavoured to rise to higher things. I would glance at my companions at those moments, but they suspected nothing, except possibly Mr Rada, if he was one of our party, who might nod his head.

Thus I moved in my orange vest through the little streets and lanes of my native city which was slowly giving up its spirit, my companions at my side as witnesses. We were cleaning the town on which refuse had fallen and soot and ashes and poisoned rain and oblivion. We strode along in our vests like flamingoes, like angels of the dying day, sweeping away all rubbish and refuse, angels beyond life, beyond death, beyond our time, beyond all time, scarcely touched by the jerkish. Our speech resembled our age-old brooms, it came from a long way back and it moved along age-old paths. But behind us others are moving up: already the jerkish sweepers are arriving on their beflagged vehicles, pretending that they are completing the great purge, sweeping away all memories of the past, of anything that was great in the past. And when, with delight, they halt in the space which appears to them to be cleaned up, they'll summon one of their jerkish artists and he'll erect here a monument to oblivion, an effigy of shaft-boots, an overcoat, trousers and a briefcase, and above these an unforgettable face behind which we feel neither spirit nor soul but which, by official decree, will be proclaimed to be the face of an artist, a thinker, a scientist or a national figure.

There has been a slight drizzle since early morning, maybe it isn't even real rain but just condensation of the fog which covers the city with grime and helps to submerge it in oblivion.

On days like this Daria would positively choke and life would seem unbearable to her, her stone or wood incapable of being worked on, and as the droplets fell inexhaustibly from the clouds so the tears began to drip from her eyes, no matter how I tried to console her.

My companions aren't in a good mood either. I hardly recognised Mrs Venus this morning. Her right eye was swollen and below it was a purplish bruise. The captain's face had lost its tan over the past few days and had gone grey. Even the foreman in his freshly laundered and pressed overalls walked along in silence.

I ordered some hot tea and the captain, instead of his usual beer, ordered a grog. 'Tell me, who gave you that monocle?' He turned to Mrs Venus.

'A better man than you,' she snapped. 'One like you I'd have torn apart before he even raised his hand!'

Mrs Venus liked to make out how tough she was, but I believe she was good-natured, and she'd paid the price for it all her life. There were clearly many men she'd loved, or at least lived with, but they'd all left her, or else she'd run away from them. She'd raised three sons, even though she probably hadn't had much time for raising them. When we were young, the order of the day was that women must devote themselves to more important duties than looking after their children. Now she lived on her own. Her flat, as I understood it, was reached by an open upstairs passage; the term 'flat' meant a single room with a cooker. Her eldest son, who was a steelworker in Vítkovice, had given her a television set on which she could follow our jerkish programmes in colour. So for those evenings when she preferred home to the company at the bar, she had a reliable companion. Besides, at the far end of the passage lived, or rather slowly died, a lonely widower who'd been incapacitated by a stroke some years back, and now and then she'd go and clean up for him and bake him a cake – so he shouldn't be left alone like an abandoned dog. – Kafka

'Yeah, maybe if two other blokes were holding me down,' the captain growled.

Normally there was nothing eccentric about his speech. Mostly he'd conceal the oddity of his thoughts. He wasn't really a captain, he'd merely worked in the shipyards before he lost his hand. But his real interest was not ships but inventions. That's what he softly told me on the second day we were sweeping alongside each other: he'd think up machines which would improve people's lives. Unfortunately, he'd so far not met with any understanding. Wherever he turned with his inventions, there were blinkered people behind desks, instructed to block real progress and prosperity. He offered to demonstrate some of his inventions to me.

I hadn't been mistaken when I'd felt his face seemed familiar to me.

It was when I was still working in newspapers. One day the editor received a letter from an inventor who'd had his idea turned down. He had devised a way of utilising waste materials, especially soot, for the removal of the Arctic and Antarctic ice caps. The editor passed the letter on to me for answering. I wrote that in this matter we were unable to help him. A few days later, however, the writer turned up at the editorial office. He was quite a pleasant and amusing fellow. I couldn't see anything odd in his appearance, anything that might make me doubt his sincerity. He merely had a deeper tan than would be usual for that time of the year, but he told me he'd just returned from the shores of Africa. Out there, even at night-time when he couldn't sleep because of the heat, he had reflected on the curious and dangerous imbalance of the planet. In some places it would offer warmth and in others humidity, and elsewhere nothing but sand or ice. During those nights he'd thought a lot about abolishing that imbalance, but his head buzzed with more crazy ideas than were found in the Academy. In the end, however, he'd discovered the fundamental mistake which nature and mankind had committed. They'd come to dislike black! Was there anything in nature that was truly black? And mankind, with the possible exception of the Chinese, regarded black as the colour of mourning. Yet black was in fact the colour which combined most completely with the basic life force, that is with warmth, whereas white, allegedly the colour of innocence, the colour of wedding dresses, repulsed heat; it was the colour of snow and of most of the poisons. Those immense white areas had to be removed from the surface of the earth, and life would then establish itself where deserts had been before, and warmth would invade the areas which until now had been frosty. It had taken him a long time to discover the right means and the right method. The means was a mixture he'd invented, a solution of soot in seven solvents and three catalysts, and the method was the melting of the polar ice. As soon as the ice caps were sprayed with his mixture they'd lose their deadly whiteness, they'd begin to soak up heat and to melt.

I realised of course that I was talking either to a madman or to a joker with a magnificent, elaborate joke. Or he might be both. A crazy inventor pulling his own leg. But I found his exposition so entertaining that I continued to listen to his vision of the world of the future, when oranges and rice would be cultivated beyond the Arctic and Antarctic circles, while in our country there would be two harvests, and breadfruit trees and date palms would thrive.

I heard him out to the end but I told him I didn't have the time to go along with him then to see how his machine for the spraying of the mixture worked. He shrugged and left, and as a farewell gift handed me a few colour photographs which showed an array of strangely shaped objects arranged on the grass. I have no technical memory, so I'm unable after all these years to recall their shapes, and the photographs were lost when I was forced to leave the paper.

A few days later he turned up again. Had I noticed that there'd been a fresh fall of snow? He'd borrowed his neighbour's car solely for the purpose of convincingly demonstrating his equipment to me. Once I'd seen it I'd realise its revolutionary significance and would maybe write an article about it after all.

The elderly Tatra car took us all the way to Kralupy. There, on the outskirts, immediately behind the railway crossing, we stopped. It was a small house, and evidently a bachelor establishment. On the wall facing the front door hung a framed photograph of a white-haired man: unless I was mistaken it was a picture of Edison, and below it in large letters the famous inventor's statement: 'My work is the work of peace!' A desk below the window was covered with cartridge paper with drawings on it and some rolled-up plans; on the shelves stood several skilfully-made model ships. We went out by the back door into his yard.

I noticed that the snow which had fallen that morning had none of the usual deathly whiteness about it, but was dirty grey. My guide didn't even look about him but hurried to a shed behind the house, opened its wide double door, and wheeled out his machinery. Unlike the house itself this was an object of impressive appearance. It reminded me of an ancient fire engine: all brass and gleaming metal parts. It might equally well have been a perfect artefact for some exhibition of art. The long hose was fitted with a nozzle.

He wheeled the assembly into the garden, uncoiled the hose and began to pump some handles. A smelly mist issued from the nozzle. I watched the mist settling on the snow, but that dirty snow, instead of getting blacker, seemed to be getting lighter. No doubt there was some chemical reaction between the artificial mist and that chemical mess that had dropped from the sky. Thus we found ourselves in the middle of a near-white island while all around lay black clods of snow. I didn't say anything, and he too was silent. In his eyes I saw neither disappointment nor the joy of a perfectly played practical joke. After a while he stopped pumping, coiled up the hose, and wheeled his shining equipment back into the shed. I seized on the moment when he was inside and quickly walked along the railway line to the station. As I walked through the black snow I thought to myself that even if that man was crazy, he was no crazier than the rest of humanity which, in its eagerness for comfort, was spraying the world with a black mist in the belief that this was the direct road to the Garden of Eden.

It would have been embarrassing if he'd recognised me too, but he didn't seem to remember me. He had been too obsessed with his own mission at the time to take note of the face of someone who served him, at best, as an intermediary.

I promised him I'd come and look at his inventions as soon as I had some time, and he did not press me any further.

'For all you know your Harry may have been with me,' Mrs Venus said. Her face seemed even more swollen than in the morning and she was gazing at us with her right eye like an owl. 'He's not like you, he doesn't only go in for machines!'

'He can do better than you, you old hag!' The captain took a swig of grog, pulled out his pipe and filled it with his good hand.

Last Monday it rained even harder than today. We had to stop work before time was up, and as we were only a short distance from where the captain lived this seemed a suitable moment for a visit.

He led me to a house which looked even more dilapidated than the one where, years ago, he had demonstrated his equipment to me. He unlocked the door and hung up his captain's cap on a rusty nail behind it. The walls of the hall were damp and hadn't been painted for a long time; everywhere lay heaps of dusty objects and scattered pieces of clothing. The room's appearance and dimensions suggested a ship's cabin. Over his bunk hung various drawings, mostly of windmills. Nowhere did I see anything that suggested our first encounter. Perhaps I was the victim of some fixed idea and the captain had nothing in common with that young man years ago. No doubt the number of unsuccessful inventors in the world was increasing like that of unsuccessful poets.

He opened the bottom drawer and took out some folders of plans. He'd lately concerned himself with the most effective way of using wind power. He unrolled the first sheet and I saw a dreamlike ship whose deck was taken up by turrets carrying windmill sails, five turrets in all. He showed me further drawings, among them a windmill bus and a flying windmill, all these craft driven by wind. The drawings were meticulously done, the individual parts all bearing letters and numbers: I recognised the drive assembly, the transmission gears and the blades of the propellers as I knew them from childhood from my father's drawings. Other drawings had landscapes dotted with wooden turrets towering picturesquely above the tops of the trees.

It struck me that the captain was not so much a madman, not so much a joker, as a poet at heart. What else could a real poet do when he realised that crowds of jerkish word-mongers and image-mongers had already flooded the world with their rubbish? What else could he do in the face of the monstrous palatial blocks choking the earth but build his windmills which rise up silently and leave behind neither noise nor smell?

I asked him how much time he spent on his inventing. He said not so much now. He was usually too tired. At one time his head used to buzz with so many ideas that there weren't enough days and nights to put them down. Then he'd got married. He'd thought his wife would support him in his endeavours, but what woman could work up an enthusiasm for something that brought her no practical advantage? She'd begun to nag him, she even threw out his drawings and models. Finally, when their son was three, she'd run off. The captain spat towards the corner of his cabin and opened a cupboard which was full of strange objects. He'd wanted to go back to his old drawings but he'd suddenly discovered that there were stones rattling in his head. He was going downhill. One day, when he was cutting a sheet of metal with a welding torch, he'd handled it so awkwardly that the cut strip fell and crushed his hand. They had to amputate it at the wrist. So he'd been transferred to storekeeping. There, now and again, some idea would come to him. He hadn't heard from his ex-wife for many years, but she'd not had a good time either. The fellow she'd run off with beat her, he knew that from his son. Maybe she'd come back some day. He wouldn't drive her out, she'd find her bed all ready. He pointed to the upper part of the bunk, and it was only then that I noticed that the check bedcover had a thick layer of dust on it.

'How old is your son now?' it occurred to me to ask.

He looked at me in astonishment, and Mrs Venus answered for him: 'Why, Harry's off doing his military service now.'

In the dim saloon bar it was getting darker still and the

raindrops were beating noisily against the windowpanes. But this was nothing compared to the drops which would beat a tattoo on the roof of the attic studio, where on days like this it got so dark we became invisible to one another, so we could find each other only with our hands and our lips and our bodies. Then, all of a sudden, she'd be overcome by tears, and as we were saying goodbye, as she was kissing me with moist lips in the doorway of the building, she begged me not to be angry with her, that it was only those clouds which had so depressed her, and she promised she'd write me a letter.

I've always wanted to get a letter from which I could see that I was being loved, and indeed she sent me one written on a rainy evening, or maybe late at night when the wind had dispersed the clouds.

> My darling, my dearest, at this moment I'd leave everything, I wouldn't take anything with me, and if you said: Come! I'd go wherever you commanded. I realise that one pays for this, but this is right because one should pay for it. But even if I were to die, even if I were to go out of my mind, which to me seems worse still, I'd go . . .

I was alarmed by these promises and resolutions, but at the same time I was flooded with a happiness, like the warmth of sunbathing.

She also wrote to me that she loved me to the point of feeling anguish and pain, that she experienced a terrible pain because I was not with her at this moment, just now when everything that was good in her was crying out to me.

That's how she called me to her, and I knew that I had always longed for just such a woman. It gave me so much happiness that the reality of her pain and despair did not impinge on me. Or else I was too old to share her hopes without fear. Was I afraid we would end up like all those whose longing dies away and who can then scarcely bear to lie down by the side of each other night after night? Or was I not so much afraid as simply unable to brush my wife out of my life, my wife of whom I was still fond and who, after all, was supposed to belong to me to the end of my or her days?

If there were a devil, she chose a suitable quotation for me, it wouldn't be he who decided against God, but he who didn't find eternity long enough to come to a decision.

How can a person win love if he can't come to a decision?

My wife suspects nothing, she trusts me. But she has tormented dreams. She is walking with her class across a snow-covered mountain plain, suddenly all of them increase their pace and she can't keep up with them. She remains alone in the wind and frost, looking in vain for the way. Fog descends. She realises she won't ever find her way out again. At other times she climbs a rock with her friends, and when she is at the steepest point they all disappear. Rigid with vertigo she presses herself to the rockface. She can't move up or down, she calls for help, but no one responds.

She tells me her dreams and searches for an interpretation. She goes all the way back to her childhood, when she used to be on her own, unable to be close to anybody.

I know that she is wrong in the interpretation of her dreams, but I keep silent, I leave her at the mercy of her anguished visions.

But how can a man still believe in love if he has no compassion?

The foreman finished his second beer and unbuttoned himself. I realised that he was not so much worried by the change in atmospheric pressure as by the fact that he might lose his bonus. He ordered a third beer and announced that he'd made up his mind: he'd finally teach that Franta a lesson!

Franta is that young idiot with the tic in his face, the one I don't understand a word of when he speaks. To my amazement he is also a foreman, he even drives a car and it looks as if he is checking on our work, not by official authority but so he can grass on us. Everyone hates him. Whether because he's a cripple or because he's a grass I can't judge.

Mrs Venus told me that he'd recently had an operation. They'd taken his manhood from him. Franta did indeed have big breasts and his incomprehensible talk was in a falsetto. Last week, the foreman was now telling us angrily, that cripple had grassed on him, that he'd gone to have a beer when he'd claimed he was seeing the doctor. 'I saw that shit at the final stop of the number 19 yesterday, in that bloody refuse truck of his, so I grabbed him by his collar and dragged him out on the pavement and said to him: "You'll kneel down right here and ask my pardon, you swine, or else bring a pot along to collect up the bits of your bloody face!" He had to get down into the mud and repeat after me: "Mister Marek, I apologise to you, I'll never say a word about you again." "Mister," I made him say to me, because to him, and to him alone, I'm no Comrade!'

The foreman is an ex-NCO who served some time at the airfield; that time he obviously regards as a heroic and happy one, and he is fond of reminiscing about it – which helps me to recollect my own childhood days. I envy him his memory. Not only does he remember a mass of stories and sayings, but he also knows the names of all the streets in our district, and that's several hundred. He is as expert about the names and closing times of all the taverns as he is about street-cleaning technology. And they put him on an equal footing with that cripple.

'You should have made him stand a round of beer,' the captain remarked. 'He'd remember that all right, having to dip into his own pocket.'

'I wouldn't accept one from him,' Mrs Venus said. 'I'd sooner stick to water.'

'He's a poor wretch,' Mr Rada cut in from the next table. 'What do you want from him?'

'That one?' The foreman became heated. 'He's a cunning little bastard, he knows very well that if they cut my bonus his will go up. Who d'you suppose grassed on us last month, the day we had that downpour, when we left out Lomnického?'

'He's a poor wretch all the same,' I joined in.

'You didn't know him,' Mrs Venus said, her swollen eye flickering between Mr Rada and me, 'before they did that operation on him. By the time he got down to work it would be midday, and out in the street the moment he'd catch sight of a skirt he'd whip out that thing of his!'

'Creatures like him should be done in at birth.' The foreman knew no pity.

'How could they do that?' I objected.

'And why not? You only bugger about with them all your life, and there's no time left for normal people. Aren't I right?' The foreman turned to the others. 'And a decent bloke's got to work till he croaks.'

'And who'd decide who is normal?'

'Leave it to the doctors; they can tell pretty well nowadays. Let me tell you,' the foreman decided to cut short the discussion on euthanasia, 'that if that damned pervert grasses once more on any one of us, I'll catch hold of the bastard and kick him all the way down to the Botič stream and there I'll hold his bloody head under the water till he sees reason.'

Two and a half thousand years ago it is believed that the Greeks in Asia Minor, whenever their community was threatened by the plague or some other disaster, picked a cripple or otherwise deformed person, led him to the place of sacrifice, gave him a handful of dried figs, a loaf of wheat-flour bread and cheese, then struck him seven times on his genitals with a scourge, and to the accompaniment of a flute burnt him to death.

It was another rainy day, but at the beginning of spring. On the window-sill of the noble town house opposite two drenched pigeons were huddling together, and we were also huddling together, exhausted from love-making. I was beginning to get up because I wanted to get home, where my wife and children were expecting me, my unsuspecting and deceived family and my neglected, abandoned work. By now she knew that cautious movement which was the beginning of my moving away from her, but she didn't, as usual, say: Don't go yet! She just started to cry.

I asked what was wrong, but she only sobbed and pushed me away from her. It had been getting too much for her, she no longer had the strength for those perpetual goodbyes, for that coming together and breaking apart, she wasn't cut out to be a two-man woman, she couldn't bear the deception, the pretence sickened her, she wanted to live according to her conscience, she wanted to be with the one she loved.

But surely we're almost continually together.

How could I say something so outrageous when every night I was in bed with another woman?

But that is my wife!

How did I dare say this to her? She was shaking with sobs. She'd never wanted to live like that, what had I made of her? A whore who wasn't even entitled to see me when she felt depressed or when she needed me but who had to come running the moment I felt like it, whenever I could find the time for her.

I didn't say anything, I was so taken aback by her grief and anger, and she screamed that I should say something, why didn't I defend myself, why didn't I try to convince her that she was mistaken, why didn't I tell her that I loved her, that I cared for her?

Then we made love again, night descended on the palace outside our window, the drenched pigeons had disappeared. She wanted to hear again and again that I loved her. I kept repeating it with a strange kind of obsessiveness. We made love with the same obsessiveness, and she whispered to me that we had been predestined for each other, that we were resisting our fate in vain, that I was resisting in vain when I longed for her so much.

And I didn't say anything. I embraced her, I melted into her, and I tried to dispel the unease which was growing within me.

But I didn't want to live like that permanently. When I got home I told my wife about the other woman.

It was getting on for ten o'clock, the time when we normally left our hospitable tavern. The foreman, who was a great one for precision, looked closely at his watch: 'One more beer,' he decided, 'and then we're off, even if it's pissing like from a fireman's hose.' And to comfort us he related how exactly thirty years ago it had rained just like this all through the summer. He was encamped down beyond Kvilda, at the back of beyond.

Luckily he managed on the second day to pick up a pretty dark-haired girl from accounts at the timberyard. He'd stopped at her office in the morning, and within half an hour he'd done all the calculations for her that she'd have spent the whole day on, so that they could get down to the real business.

The foreman was a good raconteur, and the standard of his story-telling rose with the interest of his listeners. In me he found an attentive listener, for which he rewarded me not only by addressing me more often than the rest but also, as a sign of his favour, by occasionally giving me the better and more profitable jobs. His most grateful listener, however, was the youngster, either because at his age he was the most eager to hear other people's stories or because fate had prevented him from experiencing most of the things the foreman recounted.

I knew by then that he hadn't been sickly from childhood. As soon as he'd finished school he'd let himself be lured by favourable terms into a chemical plant, where they offered him a flat within a year and special danger pay straight away. That danger pay was not just a lure. He'd hardly been at the plant five months when an incident occurred, which is the term used in the jerkish press for an event which costs the health and even the lives of an appreciable number of workers. There'd been an escape of poison gas. Two women died instantly and the young man was discharged from hospital after six months and pensioned off. His liver and kidneys were damaged, and he'd better forget about women altogether. Nevertheless he'd taken a liking to a tram driver called Dana, admittedly the divorced mother of two girls and his senior by ten years, or maybe it was just because of that that he thought he had a chance. Apparently he'd been courting her for a year and he'd been cleaning the city's streets for that period in order to earn a little extra money so he wouldn't come to her as a pauper.

The rain thirty years ago had been an obstacle to the foreman's intentions until he remembered that a little beyond the airfield there was a rusty old Messerschmitt which had been wrecked during the war. Its innards had of course been torn out, but if you pulled the canopy shut and put a rug on the floor it was almost a hotel. First time they did it the dark-haired girl had hardly taken her skirt off when she let out a terrible shriek because a snake was creeping out from one of the holes in the instrument panel. There was a whole nest of vipers there, and the foreman had to get rid of them all and stuff up the holes with tow before he could get to the most delicious hole of all. 'Let me tell you,' the foreman concluded, 'one thing I've learnt in my life more than once: a bed isn't everything!'

It was nearly a quarter past ten and it was still raining outside. Listening to other people's tales, whatever they are, I sometimes feel like a debtor, like an eternal dinner guest who never offers any invitations himself, but usually I cannot bring myself to demand the attention of others.

A few years ago my wife's sister was moving to another flat. She asked if I would help her. The woman who'd let her have her one-room flat was quite mad, she'd piled it high with junk she'd picked up at rubbish dumps, but she was anxious about it and wouldn't let the removal men touch it, and so she didn't know how to move her things out.

How many things can you get into a room? I thought my sister-in-law was exaggerating. I took the words 'rubbish heap' figuratively. I promised to move the lady's things bit by bit in my car. Even outside her door I smelt a strange odour wafting from inside. The instant she let me in the smell of rot and mildew hit me violently. The woman, however, was neat and clean, the hand she held out to me was scoured white. She showed me in. I walked a narrow path between crates, boxes and masses of parcels until I reached the window and asked if I might open it. A wave of fresh air full of smoke and exhaust fumes rushed inside, but the atmosphere of decay which persisted here was not to be drowned. Then I helped the woman finish her packing. We tied up children's copy books and stacked them in a crate together with burnt-out lightbulbs and an unmatching pair of sandals without straps, bits of worn-out cork tiles and armless dolls, old envelopes, the shells of radios, rusty saucepans, a broken chandelier and a glass marble. The woman had clearly spent her life collecting and storing other people's rubbish, which possibly gave her a sense of hope or security. For five whole days I drove to and fro. She thanked me and promised me eternal salvation for my trouble, a salvation I'd soon experience because the time was nigh when mankind would assemble for judgement in the place called Armageddon. I felt like asking her why in that case she was keeping all those things, but there was no sense in putting this question to a crazy woman when I might just as well ask anyone else or myself.

As I was carrying downstairs what must have been the fiftieth package at least I couldn't resist the temptation to untie the string and to tip the contents into the nearest dustbin. I covered it up with some empty paper cups and kitchen waste from the bin next to it, and drove off with the rest of the junk to my sister-in-law's flat.

About an hour later I returned for the next load, but I had to wait a long time for her to let me in. She was standing in the doorway as if hesitating whether to admit me. 'You, you . . .' she said to me. 'And I trusted you!'

'What a hope,' the foreman spoke up. 'Let me tell you, I've learnt this more than once in my life: you won't get any thanks from a woman!'

Wisps of fog were drifting outside, rising from the pavements and the sodden lawns. In the telephone box outside the tavern a girl was smiling prettily down the instrument at someone.

I too used to smile. I thought that I was really seeing the woman I loved and that I could touch with my eyes what she was seeing just then. She told me: outside my window a raven is freezing on a branch, he's telling me something but I can't hear him. I was freezing as much as that raven. I had to breathe on the glass to see out. On a rime-covered tree there actually sat a raven. What could he say? Nevermore, nevermore. I thought I understood him: we'd never find anyone to love so much again.

The girl stepped out of the phone box. My companions were still lazily hanging about the tavern door. I lifted the receiver. I hesitated for a moment, but I so needed to hear a familiar voice that I dialled. Lída said she was pleased to hear me and wanted to know where I was calling from, what I had just been doing and if I wasn't cold. She was looking forward to my coming home. I would have liked to say something nice to her, to my wife, to address her tenderly as I used to: Lída darling, or at least Lída dear, at least ask her what she was doing, what she was thinking about, but I was unable to say anything other than that I'd come straight home after visiting Dad at the hospital.

I remained in the box for a moment. My garish vest was brilliantly reflected in the glass. I fished in my pocket for a coin. That other number so vehemently forced itself on my mind that I repeated it in a whisper.

I stopped fishing for that coin. I watched my companions marching slowly uphill to the little park where we'd left our tools in a small shed. Mrs Venus caught sight of me and waved.

Some other time, my love, but I'm not silent because I'm not thinking of you, it's just that I have nothing new to say to you.

And you think that this silence, the way we live now, is good? ✗

I don't know if it's good, but I don't know anything better.

You don't know anything better? Just look at yourself, the stuff you're wearing, this masquerade. Have you gone in for repentance or what?

No, it's perfectly honest work. I can think while I'm doing it.

You can think, can you? How nice for you. And what about me? Are you at all interested in what's happening to me? How I've been feeling? After all those years I haven't even merited a single phone call from you.

We had a lot of phone calls with each other. At least a thousand!

Don't count them up. I don't want to hear numbers. Anyway, that was before. Afterwards you didn't ring even once.

We'd said everything to each other. We were exhausted from those conversations. What else was there to say to each other?

You're asking me? You might at least tell me whether the whole thing meant anything to you.

You know very well what you meant to me.

I don't know anything after the way you behaved. I always thought . . .

What did you think?

Never mind. I didn't want to believe it. After all you'd told me when we were together, how could I believe that you'd chase me away like some . . .

Please don't cry!

Tell me at least, did you love me at all?

You know I did.

I don't know anything. How am I to know?

An old woman was approaching the box. Perhaps she didn't even want to telephone, but to be on the safe side I opened the directory and pretended to look for a number.

If you'd loved me you wouldn't have behaved the way you did!

I was crazy about you.

Don't be evasive. I asked you if you'd ever loved me. If you're capable of loving anyone.

Don't torture me!

Me torturing you? Me you? Tell me, my love, what have you done to me? At least explain to me what was good about it.

I just couldn't carry on like that. Forgive me, but I couldn't go on living like that!

And me, how am I to live? You never thought what would happen to me, did you? How can you be silent like this, it isn't human! Surely you must say something to me, do something. You must do something about us!

At one time I used to write plays. The characters were forever talking, but their words went past each other, their remarks slid past one another like the slippery bodies of fish, without making contact. Did I write that way because I believed we could step out of our loneliness? Or because I needed to find a way of avoiding answers? Where words miss each other, where humans miss each other, real conflict may arise. Or did I suspect that a man cannot successfully defend himself in the eyes of another, and when he is talking he's doing so only to drown the silence which spreads around him? To conceal from himself the reality of life, a reality which, at best, he perceives only at exceptional moments of awareness?

The man who had alone survived the crash of the aircraft which hit a church tower in Munich was working as a newspaper editor in Belgrade. I was curious to meet a person who had risen from the ashes, but his sister had just died of cancer and he asked me to postpone our meeting for a few days. When I called on him later his other sister was gravely ill with the same disease. 'The doctors are giving her no more than two months,' he said to me. 'They told me this morning. You know what is odd? I went out into the street and I didn't hear anything. There were trams and cars moving about and people talking, but I didn't hear any of it. There was the same sudden quiet then, after the crash.'

I caught up with my companions. The youngster passed me my shovel, which he had carried for me on his handcart, and Mrs Venus said: 'Bet that wasn't your wife you've just phoned.'

Right by the kerb I noticed a dead mouse. I picked it up on my shovel and flung it on the rest of the rubbish.

My wife was amazed by what I told her. She couldn't believe that I'd lied to her for so long. I said what most men would probably say in such a situation, that I had hoped to spare her needless suffering because I'd believed it would soon come to an end.

But you don't want to end it? she asked.

I said that I loved the other woman, that I'd never loved any woman the way I loved her.

But I thought you loved me more than anybody else! Tears flooded her eyes. Then she wanted to hear details. Any kind of truth was preferable to silence. I was to tell her where she'd gone wrong and how she could put it right.

I poured out all my complaints and self-exculpating explanations, but after a while we were merely rehearsing who did the shopping, who the cooking, the laundry, the washing up and the floors, until I was horrified by the poverty of my own speech. I fell silent, but my wife wanted to hear something about the other woman and I, suddenly freed by my newly-discovered openness, began to praise the qualities and talents of my lover, to describe the uniqueness of what we were experiencing. But as I was forcing all this into words I transformed the experiences which had been mine only, and which had seemed inimitable and unique, into something common, categorisable and conventionally melo-dramatic. Yet I was unable to stop talking, and my wife listened to me with such involvement, such readiness to understand me and maybe even advise me that I fell victim to the foolish idea that she might even share some of my feelings. But she was merely hoping that if only she received my confession and listened to me attentively she might transform my words on how we had drifted apart into the first act of a mutual drawing together. She would confront the urgent attraction of the other woman with her own patient understanding.

When – suddenly not too convinced that this was what I truly and urgently desired – I suggested that I might leave home, at least for a time, she said that if I wished to leave her and the children she wouldn't stand in my way, but if after a while I decided to return home she couldn't guarantee that they would be able to have me back. I was far from considering what I would wish to do after a while, but I thought I could see in her eyes so much regret and disappointment, and anguish at the thought of impending loneliness, that I did not repeat my suggestion.

We didn't go to bed until the early hours. I couldn't have slept for more than a few minutes because daybreak had not yet come, but when I woke up there were muted sobs by my side.

She was crying, sobbing steadily and persistently, her mouth buried in her pillow so she shouldn't wake me.

I would have liked to caress her or say something kind to her, to comfort her as I always did when something depressed her, but this time it was me who'd crushed her. Unless I changed my decision I had become the one person who couldn't comfort her. I suddenly realised that the position I found myself in tormented me rather than gave me a sense of liberation.

In the morning I was awakened by a crash, by the sound of splintering.

I found my wife in the hall: by her feet were fragments which I recognised as those of the only piece of sculpture we'd ever had in our home. The angular bird's head was shattered and its human eyes had rolled God knows where.

For an instant we were both silent, then my wife said: 'I'm sorry. I had to do something.'

And I, in a sudden flush of compassion, without reflecting that the previous day I'd been determined to do the opposite, promised her that I wouldn't leave her, that I'd stay only with her. We had had our children together, and surely we'd once linked our lives together till death did us part.

Shortly afterwards we went to see our daughter's art teacher. He was exhibiting his paintings in a small-town gallery. We walked round the pictures, which somehow all seemed to express the loneliness of men, and I tried to suppress my nostalgia. In the evening some visitors arrived. They were nearly all painters and they talked a lot about art, which reminded me of the other woman. They took their observations seriously, and seemed to me to be genuinely seeking a meaning behind their activity, but all talk seemed unnecessary at that moment, it was no more than a substitute for life, for movement, for passion. I fled the company and went down to the riverbank. My wife found me there and wanted to know if I was sad, if I felt nostalgic. My wife, that voluntary healer, promised me that things would be good between us, we'd start another life, and I'd be happy in it. She wanted to know what I was planning to write and to hear what was on my mind that instant, she talked about sincerity and about living life in truth. I was listening to her and I felt as if something were snapping inside me, as if every word were a blow which cut something in two. I was surprised she couldn't hear the blows herself, but simultaneously it seemed to me that the despair was fading from her voice. I had always hoped that she would feel comfortable with me, that life's hardships would not weigh her down too much – her relief gave me at least some satisfaction.

The street was still wet but the air had been cleansed, and as we stepped out of the shade of the residential blocks we even felt the rays of the autumn sun which somehow dispelled our gloomy mood of the morning. The youngster was whistling a Gershwin tune and Mr Rada all of a sudden showed me a slim little book on the cover of which was a street-sweeping truck and a broom, while its title to my surprise promised a critical essay on the personality cult. 'Do you know it?'

I'd never seen the book before in my life.

'An interesting reflection on how we used to deify ourselves and physical matter.' He opened the book and read aloud: 'Here lies the root of the cult, here is that proton pseudon: that the miserable, mortal, ephemeral human ego declares of itself: *Ich bin ich. Das Ich ist schlechthin gesetzt.* I am the finest flower of the materialist God!' He shut the little book again and I caught another glimpse of its cover. On the sweeping truck, as I now noticed, lay a big human head.

'And what are we really?' I asked Mr Rada, and at that instant I understood the connection between the cover picture and what I'd just heard.

The youngster was still whistling that familiar tune and I felt irritated at not being able to think of the words that went with it.

'It's "The Man I Love", of course,' he told me, delighted at my display of interest and my acquaintance with the composer, and immediately he sang to me the four-beat tune: 'Some day he'll come along, the man I love.' He asked: 'You like Gershwin?'

I told him that thirty years ago a black opera company had come to Prague with *Porgy and Bess*; it had been the first visit for a long time of any company from the other side of our divided world. Getting tickets required a miracle, but I'd been lucky.

The memory took me away from the swept street. Not that I could recall anything of the performance which had then delighted me, but I could see before me the little street in the suburbs of Detroit, where a lot of black children were shouting on the sidewalk and a white-haired black man sat in a wheelchair in front of a dingy low house. Someone was playing a trumpet, or more likely had put on a record with Louis Armstrong or somebody, there was rubbish everywhere, bits of paper, advertising leaflets and Coca-Cola cans, and in the hot air hung a smell of onions, slops and human bodies.

I was seized by nostalgia for that country. Suddenly I was seeing myself in my orange vest pushing that miserable handcart. Of course I needn't have worn that particular vest, but they made me wear some garishly coloured jacket to make sure everyone recognised me from afar and gave me a wide berth. This was now happening to me, even though, having been put into a colour-marked jacket in childhood, I longed for nothing more than to get rid of the mark of disinheritance.

'We used to play him a lot,' the youngster said. When he saw my surprise he explained: 'We had a jazz band, you know, before I got my liver all buggered up.'

The captain rolled up the sleeves of his grubby pullover. 'I may have something useful for your garden,' he said to the foreman.

'So long as it isn't that greenfly spray of yours.' The foreman was alarmed. 'Made my greenflies scamper about like squirrels and screwed up my roses completely.'

'We used to play Duke Ellington, Irving Berlin, Jerome Kern, or Scott Joplin ragtime,' the youngster said enthusiastically, 'but we liked George Gershwin best, and he also came across best because people had heard his stuff before.'

'And now you don't play at all?'

'Not a hope. Couldn't blow now. Know what impressed me most? That he'd never had any special schooling, and look at the music he wrote!'

'Did you write any yourself?' I asked.

'We all did. We just had jam sessions and something or other would come out of them.'

From one of his enormous pockets the captain produced a piece of collapsed rubber fitted to a small bellows. He squeezed the bellows a few times and the rubber swelled up into a small balloon.

Now balloons were something the foreman was interested in.

'What kind of bird-brained contraption is this then?' he asked, leaning his broad shovel against the wall of a house. He couldn't know how appropriately he'd described the device, for it was actually intended, as we were informed, for scaring birds away. The balloon with the bellows also included, on one side, sails like a windmill's, and, on the other, a whistle. The windmill, by means of the bellows, would blow up the balloon, and once the air pressure in it exceeded a certain limit a valve would open and the whistle would emit a short but powerful blast, which would scare away any flying intruder.

Using his hook the captain pulled from a pocket an object reminiscent of a small organ pipe and with his sound fingers he screwed it into a thread at the end of the balloon.

We were all intently watching his antics, but the expected blast did not materialise: there was only the hiss of escaping air.

'How is this superior to an ordinary rattle?' the foreman asked doubtfully.

'Hasn't it occurred to you that a rattle goes all the time and the little bastards get used to it?' The captain once more began to squeeze his bellows and we, now all leaning on our tools, were watching the balloon filling up.

'And if there's no wind?' the foreman asked with interest.

At that moment there was a brief sound of bursting, rather like a distant shot, and what had just been a balloon was no more.

'You know, they let us rehearse at the works club twice a week,' the youngster reminisced, 'and we could stay there as long as we needed to. Sometimes we'd fool around till the early hours of the morning, just stretching out on the tables for a moment if we felt like a rest.'

'Weren't they waiting for you at home?' I asked in surprise.

'At home? But I didn't live at home!'

'If there's no wind,' the captain replied to the foreman, 'it works by electricity.'

'If you felt like it and could spare the time,' the youngster suddenly remembered, 'the boys are playing in Radlice this

Sunday.' He fished about in his wallet and pulled out two tickets. 'Maybe you'd like them.'

I objected that he'd got the tickets for himself, and while we were sweeping up the leaves and conkers which had dropped from a huge horse-chestnut tree he explained to me how to get there.

I sometimes feel nostalgic for America. Even in my dreams I wander among the skyscrapers or drive along highways through endless landscapes, always full of expectation. Yet nearly every one of these dreams ends sadly: I'd stayed on in that country, beyond the sea, I'd never return home again, to the place where I was born and where people, or at least some of them, speak my native language.

They've put me in a vest in which I feel restricted. I could take it off, or even with a fine gesture chuck it away and go somewhere where they won't force one upon me, but I know that I won't because by doing so I'd also be chucking away my home.

Franz Kafka was certainly one of the most remarkable writers who ever lived and worked in Bohemia. He used to curse Prague and his homeland, but he couldn't bring himself to leave, he couldn't make up his mind to tear himself away from them. His seemingly dreamlike plots unroll in an environment which appears to have little connection with any real place. In reality his native city provided him with more than just a backdrop for his plots. It pervaded him with its multiplicity of voices, its nostalgia, its twilight, its weakness. It was the place where the spirit could soar up to any heights, but it was also the place where there was in the atmosphere a barely perceptible smell of decay, which more particularly affected the spirit.

Kafka spoke perfect Czech, perhaps just a trifle stiffly, but he wrote in German. But he was not a German, he was a Jew.

Not a single Czech literary historian has ever found in himself enough generosity, courage or affability to range him among the Czech authors.

The sense of exclusion and loneliness which repeatedly emerges from his prose writings certainly stemmed from his disposition,

from the circumstances of his life. In fact he shared it with many of
his contemporaries. But Prague greatly intensified it. He longed to
escape from it, just as he longed to escape from his old-bachelor
loneliness. He failed to do so. He was unable to liberate himself
except by his writing.

If he had succeeded in liberating himself in any other way he'd
probably have lived longer, and somewhere else, but he wouldn't
have written anything.

Home had become a cage for me. I needed to break out, but
whenever I went out while my wife was at home I could see fear in
her eyes. She never voiced it, suspicion was not part of her nature,
she was trying to trust me as she'd done before, as she trusted
strangers, but her eyes would follow me wherever I moved. When I
returned she'd run out to meet me, pleased that I was back home
again and welcoming me tenderly. And she, who'd never been too
concerned about how I spent my time, what I was thinking about,
what I ate, would ask if I wasn't hungry, and during supper she'd
shyly reflect on where we might go together so we should enjoy
ourselves, and she'd agree in advance with whatever I suggested.
She'd never been like this before, she'd known how to pursue her
own interests and have her own way, but now, humbled and
humiliated, she was trying to live up to her idea of my idea of a
good and loving wife, and her slight gaucherie both shamed and
touched me.

She was not endowed with directness. I always felt that she
moved more freely in the world of ideas and theorems than among
people. In dealing with people she lacked naturalness. And yet she
wished she had it, she needed it in her profession, which required
her to gain her patients' confidence. I noticed her trying
desperately to achieve what others had received as a gift. I knew
that she wanted people to be fond of her. She is happy whenever
others appreciate her good qualities or her ability, and she hastens
to repay them for it by deeds, or at least by words so eager that she
embarrasses them. I'd wanted to help her not to feel isolated
among people, and now I had brutally pushed her back into the
corner from which she'd tried to escape.

Of course she had a lot of acquaintances and colleagues who respected her, but she had few real friends. The children were growing up and the day when they'd be leaving us was approaching. If I were to leave her as well, who would look after her as she moved towards her advancing years, who would walk by her side?

But could I still do it?

We are lying next to each other, we embrace. She wants to know if it was good for me; behind that question I suspect a multitude of suppressed and anxious questions and I ask her not to ask me anything. She says that she loves me, we'll be happy together yet, and she falls asleep, exhausted, whereas I am sinking into a strange void between dream and wakefulness. I am fighting against sleep, against the state when I shan't be able to drive away the voice which begins to speak to me.

At one time it was my wife who spoke to me. She'd wait for me at street corners in dream towns, she'd miraculously appear in a moving train, she'd find me in strange houses and in the midst of crowds. By some miracle we'd jointly discover forgotten box rooms, or a ready-made bed in a deserted corridor, or a hidden spot in a garden or a forest, and there we'd whisper tender words and verses to one another, there we'd embrace, and in my dream, as usually happens, we'd make love more passionately and completely than in reality.

Then she began to disappear from my dreams and other women appeared in them, but in their embraces I felt treacherous and unclean, and when I woke up I was relieved to find my wife lying by my side. Sometimes a different dream would recur repeatedly. I was aware of my age, of my approaching old age, and I realised that I'd remained alone in my life, that I'd failed to find a woman with whom I'd beget children, and that depressed me.

What speaks to a man in his dream is the secret or suppressed voice of his soul. This dream, I tried to explain to myself, echoed the memory of the time when I was growing up and when I was afraid I'd never succeed in finding a woman's love. But had I understood my soul's voice correctly?

Now I dreamed that I was waiting under my plane tree and I knew that people might come from different directions. I wouldn't therefore remain alone. Simultaneously I was afraid that the two women I was waiting for might meet. True, they both belonged to me, but they certainly did not belong to each other. It was my lover who arrived first. I hurriedly led her away, then we strayed through ever more deserted regions, looking for a place where we could be together quietly. But each time someone would turn up and watch us intently. In the end, however, we found some place of refuge, we made love in strange and inhospitable surroundings, snatched out of the world around us, the way it can only happen in a dream, intoxicated with each other, but just as the instant of greatest pleasure was approaching my wife suddenly appeared through some hidden or forgotten door and I tried in vain to hide the other woman under a blanket that was too short. Lída stood in the door, staring at me with desperation in her eyes. She didn't reproach me, she didn't scream, she just stared.

At the last house, just where the slope of Vyšehrad hill begins to drop steeply, our foreman glanced up at the closed windows and reassured himself with satisfaction that there was no sign of life behind them. 'They're all in gaol!' he informed us. Then he told us the name of the owner of the place and that the fellow had worked in long-distance haulage and had smuggled precious metals. When they'd nabbed him they'd found two kilograms of gold and half a million dollars in cash at his place.

'Half a million?' the youngster squealed. 'You're exaggerating!'

'I got it rock-solid reliably from a mate in the Criminal Branch,' the foreman said, offended. 'They found three and a half tons of silver alone. From all over the place, from Poland to Vienna. And everything for dollars.'

'Wish you'd told me about him sooner!' The youngster was leaning on his scraper, red with excitement. 'My doctor was saying . . . Fact is, in Switzerland they've got some drug, dearer than Legalon even. If I had that, the doctor says, I might get my liver right again.'

The social hierarchy

'And why,' Mrs Venus asked, 'can't they get it for you at the centre?'

'The doctor said I'd have to be at least a National Artist.'

'That's how it is,' the foreman agreed. 'Those who're entitled to Sanops treatment can get any kind of pills; if they swallow them they can stuff themselves and booze at their receptions as long as they like. But people like us don't stand a chance. I can tell you from personal experience: if you're an ordinary person no one gives a monkey's fart for you! Mortally ill? Well then, die! At least they save money on you!'

'I only thought,' the youngster said, 'if I'd really known sooner . . .'

'What then?' the foreman snapped. 'A crook like that would have shown you his arse!'

Our days passed relentlessly. Sometimes I'd ring Daria and we'd talk until the freezing cold drove me out of the telephone box, or we'd walk in the Šárka hills, climbing up the dusty slopes together, and she'd urge me to tell her what was going to happen to our lives, and she'd complain that I'd treacherously abandoned her.

Then she phoned one day and asked me to come to the studio at once. Her voice sounded so urgent that I was alarmed.

Come in quickly, she welcomed me, I've been waiting for you. She told me she'd had a dream, a dream like a vision about the two of us, and she realised that we belonged to each other, that it was fate, and that there was no point in resisting it.

When we embraced, when we embraced again, I didn't think of what would happen, of what I'd do, of what I'd say, where I'd return to or where we'd go together; I was only conscious of her proximity, of the bliss of her proximity.

I returned to lies once more. There is nothing by which a person can justify a lie. It corrodes the soul just as much as indifference or hate.

Night after night I lay awake for hours on end, reflecting on how to save myself. If I did fall asleep I'd wake up after a few hours and at once I'd hear that fine sand which was corroding me internally. In desperation I composed defence pleas and explanations, but I never uttered them, knowing full well that I had no defence. Man doesn't live to defend himself, there are moments when he has to act or at least to admit his helplessness and keep quiet.

For action I lacked the necessary hardness or blindness, and I also lacked the requisite self-love. I know that to remain with one's past partner when one has come to like another person is considered weakness or even a betrayal of ourselves and the person we now love.

We remove discarded articles to a dump, and these dumps grow sky-high. And so do the dumps of discarded people who, as they grow old, are no longer visited by those dear to them, or by anyone except perhaps others who have themselves been discarded. They still try to conjure up a smile and to fan some hope inside them, but in reality they already exude the musty smell of being discarded.

And you'd discard me like that? Daria would ask. At other times she'd say: It's their own fault. Everyone is responsible for his fate and also for his own downfall, no one else can save him.

By writing, Kafka not only escaped his torments, but only thus was he able to live at all. In his notes, letters and diaries we find that he never tried to put into words what he thought of literature. People normally express themselves about the world around them, but for Kafka literature was not external, not something that he could explore or separate from himself. Writing to him was prayer – this is one of the few statements he ever made about what literature meant to him. He switched the question to another sphere: what was prayer? What did it mean to him, who had so little faith in any revealed or generally accepted God? Most probably it was a way of personal and sincere confession of anything on a person's mind. We turn to someone whose existence and hence also whose language we can scarcely surmise. Perhaps just that is the essence or the meaning of writing: we speak about our most personal concerns in a language which turns equally to human beings as to someone who is above us and who, in some echo or reflection, also resides within us. If a person does not glimpse or hear within himself something that surpasses him, that has cosmic depth, then language will not make him respond anyway. Literature is not intended for him. Such a definition has the advantage of including both the author and the reader. Literature without those who receive it is nonsensical anyway, as would be a world where no other language was heard than jerkish, where language could no longer make anyone respond, not even someone above human beings.

The winter was barely over when I developed some strange illness. My lips, tongue, palate and the entire inside of my mouth were covered by sore blisters, so that I couldn't swallow anything without pain. I was feverish, I lay in a silence not penetrated by a voice all day long. My wife came home in the evening, she was kind to me, cooked me some porridge and told me about a seminar she'd attended and where they'd commended her paper.

On the third day I got up, dressed and set out to the telephone box. It was a clear and mild morning, and through the deserted street wafted the fragrance of spring flowerbeds.

I got through to my lover.

You're ill? she asked in surprise. I was afraid you'd made a clean breast of everything again and you weren't allowed to see me any more.

She wanted to know how much my mouth hurt, what I did all day when I couldn't do anything, if I was thinking of her. As for her, she'd received a commission, at least she'd be able to complete it undisturbed. She had such a chunk of stone at her studio she couldn't even move it, that stone was almost like me, except that with the stone a girlfriend could give her a hand. She went on for a while to talk about her rocky burden, i.e. about me. Suddenly she was afraid I might catch cold in the box, promised to write me a letter and ordered me back to bed.

Her voice was coming to me softly from a distance, her lips settled lightly on my aching mouth, her tongue was touching my sick tongue, and I was shaken by shivers. I wanted to be with her, to watch her hammering into her heavy stone, to let myself be lulled to sleep by those sounds, to wake up and find her close to me.

Two days later a small package was delivered. On top of it was a letter and a bag of herbs she'd dried herself. Camomile, horehound and silverweed, our heads in the dry grass, we were lying in a meadow and making love. I was to brew it all up together and gargle with it, but, even more important, I should find peace within myself, so my soul could be in harmony with my body. Although illnesses were seated in the body they really came from the soul, which writhed in spasms unless one learned to listen to it and enclose and restrain it by one's actions.

I read the letter all the way through, and only then freed a little figure from a protective wrapping of rags. She'd made it for me, two naked bodies leaning against a tree. A man and a woman, Adam and Eve, Eve not ashamed of her nakedness and not offering Adam the fruit of the tree of knowledge. The serpent was also missing. It wasn't Adam and Eve, it was the two of us in the Garden of Eden which our love had unlocked for us.

When I was well again she explained to me: I have seven bodies, and the person who, even only once, gets through to the innermost one will trap me and I'll belong to him totally and always.

I asked: What does that innermost body look like?

You're right, that isn't a body any longer, that's the last shell of the soul. It's thin and transparent.

In this way she wanted to tell me about the fragility of that shell. So what is it like inside?

When I was fourteen the first atomic bomb was dropped on the earth. Some time later I read the book of a Hiroshima doctor who'd experienced the explosion: factually and dispassionately he described the destruction which had befallen the city and its people, but understandably enough he didn't mention any souls. But I was pondering then about what happened to the human soul at the epicentre of an atomic explosion. Even if the soul was non-corporeal, even if it was only space enveloped by matter, even if it was of an entirely different nature, could it really survive that heat? Who could visualise a soul at the centre of the sun or some other star?

You're always racking your brain with pointless questions. What's the use of it?

Tell me at least what you think happens to a soul which cannot stand the pressure of the world around it and bursts or shatters into fragments which no one can ever bring together again?

Don't worry, it doesn't perish. Maybe a new soul springs from each fragment, like a tree from a seed. Or else all the fragments combine together again in another time, in another life, coming together like droplets in a fog. Better ask what you should do so the souls around you don't perish.

I'm asking that one too.

Better still, don't ask any more questions. Try to be a little less clever. Be with me now and don't think of anything at all!

She told me about the Kampucheans, who danced, sang and didn't worry about the future. They knew that God was near, but they didn't ponder about him. And look at the things they managed to create even in ancient times! She tries to give me an idea of the hundreds of sculptures lining the road to the Victory Arch at Angkor Tham, she even picks up a pencil and from memory draws the likeness of a leper king, his face full of contentment.

A pity, she regretted, you weren't there with me. But one day we'll go there together.

I don't know how we can go anywhere; it's ten years since they took my passport away.

Don't be so practical!

Even if I'm not, the men at the frontier will be.

Apply for a passport then. Surely we must go somewhere together someday. There should be a sea there and warmth, so we can stay together all the time.

I'll apply for a passport so we can travel to Kampuchea

together, where the people are happy and carefree, where we'd be so far away that no voice other than hers would reach me.

No voice reaches me anyway.

All around me fog is spreading, what is left of the world loses its outlines. Now and then the fog curtain tears and we catch a glimpse of the landscape bathed in a reddish evening light, in a heavy rain the surface under the windows of the little hotel is ruffled and across the street gleams a plump baroque turret, from a fresco washed pale by time an interceding Holy Virgin is smiling at us, maybe we shan't be altogether damned, the beeches are donning fresh greenery before our eyes, they turn golden, and red, a leaf floats downwards and we sink down with it, we're lying in the grass, we're lying in the moss and in the sand, above our heads flocks of migratory birds are flying, as well as clouds and time, only time stops still for an instant in repeated cries; and we light the gas stove because it is cold in the room, we move the bed right up against its hot body, in our brief intervals we tell one another about the days when we didn't know each other, about yesterday, about a girlfriend's exhibition, about our meetings and dreams, we talk about Diane Arbus's photographs and her ugly world, about ugliness in art, about Hesse's *Steppenwolf* and our hidden potentials, about ancient Mexican art and its influence on Henry Moore, and of course about Zadkin and Giacometti, about Camus and Tsvetayeva, about my book of short stories and about books by my friends which I had lent her in manuscript, we fry bits of meat in the only pan, we eat together at the low table, we drink red wine, while the snowflakes swirl outside the window. In the room there is a fragrance of clay, paint and her breath. In the evening we go out to the little park on Kampa island, we still can't tear ourselves away from each other, we kiss on the swept path under the bare trees. A little old woman with the head of a crow, as if modelled by her fingers, croaks at us: That's a fine thing, that's a fine thing! Adding something about our age and we should be ashamed!

And all the time I have my work, there are people in the world whom until quite recently I wanted to see, our daughter Beta wants to draw my portrait, our son Peter has invited me to a concert, my wife has at last found a decent job, but I have no time to celebrate it.

Beta experiences her first love, she is experiencing her second love, a drug addict who adores Pink Floyd and sniffs toluene. My wife is alarmed and asks me to intervene somehow. I talk with my daughter until late at night, she understands everything, she agrees with me, she'll soon find another love, but I still have the same one, so am I also an addict? I inhale that mist, my blood absorbs those intoxicating droplets which dull my reason and willpower. I see nothing before me or around me, I see only her, I live only for the present moment. Am I to rejoice at the gift that's been granted to me or am I to despair at my weakness, at being unable to resist the passion which is corroding me?

I can't make up my mind, I can't renounce my passion, nor can I draw the consequences from it. I cannot depart altogether nor arrive altogether, I am unable to live in truth. I've hedged myself in with excuses, I'm having every sentence I utter examined by a guard dog. I've accommodated a whole pack of them within me. I pick my way between them, their barking at times deafens me and their soundless footfall frightens me in my dreams. One of these days one of them will approach me from behind and sink his fangs in my throat and I shan't even cry out, I'll remain mute forever, as I deserve to be.

How long can I stand it, how long can it last?

Till death, my darling!

You really believe that?

Or till I leave you because you never make up your mind to do anything. She starts crying. She is crying because I cannot make up my mind, because I am too circumspect, because I put principles above love, because I am shuttered against life like a stone, even more shuttered because a stone can be worked, a stone can be turned into a shape, she is crying because I am harder than if I were made of stone, I'm playing a cruel game with her and I torture her as I have never tortured anyone before, she is crying because I am good, because I stay with her as no one before managed to, she is crying because everything in her life is turning into suffering.

I know that she has surrendered herself to my mercy, and I am terrified by the thought that I might disappoint her.

The spring sun is shining on the little terrace under the wooden steps, from the washing line comes the smell of nappies and over the wall of the house opposite we can see the monastery roof with its ornament of a maple-wood halo.

Daria is sitting alongside me in a freshly-ironed white blouse and a chocolate-coloured velvet skirt, she's dressed up because this evening we're going to a concert. She seems to me so beautiful, so precious, as if I'd gone back forty years or so and gazed in adoration at my mother. Except we're getting up, climbing a few steps, and she is stepping out of her clothes and her exalted untouchability and stepping into my embrace, and I feel as if the thin walls of my veins are bursting from the barely tolerable surge of delight.

We're lying next to each other in the descending night. Somewhere out of sight beyond the palace and the river the musicians are getting ready for a Beethoven concerto.

What would you like most of all?

I know what I am expected to reply but I ask: Now or altogether?

Now and altogether, if there's any difference.

To stay here with you, I answer, to stay with you now.

And altogether?

I'd like to know what happens to the soul.

You'd really like to know that?

I embrace her. She presses herself against me and whispers: You always want to know so much, my darling, do you always have to find out something or other?

It was you who asked.

Be glad that there are things which can't be known – only surmised.

She holds me so tight I groan. What do you surmise?

Don't worry, the soul doesn't perish, somehow it lives on.

In another body?

Why in a body at all? I see your soul as a pillar. It looks stony but it's made of fire and wind. And it towers so high that from down on the ground you can't see the top of it. And up there it is smiling.

That pillar?

Your soul, darling. Because you have a smile inside you, even if you think you've only got grief, and that's why I feel good with you. Then she asks: Have you applied for a passport?

In the woods liverwort and anemones are out again, no one but us ever goes there. She makes love to me in a way that blots out my reason. She wants to know: Don't you feel good with me?

I do feel good with you. I've never known anything like it before.

But you're not entirely with me. And she asks: How can you live like that?

Like what?

So incompletely, so divided.

She is waiting for a sign that I've made up my mind at last, but there is no sign. She asks: Are you going away with me somewhere in the summer?

How can I arrange things so that I can go away with her? What lie can I invent? I am gripped by cold fear.

Are you capable of doing anything for me at all?

I'll apply for a passport but I am tired. Worn down by love-making and by love and by reproaches, by longing and by my own indecision, worn down by my ceaseless escapes, the passion of my lover and the meek trust of my wife.

I can scarcely believe it, I am given a passport, the wild roses are beginning to bloom. Far and wide, no one lies down under them. The petals are soundlessly floating down on our naked bodies and bees are buzzing above us. She asks: Are you also feeling happy, darling?

I am feeling happy with her, and she whispers: Are you going away with me to the sea in the summer?

It has been calculated that if all those murdered in Kampuchea were stacked up on a pyre with a one-hundred-metre base that pyre would be taller than the country's highest mountain.

I have found another remark by Kafka on the mission of literature: What we need, he wrote, are books which strike us like the most painful misfortune, like the death of someone we loved more than ourselves, books which would make us feel that we've been driven out into the forest far from another human being, like suicide. A book must be an axe for the frozen sea within us.

With his honesty Kafka could write only about what he had himself experienced. He recorded his lonely road into the depths. He descended as far as anyone could descend, and down there came the end, the end of his road and of his writings. He was unable to sever himself from his father, nor did he bring himself to complete adult love – that was his abyss. At its bottom he saw a person he loved, and as he descended that person's image drew closer and at the same time began to disappear in the dark, and when he was close enough to reach out with his hand he had no breath left and was engulfed by unconsciousness.

His abyss, however, is like the abyss into which we all descend or into which, at least, we gaze with curiosity or fear. We can see in it a reflection of our own destinies, of ourselves endeavouring in vain to reach adulthood, in vain reaching out to another being and to the one who is above us. Except that I don't know if we are still capable of descending to any depth, whether we are not so pampered or so spoiled that we can no longer recognise honesty when we see it and stand before it in admiration, whether instead we are not trying to diminish it, to question it and to adapt it to our own ideas. Honesty then becomes for us an inability to live or even a source of mental disorder, courage becomes pitiable weakness. Only a weak person, one incapable of living according to our ideas and demands, seems acceptable and comprehensible to us. Indeed, we pity him for his loneliness, his vulnerability or his sick body. For the way he suffered, for being, compared to us, unhappy. We do not even perceive what that painful descent into the depths brings. The lonely diver sees in one instant what most of us who pity him don't see in a whole lifetime.

The highest mountain in Kampuchea is in the Kardamon range not far from Phnom Penh and is called Ka-kup. It is covered in primeval forest and is 1,744 metres high. Our aircraft struck the treetops and crashed into the undergrowth. We managed to jump out of the split fuselage before it caught fire. We tore our way through the dense vegetation and she was looking for a spot where we could lie down safe from snakes and scorpions. But whenever she found one, whenever she found a cleared spot, it was full of dead bodies.

I said: We'll have to find another country for just the two of us to be together.

Just then two soldiers with red tabs on their muddy uniforms emerged from the jungle and one of them said in a language which surprisingly we understood very well: Better find another world.

The two soldiers burst into shrill Khmer laughter, they laughed till they shook, and then they began to shoot at us. At the last moment I realised that in a world where five thousand million people lived, most of them starving, what did anyone care about us two?

By midday we were at the end of our stint. 'Took us a bit longer today,' the foreman said, looking up at the sky which was once more hidden by clouds composed of steam and sulphur dioxide. 'Let me tell you, there are months when I have people coming and going like in a taproom, everybody just out for quick money, and the streets like a pigsty. Everything has to have its – you know. But you lot, hats off! They've noticed it even at the office. The other day they went through my whole district without finding a single fault. Only that bloody castrated bastard's running us down wherever he can.'

We were walking along in a disorderly column – on one side residential blocks, on the other a little park with massive maples and lime trees, from whose tops every gust of wind brought down a shower of tired leaves. The youngster stopped and looked into the park, perhaps walking up the slight hill had tired him or else he'd caught sight of someone he knew on the gravel path, or else he needed to let his eyes linger on something at least a little way above the ground:

> And it may happen to a sweeper
> as he waves
> his dirty broom
> about without a hope
> among the dusty ruins
> of a wasteful colonial exhibition
> that he halts amazed
> before a remarkable statue
> of dried leaves and blooms . . .

These verses suddenly came to my mind – as well as the voice of the man who'd spoken them.

'There's money to be made in other places too,' Mrs Venus said. 'I know a fellow got into a gang that collects the mess in trucks in Slivenec. After all, they shift it from there by the cartload!'

'Don't tell me that,' the foreman got excited. 'You wouldn't stand a chance there, it's the private preserve of the Demeter gang and nobody can winkle that lot out, not even the public prosecutor.'

In the crowded bar at the bottom of the street we were lucky enough to find room at a table from which a gang of bricklayers from a nearby building site was just getting up. Our foreman jerked his head towards them: 'My girl's been waiting for a flat for seven years, and she was told at the co-op she'd have to wait at least another seven years. So when I see those pissed malingerers I feel like kicking their teeth in. And who knocked you about like this?' He turned to Mrs Venus. 'Don't you tell me you slipped on the stairs!'

'But I did,' said Venus in a voice I still admired. 'Now and again my legs give way under me.'

'If I was you, Zoulová, I wouldn't stand for it. You go to the centre,' the foreman advised her, 'get them to confirm it and then go and report it as grievous bodily harm. They'll throw the book at him, so much he'll never be able to pay up in full.'

'But it was my brother-in-law!' Mrs Venus objected.

'Which one?'

'The one from Ostrava, of course, the brother of my Joe that died a couple of years ago. Always turns up at my place like this. Once a year.'

'Still working down the mines?' the foreman wanted to know.

'That's what it was all about,' Venus explained. 'He's just as stupid as Joe was. His lungs are all shot to hell, full of coal dust. And the same doctor, that murderer that did my Joe in, told him he couldn't send him to a disabled home, they wouldn't authorise that, and if he wrote down what the matter really was with him they'd put him on surface jobs where he'd be cleaning lamps for bugger-all, and then he could whistle for his pension. Exactly how that murderer chatted up my Joe. In another year, he promised him, we'll put you straight into a disabled centre, that's what that shit promised him when the poor bugger couldn't even walk up a few steps. Six months later he was past caring whether he was declared disabled or not. I told my brother-in-law: Vince, look at what happened to Joe. Are you stupid or what? What bloody use is money to you when you're pushing up the daisies? That made him angry. So I said to him: You're all alike, you men, brave enough to hit a woman all right, but when it comes to standing up to the deputy you'd sooner shit yourself!'

'Men aren't all alike,' the foreman protested.

'Don't tell me that! How long were you in the army?'

'Twenty-five years.' There was a ring of pride in the foreman's voice.

'And how often were you in action?'

'No one to fight,' the foreman said dryly.

'Who told you that?'

'A soldier fights when he's ordered to,' he told her. 'If there's no order he can do bugger-all.'

'Women would fight even without an order,' Venus snapped. 'Why d'you think they won't give women weapons? And what are you grinning about?' She turned on me. 'No doubt you were a real Ho Chi Minh!'

'Now watch your tongue, Zoulová!' the foreman admonished her. 'You know that I've always stood by you people. There'll soon be an opportunity for you to realise it.' We all of us knew that the post of radio dispatcher was about to be vacant at the office and that the foreman was firmly counting on getting it. 'You'll get tired of wielding that broom one day.'

'So what,' Mrs Venus snapped. 'I can just see you letting me drive a carriage with golden wheels!'

I noticed that the captain was enjoying the argument.

The crazy inventor had called on me once more at the newspaper office. That was when foreign soldiers were trampling through Prague. He sat down on a chair. The recent events had led him to concern himself once again with his soot solution. He'd changed the proportions of his seven solvents and added two catalysts. Now he was certain of the result. The ice would turn to water, to whole oceans of water. Did I understand the consequences? Did I realise which countries would be flooded if the ocean levels rose?

My first thought was The Netherlands, but he produced from his pocket a map of Europe on which he'd carefully cross-hatched the territory which would disappear under the sea. True, parts of The Netherlands and the Jutland peninsula would be affected, but worst affected of all would be the lowlands in the east, complete with all their gigantic cities.

I conjured up a vision of only the head of the Bronze Horseman showing above the waves, and even that was slowly disappearing:

> 'Here cut' – so Nature gives command –
> 'your window through on Europe; stand
> firm-footed by the sea, unchanging!'

Ay, ships of every flag shall come
by waters they had never swum
and we shall revel, freely ranging.

'Do you understand now?' he asked, folding his hands as if in prayer.

A siege! The wicked waves, attacking
climb thief-like through the windows; backing
the boats stern-foremost, smite the glass,
trays with their soaking wrappage pass;
and timbers, roofs, and huts all shattered,
the wares of thrifty traders scattered,
and the pale beggars' chattels small,
bridges swept off beneath the squall,
coffins from sodden graveyards – all
swim in the streets!

I understood. His mind may have been disturbed, but there burned within him the flame which the rest of us, from cunning or from common-sense, were stifling.

I had always hoped that life's flame would burn pure within me. To live and at the same time have darkness within one, to live and exhale death, what point would there be in that?

But what kind of flame had there been burning within me these past few years? I couldn't answer my question, I'd lost my judgement. Everything that had surrounded me in the past, everything that had been significant and had filled me with joy or sorrow, had gone flat and like a strip of faded material now drifted at my feet.

In the evenings my son would play to himself the songs of his favourite singers. The words of these songs persistently and vehemently protested against the unhappy state of our society. He was clinging to protest, which was one-sided, as though he wanted subconsciously to make up for the one-sided way in which I had turned my back on any injustices which might keep me from my private region of bliss.

My daughter was now often coming home late, smelling of wine and cigarette smoke and talking cynically about love. Was she not finding the love she was seeking because I had found it, or, on the contrary, because she was seeking it where I remained blind?

My wife went regularly to her psychoanalyst. She too was descending into her depths, looking about herself there, confident that she was accompanied by the light of a wise guide, and she arrived at unexpected conclusions about herself and about me, about her relationship with her mother and about my relationship with mine. She was pleased that she had at last learnt to understand herself and therefore to improve herself. She felt sorry that I didn't wish to do something similar, that I didn't long for self-understanding, that I persisted in erroneous ideas about myself.

Those I love know how I should run my life, they know what's right in life, they know their hierarchy of values, only I blunder about in uncertainty.

I did not doubt that my wife had long surpassed me with her knowledge of the hidden mysteries of the soul and the motivations of human passions and emotions. She was developing an interest in ancient myths, she studied books on the customs and ceremonies of savages whose native countries she'd never seen and most probably never would see, and she tried to convince me that what people, including we two, were lacking was ritual. For years we hadn't courted one another much, and as a result a mundane element had invaded our relationship. She asked me if she might read part of her study on sacrifice and self-sacrifice to me, and I told her I'd be glad to listen to it. I lay down on the couch, my head next to the armchair she was sitting in, and tried to listen to her attentively, but I was overcome by fatigue and the sense of the words drifted away. Now and again I looked up at her, at my wife, with whom I'd lived and not lived for nearly twenty-five years. I was aware of her keen involvement and I tried to catch the meaning of at least some of the sentences. At one point she looked up from her paper and asked anxiously if she wasn't boring me, and I replied hastily: No, the problem of sacrificial lambs interested me – if only because of my own childhood experiences – as did the sacrificial rites of the Ndembas and the Indian Khonds, although I was amazed by the amount of brutality or sadism that was hidden beneath human nature. She seemed satisfied and continued with her reading, her fingers having first tenderly touched my head. I was suddenly conscious of her closeness and I felt depressed by not being able to give her my full concentration and to stay with her. I felt guilty for my inattention. It was a childish sense of guilt: my mother was bending down over me lovingly while I, in order to conceal my feelings, pretended not to notice, pretended to be asleep. I felt tenderness towards her and also regret that I'd let her talk for so long, that I'd let her address me for so long while I wasn't listening. I would have liked to embrace her and tell her everything that was troubling me: Forgive me and stay with me like this always! And to call on myself: Stay with her, after all she's your wife. And on my soul: Come to rest! And to ask the other woman: Let me go without anger and without a sense of wrong. And aloud I said: You really did a good job there. And she smiled at me with her old girlish smile.

'I once got on a ship that was skippered by a woman,' the captain reminisced. 'In the Baltic it was.'

'What was her name?' the foreman wanted to know.

'The woman's? I don't know. The ship's name was the *Dolphin*, she belonged to the fishing combine. We had put her engine through sea trials after a general overhaul, so we took her out without cargo, only about six fellows, that woman and myself.'

'She was the only woman with six fellows aboard?' the foreman asked, hoping for a story of erotic entanglements. But the captain had other things to relate. They'd left Warnemünde on a northerly course, then they'd turned east by thirty degrees because otherwise they would have soon found themselves in the Danish port of Gedner. There was a north-westerly blowing and it was raining, visibility was down to about 300 metres. After an hour or so they spotted something floating in the sea. It seemed incredible, fifteen miles offshore, but it was two people, a man and a woman on rubber mattresses, both of them only in swimsuits.

'Carried out by the wind?' asked the youngster.

'I just told you the wind was onshore. They wanted to skidaddle to Denmark. They'd got through the cordon at night, the foul weather helped them.' Whenever he left the realm of his poetry the captain was logical and matter-of-fact.

'As soon as they spotted the ship they paddled away from us like people possessed, but the woman captain ordered the boat to be lowered and had them brought aboard. The poor wretches were frozen stiff, but even so they begged to be left in the water, all they needed now was half a day, but the old woman decided she had to hand them over.'

'What happened to them?' I asked.

'How should I know?' the captain replied. 'If I was those people I'd build myself a boat that no one could keep up with. Except that that sort haven't got a clue about engineering. They just try to swim across: backstroke, breaststroke. And they're never seen again, unless the sea throws them up on the beach, all gnawed.' The captain pushed his cap back and took a swig. No doubt among his designs there was the blueprint of a small submarine driven by compressed air or a propane-butane bottle.

'Well, we none of us have a written guarantee for our lives,' the foreman remarked in an attempt to regain the centre of the stage.

'I wonder they even try it' – the youngster sounded surprised – 'when they must know it's useless.'

'Because they're idiots,' the foreman again intervened. 'Everyone thinks he can make it. Stupid!'

'Maybe they're not the only stupid ones!'

'Who then?' The foreman seemed surprised at my remark.

'If they were allowed to board a ship they wouldn't try that kind of thing.'

'Can't have just anyone boarding a ship and sailing wherever he pleases, can we now?' He turned to the others. 'When I saw they weren't going to let me out I'd sit tight on my arse and wait.'

By a miracle we got a little room with a two-tier bunk in a small brick house at the spot where the neck of the Dar peninsula was narrowest. From the little garden, where blackcurrants were ripening, you could see the surface of the inland sea, above its surface coloured masts and sails, above them seagulls, and above them the sky which, for most of the days we stayed in this normally rainy area, was cloudlessly blue; on the other side, immediately beyond the road, was a gently rising field of wheat. If you climbed up to the nearby ridge you could see the sea proper. We took a brightly-coloured bus to a stop called Three Oaks and walked down a sandy path to the beach, which was as spotlessly clean as everything else here. There we rammed into the ground a few sticks we'd collected which had been leached out and bleached by the sea. On them we spread a piece of yellow material, which was soon covered by small, metallically shiny black beetles. We buried a bottle of lemonade, spread a blanket on the sand and lay down on it. Thus we lay there hours, in immobility and mutual proximity. I had never before been able to stay by the water for even a few hours, I was frightened by the void of laziness. I could not be totally lazy, just as I could not love totally or surrender to work totally, though this last perhaps more than the rest. I always had to escape from the reach of the black pit which I invariably saw before me as soon as I was quietly relaxing anywhere, but here I saw only the sea, only the sky, only her loving features. Time here was slowed down. Sometimes during its retarded flow I read Kierkegaard or the story of Adrian Leverkühn as the ageing Thomas Mann had invented it and was telling it at the same slow and leisurely pace. Sometimes I read to her aloud and she listened with the concentration of a person who did everything she did in life with total completeness. But when, in that sun-scorched wasteland, where countless naked bodies were indulging in total inactivity, I read to her that action and decision in our – that is Kierkegaard's – age were just as rare as the intoxication with danger felt by someone swimming in shallow water, so the rule that a man stands or falls with his action no longer applies, I observed in her concentration an almost excessively attentive and enthusiastic agreement, and I realised that these sentences I was reading told against me, that I was merely continuing her silent, ceaseless and scarcely disguised evidence for the prosecution. We argued about the philosopher's theses, pretending that we were not talking about ourselves or about our conflict. We argued until the moment when I shook the sand grains out of my book and put it back in my bag. Then we just lay, our naked bodies touching each other, and gazed on the white crests of the waves which managed to touch each other without causing each other pleasure and pain. Not until evening did we get up, climb the sand dune along the line of dustbins towering there, metallic, among the flowering wild roses, and return to the road.

The evenings were long northern evenings. When we'd eaten we went back down to the beach, which by then was deserted. She sat down cross-legged on a rock, gazing at the seemingly cooling sun, while I looked at the dark surface of the water, noticing the menacing cordon of ships on the distant horizon, a cordon designed to block even here the freest and most unfettered area of water, and I also looked at her sitting there statue-like, perceiving how in the silence of the sea, in this marine solitude, she was receding, changing into an unfamiliar being that lived in inaccessible regions, and I couldn't decide if I was feeling sadness or relief.

We also borrowed bikes and set out early in the morning, not along the road but along sandy paths, along the footpaths which intertwined on the narrow ridge which rises above the sea.

The waves roar and the wind howls, we stop to embrace, to sit down and look across to the distant shores. Then we continue in a westerly direction and our bikes sink so deep into the sand that we have to carry them. Before us lies a dark green expanse of heather, we turn into it; the soil here is black, our path is blocked by an ever thicker tangle of roots, the air is full of whining mosquitoes, our little path has almost disappeared, we don't know where we are, whether to turn back or go on, path or no path. Our bikes are useless now, we wheel them along, I try to discover the way ahead while she sees the shapes of spirits in the twisting branches and hears the whispering of the dead in the sighing of the wind, the last breaths of suicides and the vain shouts of the drowning, there is a wizard crouching in the undergrowth whose body lacks a soul, and over the treetops the carrion crows circle, soundless and dark. We circumvent pools from which gas bubbles rise up and eventually reach the road. Now she is riding in front of me, her hair, which would be almost grey by now if she didn't give it a blonde rinse, shines around her head. We are approaching Bad Müritz, where half a century ago our fellow countryman, the unsuccessful lover Franz Kafka, was preparing for his fall into the black pit, where his brittle soul concurred with his sick lungs that they would give up the exhausting struggle.

We are riding through the streets from which they haven't yet driven out the *fin de siècle* spirit as they have done so thoroughly from our native city, thirstily we drink beer at a pavement stall, hungrily we sit down at a battered table in a shabby café. We sit opposite each other, far from our near and dear ones, in a strange café in a strange town, we eat cakes, we are silent, we look at one another, and I can see in her eyes a devotion I didn't believe I'd ever find anywhere, I can feel it invading me deeply, pervading me, settling into every cell of my body. I don't know how or when I'll end my struggle, but at that moment my soul is still capable of rising up, of making one last flight to where it belongs, to the place of its longings, to the regions of blissful paralysis from the proximity of a loved being; after that it will fly out to this battered and by now deserted little table, for a last time briefly smile with sudden relief, and then accept its fate.

Later we stand in the cathedral of Güstrow before Barlach's rising angel. I can see my lover going rigid, rising up to those exalted shapes, moving away from me into heights which I cannot conceive, which my vision cannot reach, where only angels and perhaps the souls of great artists reside. I move away, unnoticed, and sit down in a pew in a corner of the cathedral and wait for her to come back to me.

Nach der Rede des Führers am Tage der Deutschen Kunst in München haben die zuständigen Stellen nunmehr beschlossen, das von dem Bildhauer Ernst Barlach im Jahre 1926 geschaffene Ehrenmal für die Gefallenen des Weltkriegs aus dem Dom in Güstrow entfernen zu lassen. Die Abnahme wird in den nächsten Tagen erfolgen. Das Ehrenmal soll einen schwebenden Engel darstellen und war schon seit langem ein Gegenstand heftigster Angriffe.

(Following the Führer's speech on the Day of German Art in Munich the appropriate authorities have now decided to remove from the cathedral in Güstrow the memorial created by the sculptor Ernst Barlach in 1926 for the fallen of the World War. The removal will take place during the next few days. The memorial, designed to represent a hovering angel, has long been the object of fierce attacks.)

When eventually she returns to me she has tears in her eyes.

Do you think you could manage an angel like that?

I don't know. I'm probably not sufficiently obsessed – by stone or by wood.

I don't ask her what she is possessed by, I know. But I also suspect that there is a burning ambition in her, at the price of exhaustion if need be, to ensure that those who view her work go rigid.

The next day she walks down to the edge of the beach, where the sand has soaked up the seawater, and her fingers, used to creating shapes out of shapeless matter, there create a sand relief of a creature resembling a winged centaur rather than an angel. That creature has my features, except that perhaps it smiles more in all directions. Small groups of sunbathers gather around her and with admiration watch her work taking shape, but she pretends not to notice them, she only wants to know if I like her sand sculpture.

I like it and it's like me, I answer, in order to amuse her with my pun. My only regret is that this strange creature with my face will not survive the next tide.

What does it matter? Tomorrow, if we feel like it, we'll make something different. At least we aren't burdening the world with another creation. This is something we are both aware of: that the world is groaning, choking with a multitude of creations, that it is buried by objects and strangled by ideas which all pretend to be necessary, useful or beautiful and therefore lay claim to perpetual endurance.

We don't need either objects or creations, she says lovingly, for us it is enough to have one another.

We are together while the day ascends, while the night descends, we are so totally together that it saps our strength, that the fire consumes us, that the heat consumes her till I am alarmed: suppose we are buried in ashes from which we won't rise again?

I have never been as close to anyone, I have never known a person capable of being so close to me, capable of such passion, of such intensity.

Maybe both of us have been gathering strength all our lives for just this moment, for just this meeting, maybe we have gravitated here in our dreams, to this small room, to this coastal spot, where water, sand and sky blend into each other, where time trickles softly and cleanly, this is where unconsciously we have wanted to come at moments of loneliness. And when our bodies are finally exhausted, when only a few last breaths are left of the northern summer's night, when I am about to climb down to my bunk, she begs me not to go yet, to stay with her at least here, and so I persevere in immobility, even though I now long to be alone, so many days of absolute proximity have exhausted me and I am longing for a moment of isolation; in the midst of a strange world into which I was snatched I now long for the undemanding routine of home. But have I got a home left? After all, I'm breaking it up myself. My daughter has left, she is a mother now, and my son is leaving very soon. And as for my wife, even if she smiles at me, where is she really at home? What is left of our love?

My yearning is growing within me, a nonsensical regret because it is backward-facing, a regret that my life, against which I want to rebel just now, is running away.

The other woman is lying by my side. She's asleep. Her breath has gone quieter, her spirit has calmed down. I try to make out her features, I bend down over her, I do not kiss her, I just look at her, at a remote creature whom, despite everything, I have not managed to absorb fully into myself, to accept fully. I climb quietly down and lie on the lower bunk, I gaze into the blackness before me. Outside a tomcat is noisily complaining and the wind is driving a thunderstorm before it. I get up and open the window wide, on the dark sky a soundless flash of lightning now and then lights up the huge plane tree in the garden.

And suddenly I see her – my wife. The lightning illuminates her, she is sitting on a bench, waiting for me. We are walking down a little path in the park, I am pushing a pram whose wheels keep coming off but we haven't got the money to buy a new one, I am pushing it along the Prokop valley.

A nonsensical yearning directed backwards, but what am I to do? There remain in me, rooted, countless days and nights together, from which time has gradually eroded everything that was not solid, leaving behind boulders on an autumnal field, boulders which can't be rolled away, even if I walk around them I can't get rid of them, I only have to turn my head and I see them: towering there like immovable milestones, they regard me like some monstrous stony eyes of the night, motionless, they wait for me to give up everything. I take a few more steps but I can feel their stony stare on my back, my legs are growing heavy, and I come to a halt. I am not going back and I am not going forward, I am standing in a void, I am standing between two fields, at the meeting point of two calls which intersect each other, I am nailed to the cross, how can I move?

And the other woman, the one I've come here with, the one I followed from weakness, from longing, from loneliness, from mental confusion, from passion, from prodigality, from the hope that I might forget my mortality for a while, now complains about my immobility, she curses it and my wife, instead of cursing me.

So here I stand, she is asleep behind me while I am waiting by the window for my wife to look up and see me. But she doesn't see me. Suddenly I am conscious that between us lie mountains and rivers, life and death, betrayal and lies, years of unfulfilled longing and vain hopes. I see my wife beginning to tremble like an image on the surface of water when the first raindrop strikes it, in a sudden surge of longing I reach out towards the window to hold her, to save her, to draw her to me from that distance, but it is in vain, the rain is getting heavier, and I become aware of the other woman looking at me from behind. What are you doing, dearest, why aren't you asleep?

I'm just shutting the window, I answer, it's beginning to rain.

I got up from the table simultaneously with Mr Rada. No sooner were we out in the street than he could no longer restrain himself from telling me what, clearly, he'd wanted to keep from the others. 'I got back from Svatá Hora yesterday. Have you heard about it?'

The fact that there had been a great pilgrimage and rally of believers had been mentioned even in our jerkish press, probably to enable the rally of believers to be portrayed as a peace festival.

'It was fantastic,' he said joyfully. Evidently he'd brought back from there the little book from which he'd read a passage to me that afternoon, or at least a taste or enthusiasm for reading from it, if necessary in the street.

We usually went together to draw our pay. I told him what paper I used to work on. I didn't mention the books I'd written. He in turn confessed to me that all his life he'd had to do something other than what he wished to do. Although he'd studied to be a priest he'd worked as a miner, a boilerman, a storeman, a stage-hand and even a lorry driver. Now, in order to help his mother, he was making some extra money by street-sweeping. What he liked about the job was that it was outdoor work, often indeed among gardens, he was a countryman. He also had a sense of doing something useful. In a city filthy with refuse people might at best find a place to sleep and store their belongings, but never one to establish a home and experience the thrill of belonging to the place, to their neighbours, to God. Today's people were like nomads, he complained, they moved from one home to another, carrying their little household gods with them. They didn't establish ties either with their surroundings or with people, often they didn't even take their children out into the country. They either killed them while still in the womb or they abandoned them in their chase after pleasure. And how were those children going to live when they had known no home? They'd develop into real Huns, they'd move through the world and turn it upside down.

But he didn't complain about his own fate. He spoke without bitterness about what had happened to him.

'There were at least thirty thousand of us there, mostly young people.' He sounded pleased, as if he'd quite forgotten his own gloomy prophecies.

At night they had sat in front of the church and in the surrounding meadows, passing the time in prayer and singing. 'Holy Wenceslas, prince of the Czech realm' – the hymn imploring the patron saint not to let his progeny perish – had been sung three times. If I'd heard what the hymn sounded like under the open sky perhaps I too after all would look forward to better days.

We were advancing down the narrow little street which runs round the park by the ramparts. Mr Rada was engrossed by what he was telling me but I couldn't resist looking up curiously to the window which the artist had turned into his showroom. The hanged man had long disappeared, there had since been a three-legged swan and later a fountain which instead of water spewed dirty sand or ash, letting it rain down on a female head whose plaster features seemed pretty, and down whose cheeks it slid like solidified tears. Now the head and the cloud of ash were gone, there was a manikin sitting on a little horse, made up, as was his steed, of plastic items evidently picked up from a rubbish heap: old containers, motor oil and spray cans, hideous toys for infants and coloured fragments of handbasins and jugs. His open mouth was a red butter-dish, in one of his eyes was a poisonously green

pot of paper paste, Koh-i-Noor brand, and in the other the
dark-haired head of a doll. At first glance it seemed that the
horseman was smiling, a mere toy, a present-day Don Quixote
riding out into the world in armour, but then I noticed the rider
was showing his light polystyrene teeth and I could make out some
bare bones. This was not the noble though confused knight but
rather the fourth horseman of the Apocalypse, as seen by Dürer.
'And behold a pale horse; and his name that sat on him was Death,
and Hell followed with him,' the horseman with the head of the
mouth of hell of Brueghel's 'Dulle Griet'.

What kind of head, I wondered, had that unknown artist? Why
and for whom was he staging these exhibitions in a little street into
which hardly anyone ever strayed? Why was death so often on his
mind?

'These young people,' Mr Rada continued enthusiastically,
'have realised that they've had distorted values imposed on them.
From childhood they've had it drilled into them that hate and
struggle are the levers of history. That there is no superior being
above man! And they came to pray and to listen to the tidings
about Him who is above us and who, despite everything, looks
down on us with love.' It was possible, he concluded, that by the
grace of God a period of rebirth was beginning, a new Christian
age.

He communicated his joy to me and supposed that I would fully
share it with him. It is certainly encouraging to hear that people
are not content with the jerkish notion of happiness. But it
occurred to me, even while he was reading to me about how man
strayed off his path by deifying himself, that man can behave
arrogantly not only by deifying his own ego and proclaiming himself the finest flower of matter and life, but equally when he
proudly believes that he has correctly comprehended the incomprehensible or uttered the unutterable, or when he thinks up
infallible dogmas and with his intellect, which wants to believe,
reaches out into regions before which he should lower his eyes and
stand in silence. We might debate for a long time about when that

fatal shift occurred (if it occurred) which gave rise to the arrogant spirit of our age, and also about how far we must go back to put matters right, but what point would there be in such an argument when there is no return anyway, either in the individual's life or in that of humanity?

'What about your brother?' it occurred to me to ask. 'Was he there with you?'

'Him?' He made a dismissive gesture. 'It might cost him his career!' His own words struck him as too harsh, for he added: 'He might perhaps just walk along in some Buddhist procession.'

Dad had been in hospital for a week. Lately, even before he was laid so low by fever, he'd complain that he couldn't sleep at night. I wanted to know why and he didn't tell me, he made some excuse about some undefined burning pain, an elusive ache. But I suspected that he was suffering from anxiety. His intellect, which all his life had been concerned with quantifiable matter, knew of course that nothing vanished completely from this world, but he also knew that nothing kept its shape and appearance forever, that in this eternal and continuous motion of matter every being must perish just like every machine, even the most perfect, just like the worlds and the galaxies. Dad's intellect realised that everything was subject to that law, so why should the human soul alone be exempt from it? Because the Creator breathed life into it? But surely He too, if he existed at all, was subject to that law. But what sense would there be in a God whose existence and likeness were subject to the same laws as everything else, a God who'd be subject to time?

Dad was standing on the frontier which his intellect was able to visualise, the chilling nocturnal fear of the black pit was crushing him – and I was unable to help him. My dear father, how can I help you, how can I shield you from fear of your downfall? I wasn't even able to burn your fever. I am only your son, I was not given the power to liberate you from darkness, or to liberate anyone.

Dad is lying in a white ward which smells of doctoring and of the sweat of the dying. They have temporarily kept his fever down with antibiotics and they have dulled his fear by antidepressants. They'd given him the middle bed of three. On his left lay a hallucinating fat man who'd been irradiated at night by unknown invaders with hooded faces, on his right a wizened old man, punctured all over by hypodermics, was dying.

Dad was sitting up and welcomed me with a smile. I fed him, then I took out a razor from his bedside table and offered to shave him. He nodded. Lately he'd hardly spoken at all. Maybe he didn't have the strength, or else he didn't know what to tell me. He'd never talked to me about personal matters, nor had he ever spoken about anything abstract. In his businesslike world there was no room for speculations which led too far from firm ground. So what was he to talk to me about now that the firm ground itself was receding from him? And what was I to talk to him about?

The dying man on his right emerged for an instant from his unconscious condition and whispered something with a moan.

'Poor fellow,' Dad said, 'he's all in.'

I helped my father to get up. I took his arm and he moved out into the corridor with small shuffling steps. I should have liked to say something nice and encouraging to him, something meaning-ful.

'I have those dreams nowadays,' he confessed to me. 'They proclaimed a beet-picking drive, and Stalin was personally in charge. I had to join, and I was afraid he'd notice how badly I was working.'

During the Stalin period they had, with the deliberate intention of hitting him where it would hurt most, found him guilty of bad work.

I might have told him that I'd always admired his ability to concentrate on his work, that I knew what outstanding results he'd achieved, but it would have sounded like empty phrases from a premature funeral oration. He knew better than anyone what he had achieved, and he also knew what I thought of his work.

We were approaching the end of the corridor – everything was spotlessly washed and polished, almost as it used to be in our home. We were on our own, although in the distance we could see a young nurse hurrying from one door to another. Only a few days earlier Dad had been irritated by the nurses, who'd seemed to him disobliging. Now he wasn't complaining. He sat down on a chair by an open window, his grey-streaked hair was stuck together by sweat. He looked out through the window, where the birches were shedding their yellow leaves in the gusts of wind, but he was probably unaware of them, he'd just witnessed an explosion at a great height and he was alarmed. 'It's stupid,' he said softly, 'to play about with it. Any piece of machinery will malfunction sometime. If they don't stop it it'll be the end. You ought to tell them!'

'Me?'

'You ought to tell them.' Dad was still looking out of the window, but he was silent again. A plane roared past overhead, it moved on, it didn't crash, it only left an unnecessary white trail of poisonous gases behind.

Had he perhaps just uttered the most important thing he'd intended to say to me? Or did he merely wish to confess a further disappointment of his – that the wonderful engines, which he'd invented and designed all his life, while lifting man off the ground, still did not lead him into the Garden of Bliss but would, more probably, prematurely incinerate him.

I helped him get up and we returned to his ward. I sat him up in his bed, straightened his blanket and told him how well he'd walked. I should have asked him, while there was time, if there was anything else he wanted to tell me, anything he hadn't told me so far, some instruction, advice or message. Was he perhaps leaving a grave behind somewhere that I should visit for him? Or a lonely person whom I should visit? But Dad was certainly not thinking of graves, he regarded it as nonsensical to waste time on the dead, and he wouldn't venture to give me any advice. He'd been disappointed in so many of his expectations, and if there was a woman somewhere whom he had loved and whom he had never mentioned to me, he had clearly decided not to burden me with her name now. He had nothing left to pass on to me.

Maybe I should have been saying to him that, if anything, I was finding some hope in his disappointments, because he'd been misled only by a self-assured intellect which thought it knew everything and which refused to leave any room for the inexplicable, that is for God, eternity or redemption. Would he even understand me, could he still hear me?

I noticed that his chin had dropped on his chest and that he had slipped down on his side. I slackened the screw behind his bedhead and brought the bed down into the horizontal position. Dad didn't wake up as I laid him down, he didn't even open his eyes when I stroked his forehead.

When I got home a young man was waiting for me who, by coincidence, had just arrived from a town near Svatá Hora. About two years ago I'd given a reading of some of my short stories to a few friends of his at his place. Since then he'd turned up occasionally for a chat about literature. He was always well-groomed, his fair hair looked as if it had just been waved with curling tongs and in his grey eyes there was some painful anxiety as if he'd taken on more of life's burdens and responsibilities than he could bear. He was interested in Kierkegaard, Kafka and Joyce, as well as in the cinema and in art. In one of the stories I'd read that evening there was a mention of Hegedušić; after I'd finished he told me that there was a short film available in our country about him. I was surprised to find a young man, who worked in the mines near Svatá Hora, being interested in a Yugoslav painter. He'd now arrived suspiciously soon after the famous pilgrimage, but he made no mention of it, which reassured me. He'd come to get my advice about his future. He'd decided he wouldn't stay in the mines any longer. He'd find some unskilled job and would try to study aesthetics, art history or literature by correspondence. The work he was doing, he explained to me, made no sense. The people among whom he moved disgusted him. If only he knew what people he'd have to move among if he succeeded in getting where he wanted to go! But I don't like imposing my dislikes on others. I merely dug out some recent article by a leading jerkish official who'd been appointed to a university chair to ensure the oblivion of all literature.

From that article I read him just a few introductory sentences on communism, which had become the highest form of freedom of the individual and the human race, and in consequence provided the writer with an unprecedented scope, whereas in the USA, that bastion of unfreedom, the greatest artists, such as Charlie Chaplin, had to escape.

My visitor smiled. He considers it more acceptable to have to listen, voluntarily and for no pay, to jerkish babbling than to destroy and pollute the landscape for good pay, to mine the ore from which others would produce an explosive device capable of turning everything into flames.

What stands at the beginning and what at the end? The word or fire, babbling or explosion?

Speaking of explosions, my visitor was reminded that in his little town some unknown persons recently blew up the monument of the 'workers' president'. The president had died more than thirty years ago, my visitor does not remember him. All he knows about him is that he brought upon us all that 'highest form of freedom of the individual and the human race', and also that, in its name, he had masses of innocent people liquidated, including his own friends and comrades. My visitor wanted to hear how I felt about the destruction of monuments. It is my impression that people don't take any notice of monuments, especially the new ones, or if they do there is nothing about those statues that could impress them. After all, what appeal can one expect of shaft-boots, overcoats, trousers and briefcases, with on the top, accounting for less than one-sixth of the whole, a face behind which we detect neither spirit nor soul? What I mind about the monuments of officially proclaimed giants is that they are ugly and mean, in other words that they disfigure their surroundings. But then it would be difficult to imagine different ones, considering whom they have to represent and given the abilities of the artists from whom these statues are commissioned for a fat fee. Besides, there are so many things disfiguring this world! If we were to destroy them all, where should we stop? To destroy is easier than to create, and that is why so many people are ready to demonstrate against what they reject. But what would they say if one asked them what they wanted instead?

The young man nodded. He hoped his studies would help him find what to aim for himself. He apologised briefly for having kept me up so late and vanished into the night.

The Buddhists have their own vision of the apocalypse. Once all our good deeds, love or renunciation no longer offset our crimes, the equilibrium between good and evil in the universe is upset. Then snakes, crocodiles, dragons and many-headed monsters will emerge from all the openings in the earth and from the waters, breathing fire and devouring mankind. This will restore the disturbed equilibrium, and harmony of silence and nothingness will reign once more.

Night and silence and nothingness. In the sleeping city distant people and near ones, friends and strangers are all swallowed up by darkness. Where in all this darkness have we lost our God?

The questioning intellect normally penetrates into the depths of the individual, the world and the universe until it encounters the boundary beyond which mystery begins. There it either stops or else rushes on, failing to realise, or reluctant to realise, that it calls out its questions into the void.

In his questioning Kafka stopped at the very first step, at himself, because even here he'd entered an impenetrable depth. In a world in which the intellect predominates more and more, the intellect which believes that it knows everything about the world and even more about itself, Kafka rediscovered the mysterious.

Unexpectedly the telephone rang. I ran out to the hall, lifted the receiver and identified myself, but there was silence at the other end. It was listening to me, silently. I replaced the receiver and lifted it again. The silence had gone, the dialling tone was buzzing.

That was you?

You aren't angry, are you, darling? Were you asleep? I'm here on my own. I was lying in bed, reading, and suddenly I thought this was nonsense: to lie here and read about another person's life. I'm sad. Aren't you?

Just now?

Just now . . . And altogether. I do something and then it hits me: why am I doing it, and for whom? Now I'm lying here, everything is quiet, but why should I be lying here? I don't need any rest when tomorrow I won't be alive anyway. You assured me that you were happy when you were with me, that you'd never experienced anything so complete. Was that a lie then?

Surely you'd have known if I'd told you a lie at that moment.

So why don't you come? Tell me what has changed, in what way have I changed that you don't even ring me? What wrong did I do to you?

You didn't do me any wrong, but we just couldn't go on. Neither me nor you. It was impossible to carry on that divided life.

And like this one can live? Don't tell me you're living. Tell me, you really believe you're living?

Surely living doesn't only mean making love.

It doesn't? I always thought it meant just that to you. So what, in your opinion, does have any meaning? Eating and sleeping? To botch up some important work, some great piece of art?

What I am trying to say is that one can't indulge in love at any price. Like at the expense of others.

You think that's what we were doing?

You don't think so?

You are asking me? You who were always ready to sacrifice me? As if I weren't a human being at all, as if only she were one. Why don't you say something? You're angry now. Wait, wait a moment, surely you admit that you've always decided against me.

I didn't decide against you, I wasn't free to decide for you.

That didn't worry you in some respects.

It worried me precisely in the respect you're talking about.

You're making excuses, you've always only made excuses. You

know very well that you never gave me a chance.

A chance of what? Weren't we together enough?

You were never only with me. Not even a week. Not even a day! You were never with me except secretly. Even by the sea . . .

Don't cry!

And I believed you. I thought you loved me and would find some way for us to remain together. At least for a time.

I did love you. But there was no way round. Surely people aren't things which you can move to another place when they seem to have served their purpose. I could only either remain here or join you.

You're so noble about other people. But you calmly moved me as far away as possible when I'd served my purpose. Wait, wait, tell me one more thing: are you happy at least? Don't you regret anything? Why aren't you saying anything? If you've no regrets about me don't you at least have any about yourself?

You think I should have regrets about myself?

Surely it's sad if a person has loved somebody and then loses him.

I know, but a person can lose something worse.

What is there that's worse for a person to lose?

Perhaps his soul.

Your soul? You lost your soul with me? You shouldn't have said that! What do you know about the soul? You're just a pack of excuses!

III

◆

The morning rises from the autumnal mists and the sky slowly turns blue. On the far bank of the river, ever since dawn, there has been a rapid procession of cars escaping for the weekend from the polluted city. Over breakfast I'd read a poem in the paper by the leading author writing in jerkish:

> *Chain of Hands*
> Who knows who knows
> where beauty is born
> where happiness seeks us
> why love trusts us
>
> People people
> maybe that day is dawning
> when children may play
> everywhere is white peace
>
> People people
> let's be ever vigilant
> they who sow the wind
> must reap the storm
>
> People people
> we're but a chain of hands
> we're but the music of dreams
> we're but the beauty of deeds

For this poem of sixty-nine words, including the title, the author needed a mere thirty-seven jerkish terms and no idea at all, no feeling or image. The substantives – beauty, happiness, love, peace, people, children – are of course interchangeable, the sense or nonsense of the rambling remains unchanged. The obligatory call for hatred of the unworthy and for love of the worthy strikes one by its clichés, even if one allows for the limited scope of the jerkish language. It's almost as if the author was afraid that among the chimpanzees there might after all be one individual who would not understand him.

Anyone strong enough to read the poem attentively will realise that for a jerkish poet even a vocabulary of 225 words is needlessly large.

On the far side of the river – you have only to cross the bridge – are rocks and woods. We used to go for walks there with the children, now someone said they'd established some huge depot there. My wife agrees that we should set out in that direction, she is happy that we're going on an excursion.

Under the bridge gypsies are playing football, the beds of a nursery patch look like an oriental carpet. My wife is walking ahead, with an energetic step. Her fears have left her, hope has returned to her, hope of a life that can be lived in harmony and love. And I still feel relief at her proximity, relief unblemished by pretence or lies, I am conscious of the lightness of the new day, upon which I am entering full of expectation.

One reason why I like walking in the country is probably that I was never able to do so in my childhood. The first thing I ever wrote in my life – I was eleven at the time and had been in the Terezín fortress ghetto for over a year – was not about love or suffering or my personal fate, but about landscape:

> As we climb up the steep slope of Petřín Hill we feel increasingly like birds rising into the air. And then, at one instant, we turn round. We see before us such a multitude of Little City roofs that we catch our breath and regret that we are not really birds and so can never alight on those roofs or see their secrets from close up . . .

At that time I didn't know yet what I was doing, I had no idea how many books had been written by then, how many minds had spoken in them. I wrote because I was dying from a yearning for freedom, and freedom for me then meant stepping out of my prison, walking through the streets of my native city; I wrote to fortify my hope that outside the fortress walls the world still existed, a world which had seemed to exist then only in dreams and visions.

I still believe that literature has something in common with hope, with a free life outside the fortress walls which, often unnoticed by us, surround us, with which moreover we surround ourselves. I am not greatly attracted to books whose authors merely portray the hopelessness of our existence, despairing of man, of our conditions, despairing over poverty and riches, over the finiteness of life and the transience of feelings. A writer who doesn't know anything else had better keep silent.

Man goes through the landscape, seeking hope and waiting for a miracle, waiting for someone to answer his questions. Some monk, pilgrim, enlightened Buddha, prophet or at least a talking bird, to tell him if he's been endowed with a soul, whose existence would not be cut short even by death, of what matter that soul was woven, what there was above man, what order, what creature or being, in what kind of big bang time had its origin and where it was heading; man passes through the landscape, waiting for an encounter, or at least for a sign, without knowing its nature.

My wife stops, she is waiting for me. I catch up with her, I embrace her. She goes rigid in my embrace, I can feel her trembling.

When I'd met her years ago I was happy that someone was interested in me. She was very young then, she probably didn't understand what I was feeling, or how impatiently I would wait for her, she was regularly late for our dates.

I'd stand on the edge of the little park not far from where she lived, in the shadow of a magnificent plane tree, or in winter under its bare branches, watching the hands of the street clock. Time and again I worried that she wouldn't come, that something had happened to her, that we'd missed one another or that one of us had made a mistake about the time. When eventually she arrived I was so happy she'd come I couldn't bring myself to be angry with her.

No matter where we'd set out for, we felt good. It seemed to me that we were jointly looking for the same signs. For her everything changed into images, as happens to children, savages or the elect among the poets, and I felt buoyed up by her side.

To this day I can feel the joy which pervaded her, her pleasure at everything we met and saw: a little flower whose name she didn't know, or the roof of the distant estate building, or the little feather lost by a bird of prey, and most of all our being close together. And it struck me that our actions, wherever they might seem to aim, were in fact aimed at just this point, at the close proximity of a person who might become a companion. At the bottom of all our hopes lies a yearning for encounter.

Daria was convinced that we belonged together, that we'd merely not known about one another, or that the right time had not yet come for us to meet in the way we'd now met. And she found this belief confirmed in the stars, in her cards, in the prophecies of an old clairvoyant whom she'd sought out on one occasion when, after all, she was overcome by doubts.

She pressed me: Why do you tell lies at home? You're only wronging me, your wife and yourself. She reminded me of Buddha's words. Apparently he said: No one's deed is lost, it comes back to him! I understand those words, I also understand her. She asks me: Why don't you come all the way to me, why do you resist so? Surely no one else can love you as I do.

Suppose we loved one another just because we do have to part all the time and then find each other anew?

She went to Greece with her husband. She was so far away that her voice came to me only as a soft whisper at night, from the region of the stars, her tenderness too was fading over that distance, and I felt easier. As though I were returning from some beautiful exile, descending from mountain heights where I'd felt happy but uneasy. How could I go back to the home that I had needlessly and wilfully left?

I went on holiday with my wife, on the way we stopped at a campsite managed by our son.

We sit together and eat porridge out of billycans, it smells faintly of burnt wood, and in the evening we sing at the campfire. Lída's voice carries above everybody else's, there's tranquillity in it, it drives out everything alien and evil that still clings to my soul. It's raining, the fire is smoking, we huddle under a single rubber coat, we touch as if embracing, and it seems to me that my lies have disappeared somewhere without trace and I'll never return to them. And I wish time would not march on, that it would delay the return of my lover whom, surely, I can't betray either, I can't just chase her away. And somewhere deep down within me something is stirring, and amidst the raindrops I can hear her rapid footsteps, I can see her emerging from the dark and hurrying down the stony path among the olives, among the fig trees, among the umbrella pines, I can see her alone, even though I know that she is not alone. In my mind, however, she lives separated from all other people, with the possible exception of the swarthy villager who pours her wine. From that great distance there comes to me the muted roar of the Minotaur. I duck under the onrush of longing. In how many days will she come back to me, if she comes back to me at all?

The days have now gone, it is only two hours' journey now, no frontier to cross, I could embrace her, provided she comes back to me.

The thought of it pushes everything else out of my mind. I walk down a path and she is coming towards me, we run towards each other, again and again we run towards each other in daylight and in darkness. At night she slips into my bed, we make love like people possessed. She moans and caresses me, I whisper tender words in her ear.

I'll pretend I'm meeting some friends, I'll get into the car and drive off. I don't know with whom I'll find her, or if I'll find her at all, I don't know if I'll make up my mind to knock at the door I've never stood before, the door I know only from her account. I'll arrive at the village which is so remote it hasn't even got a church, I'll leave the car under a tall lime tree and set out at random towards where I suspect her temporary place to be.

And there she is, coming towards me, real and alive, tanned by the southern sun, I know her from afar by her rapid life-hungry step. She recognises me, she raises her hand in greeting but we do not run towards each other, we walk towards each other, and she asks in surprise: You've come to see me, darling? We don't kiss, and she says: I've brought you a stone from Mount Olympus. And she opens her eyes wide, she embraces me with her eyes till I sigh at the thought of ecstasy to come.

We'd walked through the patch of woodland outside the city, there were even mushrooms growing by the footpath, and through the branches we could see the blue sky.

My wife wanted to know whether street-sweeping wasn't depressing me too much.

It certainly would depress me if I had to do it for the rest of my life.

What about the people who actually do it for years on end?

I don't know what to tell her about them. After all, street-sweeping isn't all that different from lots of other jobs which all have one thing in common: they are not inspiring. Sweepers pass their time just like other people, by talking, by reminiscing about better moments in their lives. Maybe they talk in order to rise above what they are doing, but more probably they just talk to make the time pass more pleasantly.

Didn't they look to me somehow marked, outcast or humiliated? I consider my answer. But my wife is asking these questions only so she can tell me about her experiences with her patients, whom circumstances had picked on as sacrificial lambs: as a result they were marked for the rest of their lives, most of them had had their self-assurance broken and their mental health had been affected.

I asked her if something like that must inevitably occur, and my wife said it did. In this manner people satisfied their innate need to find someone onto whom they'd transfer their own guilt. Sacrifices to superior powers were age-old, indeed they used to be performed with solemn rituals, and for their victims men chose those whom their society considered the best or the purest.

The ritual of sacrifice no longer existed today – disregarding the symbolical sacrifice of the body of Christ. What had persisted, however, was the need for sacrifice. People now sought their sacrificial victims in their own midst, and mostly they chose the ones who were the weakest and most vulnerable. They no longer spilled their blood, they merely destroyed their souls. The most frequent victims were the children.

Yesterday, as we were moving down the street of the housing estate, the dustbins were overflowing and everywhere on the pavement and in the road rubbish was blowing about. In front of one of the refuse dumpsters was a large red puddle. It might have been human or animal blood, if it was blood at all. On the surface of the puddle dust and dirt had formed an uneven scum in which some bits of greasy paper had been trapped. Mrs Venus turned away. I thought her Red-Indian face had gone yellow. 'Ugh, can't look at that. That's how I found her – my little Annie.'

She told me that before she'd had her three sons she'd had a daughter. Doing her shopping one day she'd left her in the pram outside. She'd already paid for her purchases when there were shrieks outside, then something crashed into the wall and the glass in the shop window was shattered. She rushed out, there was an overturned lorry, two adults lying there, blood everywhere, and nothing left of the pram. 'I was beside myself then, I'd have killed that drunken pig behind the wheel if they'd let me. But they rushed up from all sides and held me until the doctor who came with the ambulance gave me a jab of something.'

At that time she was still working at the stud in Topolčianky. And just a few days after her little girl was killed it so happened that her favourite mare, Edith, a chestnut with white socks, fell at a fence and broke her right foreleg just at the fetlock. The vet insisted that she'd never race again, in fact she wouldn't even walk again, and he wanted to put her down. She ran straight to the manager of the stud and begged him to let her look after the filly. The manager knew what she'd just gone through and took pity on her. After that she spent every free moment with Edith. She made splints for her, mixed saltpetre with water parsnip and nasturtium leaves and alternated these applications with an ointment which the vet, in the end, gave her. With that filly she could talk just as she'd talked to her little girl, the animal understood her. At night, when Mrs Venus woke up and saw her little girl all bloody and mangled on that pavement, she'd run to the stable; her filly was never asleep, just as if she knew she'd come to see her. After six months she was riding Edith, they even allowed her to enter her for their local steeplechase and she rode her herself. As she was waiting at the start she forgot for the first time what had happened to her.

'And did you win?' I asked.

'Some hope! We were doing all right as far as the third fence. But I was so excited I got a belly-ache, and then I couldn't control Edith any more, she just ran as she pleased. We finished last, by ten lengths, but we finished.'

As we walked on through the deserted little wood there was more and more rubbish on the ground, and not only on the ground – even the branches of the trees were festooned with translucent tatters of plastic. At every gust of the wind they touched, interlocked and embraced like a pair of crazy lovers, and in doing so they emitted a rustling sound and with the sound came the smell of rotting, mould and mildew.

Even the road up Mount Olympus, Daria had told me, led through rubbish, and even the way up Fujiyama, which she'd also climbed, was lined with garbage. On Mount Everest, just below its summit, lay drums, abandoned tents and plastic containers. Even a crashed helicopter is said to be rusting there.

My dear Lída is mistaken when she thinks that sweepers must feel ostracised or humiliated. They might, on the contrary, if they cared about such things, regard themselves as the salt of the earth, as healers of a world in danger of choking.

I asked if it was possible to help those who had already borne the brunt of ostracism. My wife, thankful for a question that was seeking for hope, replied that the best chance was psychotherapy. This might help to uncover the causes of their rejection by others and shift their sense of being wronged from their subconscious to their conscious minds.

The main theme of my wife's life is finding hope for other people. The pain of others hurts her personally, she suffers with every rejected person, she tries to alleviate his lot, to help him see into his own soul and to discover there what he wouldn't discover otherwise. If she feels she is succeeding she is happy, she knows she isn't living in vain.

If any theme excites me, it is probably the theme of freedom.

How can you write about freedom when you're unable to act freely, Daria objects. By which she means that I am unable to leave my wife.

I don't know why leaving someone should be a freer action than staying with them.

All right then, why didn't I stay with that dreadful woman who battened on other people's misfortunes, and leave her alone.

Perhaps my theme ought to be not so much the search for freedom as the search for action. Or maybe resolution, or determination, or ruthlessness? I'll write a novel about a hero who sweeps aside anyone standing in the way of his happiness or satisfaction. He'll go on sweeping everybody aside until somebody sweeps him aside. Maybe, if he is sufficiently determined, vicious, resolute, ruthless and at the same time circumspect his turn will not come at all: only death will sweep him aside.

A few days ago an aircraft crashed not far from the Irish coast with 325 people aboard. There was no engine failure, no instrument failure, the plane didn't strike a church tower or a mountain veiled in mist, but a time bomb exploded in it. Not a single passenger survived. Among the victims were eighty children. Floating in the water – wrote the journalists, knowing that people in their secure armchairs love reading moving or harrowing details – were dolls and other toys.

Heroes impose themselves. They'd placed a bomb aboard the plane and they were not only resolute and ruthless, but were no doubt also fighting for someone's freedom.

A lot of people talk about freedom, those who deny it to others most loudly. The concentration camps of my childhood even had a slogan about freedom inscribed over their gates.

But I am more and more convinced that an action can be free only if it is inspired by humanity, only if it is aware of a higher judge. It cannot be linked to acts of arbitrariness, hatred or violence, nor indeed to personal selfish interest.

The amount of freedom is not increasing in our age, even though it may sometimes seem to be. All that increases is the needless movement of things, words, garbage and violence. And because nothing can vanish from the face of the planet, the fruits of our activity do not liberate us but bury us.

They even held an international conference about the Apocalypse. Scientists have calculated that if fewer than half of the existing atomic warheads exploded, a firestorm would sweep over the continents and the oceans, igniting anything inflammable on earth. The air would be filled with poisonous vapours, including lethal cyanides from certain plastic materials which we ourselves have manufactured. The heat would destroy not only all living things on the surface of the planet but also the seeds in the ground. The fire would be followed by darkness. For a week after the explosions the air would be filled with such a quantity of black smoke that these clouds would block out 95 per cent of the light that used to reach the earth. If any plants had remained unburnt, they would die in the months-long darkness. During the darkness a prolonged arctic winter would begin, turning the water on the planet's surface into ice and thus destroying what remnants of life might have survived in the waters.

Between Crete and Rhodes lies the little island of Karpathos, and on it stands the small town of Olimbos. A tiny church and a few dozen houses climbing in terraces up an almost bare mountain flank. The stone houses have flat roofs and huddle together in narrow streets. Here one still finds women in dresses as black as their hair, and there is something age-old in the swarthy faces of the men. Even the silence and the sounds are age-old. This is where we'll go, the two of us together, it came to her in a flash, and as she was climbing the steep little street to the church she knew for certain that she'd be coming back here, and that I would come with her. Maybe we shall stay there and grow old. She'll lead me through ruins, among the remains of temples, she'll lead me through little villages whose names I instantly forget and whose names even she possibly doesn't know. I inhale the scent of rosemary, tamarisk and lavender, the fragrance of the hot, sun-parched soil, I hear the chirping of the cicadas and the braying of the donkeys and the pealing of bells, wedding bells overhead, and together we are conscious of what others are not conscious of: the spirit of our breath and the breath of our spirits.

I know that she is visualising her future life and that she includes me in it, that she imagines the travels we'll undertake together, as well as her old age by my side, just as if we now really belonged together forever, as if there were no longer other people alongside us. Perhaps it doesn't even occur to her that we are wronging anyone, she is convinced that our love justifies everything. Or is she just more genuine than me, does she want to accept the consequences of having decided to love me?

I love her too, I try to dispel my uneasiness, my anxiety to escape from her visions, I want to be with her. At least for a day, at least for some fraction of time.

And so we loved each other with all our strength and passion, out of uneasiness and out of loneliness, out of love, out of longing and out of despair. The fragments of time piled up into weeks, into further months. The winds blew, storms passed over, snow fell, my son began studying management science, he was increasingly interested in programmes for the management of the world in which he had to live, her daughter was growing up and had decided to become an agronomist, a downpour drove us into an abandoned basement where we held each other as tight as if we'd just met after a long separation, we waded through the tinted leaves in the park where the ravens in the tops of the tulip trees again called out their Nevermore to us. Her husband fell ill so that she had virtually no time for me, but she wrote me long letters in which she embraced and caressed and cursed me: Life without you is almost like death! My son celebrated his twentieth birthday, he was told to choose a present that was useful and would also give him pleasure, and after some reflection he asked for a Geiger-counter. My wife noticed that I was taciturn, I looked drawn, and she asked me whether I didn't sometimes feel nostalgic for that other woman. She suggested that I should ask her round some time, and then left for an indoctrination course, and I was able to stay with my lover day and night.

Next spring, she says, something decisive is at last going to happen.

Why next spring?

After twelve years Jupiter would enter the house of life for her.

And indeed in early spring a gallery owner in Geneva expressed interest in her work and offered to stage an exhibition for her.

I'd come to her attic studio as usual, and as soon as I'd opened the door I could see that something out of the ordinary had happened: cupboards and packing cases on which the soot from the little chimney-flue had settled for years now stood open; wherever I looked I saw mountains of her creations and monsters, succubi, witches, little demons, shameless displayers of their sex as well as angelic creatures without any sex, men-jackals, and ordinary drunks from a Little City tavern. Most of them I saw for the first time.

She kissed me, cleared a chair for me, told me her news, and wrung her hands in lamentation: she didn't know what to do. For a while we continued to unpack some of her earlier work from crates. She placed each on a modelling stand, inspected it carefully for a few minutes, like an archaeologist who'd just unearthed an unexpectedly large fragment, and then put it down with the rest. She didn't know if she was justified in dredging up and exhibiting such ancient work. She pointed to the head of an old woman:

she'd made that while still at school. It was her father's mother, she'd lived to the age of ninety. With her left eye she was winking while with the other one she was smiling.

I recognise the forehead, which is as high as her own, and the smile too is familiar. And that bronze youngster hanging his head, in which there is an opening for a long-stemmed flower, was a fellow student who'd committed suicide, she'd told me about him. At that time she'd wanted to make portraits of all the members of her family she knew anything about. Many of them were still in her basement workshop. Then she says: That gallery owner is inviting me to the private view and you're coming with me.

How can I go to Switzerland?

I don't know how, she says, but I do know that you'll see my exhibition.

As I get up to leave she neither holds me back nor sees me out, she wants to get on with her work.

I see her every other day, that's what she wants. I always find her at work. A new figure would gaze at me out of stone or clay eyes, and in its gaze I'd recognise a familiar passion. My lover goes on working for a little longer, while I fry up something simple for lunch, then she puts down her tools, takes off her stained smock and washes her hands. Now she doesn't want to think of work any more, only, just before we embrace, she has to tell me what she's been thinking about, who she'd had a beer with last night, what they'd told her at the agency this morning, the one that is supposed to negotiate her exhibition, and finally she must tell me her dream. Her day is so rich that she will never enter the kingdom of heaven.

I admire her. I'm sure I'd be spending weeks before the stand without finishing more than one or two things.

How can you be so sure?

Because I know how long it takes me to think up a sentence before it more or less satisfies me.

That's because you're tense, she explains to me. You try to master everything by your intellect and your strength. You don't know how to submit to life.

She doesn't force herself to do anything. What she needs most is a sense that she is free. If she doesn't feel like work she'll go out with a girlfriend and they'll get drunk, or else she comes here, she sits down, she doesn't want anything, she isn't driven anywhere by her thoughts or her imagination, she just gazes as if she were gazing at the clear sky, into pure water, into emptiness. She realises that nothing need happen, and that's also all right by her. Or else some shape suddenly appears before her, a face, a likeness, maybe just a coloured blotch which may take on form or else dissolve. She can't tell where they come from, these shapes don't seem to come from within her, she feels she's only a mediator, the executor of some higher will. She then executes whatever she has to, and she feels good while doing it. She doesn't reflect on what it will turn into. That, she feels, is not her concern but the concern of whoever put that vision into her. If I could write like that, without torturing myself beforehand about the outcome, without seeing some mission before me, I'd also feel good.

But I can't work the way you do, I'm different.

You don't know what you're like, she says with assurance.

And who does?

I do, because I love you.

So what am I like?

You're more passionate than rational.

I don't know whether I am passionate. I know that she is. Her passion will destroy us both one day.

Next time I found her in tears amidst fragments of clay. The stand was empty.

What happened?

Nothing. What should have happened? Better leave again, I'm out of sorts today!

Has anybody hurt you?

Everybody's hurting me, but that's not the point.

So what is?

How could I ask? Didn't I understand, couldn't I see? All we were doing was pointless, nothing but a self-important and vain playing at art. Nothing but desperate caricaturing and endless repetition of what had already been repeated a thousand times.

And if she'd now and then managed to catch something more, to
realise some higher clue, who'd detect it, who'd notice it? Why did
she have to choose this particular occupation, such a useless,
joyless and exhausting drudgery? She hated all art! She didn't
want to exhibit anywhere, she didn't want to show anyone her
fumblings. There was no sense in it!

What about Barlach's angel?

Yes, Barlach's angel – but they'd had it removed, hadn't they?
He survived only because angels are immortal. She's laughing
through her tears. If you'd sit for me I'd make you a pair of wings
and maybe you'd be immortal too.

I'll sit for you.

Better lie down with me!

We embrace and she forgets all her sorrow. She looks forward
to our love-making on the shores of Lake Geneva.

Three days later the organisation, or rather agency whose task it
is to organise, in other words authorise, exhibitions abroad
informed her that it would not handle her exhibition.

I want to know why she's been refused but she only shrugs.

I suspect that it might have been because of me.

It's possible, darling, they're envious of me because I have you,
they know that nobody loves them so much.

However, we composed a letter of protest to the authorities;
she'll probably not send it off. She then went out to see her
fortune-teller friend to discover what the cards had to say about
the chances of her appeal. Told that they weren't too good, she
decided to hold an exhibition in Kutná Hora instead of Geneva.

We were still walking in the direction where I expected the
depot to be. The trees all round were more and more heavily
festooned with tattered pieces of plastic. At the base of the
miserable little tree-trunks dirty crumpled bags were tumbling
about, and whenever there was a gust of wind the yellowed pages
of some jerkish newspaper rose up from the ground like
monstrous emaciated birds and weakly flapped their mutilated
wings.

Franz Kafka became a sacrificial victim by his own decision. It does not seem as if those around him were as anxious to sacrifice him as he was himself. Time and again he recorded the state of mind experienced by the victim. With few exceptions the victim resists, and even thinks up elaborate means of self-defence, but his tragic end is unalterable. In this respect Kafka certainly anticipated the fate of the Jews in our age of upheaval. His youngest sister met her end in a gas chamber. That is where he would probably have met his end too if he hadn't been lucky enough to die young.

Jewish authors, such as Kafka's contemporary Werfel, or later Bellow and Heller, keep returning to the theme of the sacrificial lamb with an obsession that is possibly subconscious and possibly prophetic. The theme of the victim of sacrifice and the person staging sacrifices, of an increasingly random victim and of the victimiser prepared to drag to the altar of his god any number of human beings, if not indeed the whole of mankind, is increasingly becoming the theme of the present-day world, of a mankind that once believed in an earthly paradise and in the beneficial effect of revolutions in leading it there.

At last we emerged from the forest. Before us, behind a high wire fence, we saw a mountain with many ridges, crevices and humps. Its slopes glistened here and there as the fragments of plastic reflected the sun's rays. Along its long crest a yellow bulldozer was moving, its scoop pushing a multicoloured mass before it. From one side a road led up to the mountain. Access, however, was barred by a red-and-white striped barrier. Just then an orange dumpster came hurtling out of the forest, an invisible guard raised the barrier, and the vehicle entered the enclosure. As it slowly climbed up the slope of the artificial mountain some fat crows rose up from both sides of the path, beating their massive wings. On the crest the garbage truck stopped, its body bright in the sunlight. Then it began to evacuate its entrails. No sooner had it begun to move off than a group of little figures rushed out from some invisible hiding place. I counted thirteen of them – if Daria had been here she'd have said an unlucky number! – men, women and children. The grown-ups had rakes in their hands, and pitchforks and poles fitted with hooks, or else they were pushing discarded prams. They all pounced on the fresh rubbish and began to dig around in it as if in a race; they flung items from one pile onto another, a few items they picked out and put aside for themselves, and others, which were evidently still useful for something or other, i.e. for sale, they flung straight into handcarts or prams.

I was reminded of the woman whose things I'd moved. Disease was eating up her soul, she believed in Armageddon, and she took delight in things she'd saved from the dustbins. Here she'd be in her element. She wouldn't have sold any of the items she found here, she'd have piled them into a heap which would have grown ever higher and wider. She'd have laboured till she dropped, not until nightfall would she have sat down by the base of her own mountain and anxiously rested in its shelter for a while. Like Sisyphus, that woman would never have completed her work, not only because the supply of new garbage will never stop, but also because an inner emptiness cannot be filled even with all the objects in the world.

We soon became aware that nothing that was happening before us was happening without a plan, and that all the running around and exploratory digging was directed by a massive bald-headed fatty in a black suit. Unlike all the rest, he never once bent down to pick up anything, but merely strolled about as their supervisor. And just then his name came to me and I surprised Lída with the information that, to the best of my knowledge, that fellow was called Demeter, and that he'd had to pay a good deal of money for the right to mine the treasures in this mountain, though I didn't know to whom. Now and again the searchers might dig up a pewter plate, an antique coffee grinder, a discarded television set, or a banknote thrown out by mistake.

When the Kampuchean victim-makers, known as the Khmer Rouge, occupied Phnom Penh they broke into the abandoned bank buildings, burst open the safes, carried out armfuls of banknotes and flung them out of the windows – not only rials but also American dollars, Swiss francs and Japanese yen, the banknotes of every country in the world sailed out of the windows, but none of those who were still alive in the city dared pick any of them up. The coloured pieces of printed paper were gently scattered by the wind. They rose into the air alongside scraps of newspaper, torn posters and blank picture postcards, then settled by the kerbs or in the middle of the streets which nobody came to sweep. The rubbish gradually rotted, unless the monsoon rains washed it away and the waters of the Mekong carried it down to the sea.

What Kafka was longing for most in his life was probably a human encounter. At the same time it represented for him a mysterious abyss whose bottom seemed to him unfathomable. But he lived at a period which, more than anything else, began to exalt revolution. Only what was revolutionary in art, as much as in the social order, seemed worthy of admiration or at least of interest.

For that reason, too, they looked in his sentences and images for a revolutionary message. But when I read his letters to the two women he loved, or at least tried to love, for whom he yearned and of whom he was afraid, I realised that if I did the same I had no hope of understanding him.

His first love lasted for more than five years. He invited her to him, he drove her away again, he implored her not to leave him unless she wished to destroy him, and he implored her to leave him or they would destroy one another. He got engaged to her and immediately afterwards he fled from her. When she kept silent and failed to answer his letters he lamented his fate and begged for a single word of favour. Encounter, coming close together with a woman he loved was for him a chance of fulfilling his life, a chance he persistently missed. The struggle he was waging with himself totally consumed and exhausted him.

Could a person as honest as that write about anything other than what was shaking his whole being, what occupied him day and night? About anything other than the struggle he was waging, even though that struggle, in comparison to the revolutionary events in the world, was less than trivial? Although he mostly speaks of himself and although his heroes are, even in their names, avowedly himself, he yet concealed the true nature of his struggles. He was not only shy, he was so much an artist that he expressed everything he experienced in images. The torturing machine, which slowly murders the sentenced man, was invented by him at the very moment when, after a bitter inner struggle, he decided to get engaged after all. A few weeks later, when he broke off his engagement, treacherously as he himself felt, he conceived the trial in which the tribunal judges the accused for an offence that is not clear to the reader and has often been interpreted as metaphysical guilt, as a metaphor of original sin.

Even in a revolutionary period there were undoubtedly other writers whose works, without our feeling obliged to search them for hidden messages about the meaning of existence, were full of images and metaphors. But in Kafka's work there is something more than just a cleverly invented image, something that moves us and grips us, something that lures us fatally on like a sheer drop.

Daria's exhibition was being set up in three reasonably sized rooms of a Gothic house. The exhibition – including twenty drawings – comprised seventy-three items. She could easily have shown a few items more or less, but that number seemed to her the most suitable. 1973 was the year her daughter was born.

For almost two weeks we packed and heaved crates with figures and paintings. Our faces and hair were covered with a layer of wood-shaving dust.

You're so kind to me, she said, brushing the dust off her jeans and embracing me. And I'm not devoting myself to you at all. Have a glass of wine at least!

She promised to make it all up to me. We'd travel somewhere that I'd like, there wouldn't have to be any water there, she knew that I didn't care for water, she'd come to the mountains with me.

I wasn't anxious to go either to the water or to the mountains, I didn't need a rest, I'd much rather work undisturbed. But I behaved like a good boy, I didn't raise any objections, I unpacked the sculptures we'd brought along, I helped to nail pedestals together and hang cords from the ceiling, I adjusted the lights, and in the evening I drove her back home as fast as I could.

My wife, it seemed to me, still had no suspicion of how I was spending most of my time. Or didn't she want to suspect? The day before the opening of the exhibition she was leaving for an ethological conference and wanted to know if I minded being left on my own for so long.

I didn't betray my relief at her going away just then. I assured her I could look after myself.

If I wished, she suggested, I might come along with her. I was sure to find the people at the conference interesting. For a while she told me earnestly about people who kept snakes or exotic butterflies, about experts on owls, marmosets and white stags. She wanted to provide some diversion for me, some experiences I wouldn't have in my solitude, and when I declined her offer I felt guilty. I was about to repay her offer of help with betrayal.

It was her husband who drove my lover out to the private view of her exhibition. He'd finally emerged from the darkness. I suggested to her that I stay at home that day, I'd seen her work anyway. But she didn't want me to leave her at such a moment. I had to overcome a cowardly wish to avoid what would be an awkward encounter, to make the excuse of being ill, or of the car being out of action. There are plenty of excuses a man can invent, but I didn't wish to lie, at least not to her, so I went.

I knew her husband only from photographs, but I instantly identified his tall athletic figure. The room was crowded by then and I don't know if he noticed me too. He was talking to a bald-headed, wizened old man, almost certainly her father, whom I hadn't met either. I didn't know any of the people in the room, I belonged solely to her, to her who was severed from all ties and relationships. I felt so much out of place that it depressed me.

She came over to me almost instantaneously. Unfamiliar, a little strange in a long poppy-crimson dress. Even her features seemed strange to me, the little lines which I'd so often touched with my lips were skilfully covered by a layer of cream and powder. She kissed me, as no doubt she'd kissed other guests as well, and whispered that she loved me. Then she asked me if I wanted to meet her husband. She declared herself as belonging to me in front of everybody – 'My lover' – and I suddenly wasn't sure whether I was pleased about it or not.

After all, why shouldn't I shake hands with you? her husband said to me and gave me a slightly injured smile. Although I'm not exactly short, he was a head taller than me, and also ten years younger. At first glance he was one of those men women run after of their own accord. He said that Daria had worked pretty hard these past few weeks, they'd scarcely seen her at home, and he shrugged as if to say: And on top of everything there's you and that's really a bit much. But instead he said he'd read my new stories, and this would have been the right moment for me to shrug but he gave me his injured smile again and walked away. I hung about near the door but lacked the courage to make a getaway. I had a feeling that they were all furtively watching me, for the moment I had become one of the exhibits. I might have a little card by my feet: Banned but active in another field. Or: The lover presented. Or simply: That's him!

In the last room Daria's sister, whom I had likewise never seen before, was setting out canapés from cartons on a little table and pouring wine into paper cups. I took a canapé but I declined the wine because I was driving back that evening.

An elderly man whom I knew from somewhere took a drink and said that it was years since he'd seen anything so free and so liberating. He was looking at the sister but I was sure he was talking to me.

That's what she's like, her sister agreed. When she was small she'd run away from home and play truant from school.

Her husband was approaching and I beat a hasty retreat. I was unable not to take notice of him, even though, to my own surprise, I looked upon him without jealousy, as if it were no concern of mine that she lay down by his side night after night. I only felt a little embarrassment, shame and perhaps even guilt. That man had never wronged me, whereas I had for several years now secretly and insidiously worked my way into his life.

She guessed my mood and hurried over to comfort me. Her husband was leaving now, he'd be taking the rest of her family with him, the whole circus would be over in a little while, there'd only be a few friends left whom she hadn't seen for years and whom she'd like to invite for a glass of wine, also the representatives of the gallery, they'd promised to buy one or two of her things, but that too would soon be over and then there'd be just the two of us.

I asked if there was anything I could do, but there wasn't, her sister had already gone to reserve two tables. I would have liked to tell her how pleased I was that the exhibition had been a success but I was somehow paralysed and she'd run off before I could pull myself together.

Her husband was still not leaving, maybe he needed to demonstrate his satisfaction. I could hear his loud, good-natured, jolly laugh. He might stroll over at any moment, slap me on the back and tell me that in spite of my gaucherie I seemed quite amusing, he'd expected worse. Indeed, he felt some sympathy with me. On top of all my problems I'd landed myself with his wife! Perhaps we should finally settle this business.

I thought I was choking in that close and stuffy space.

Outside I was surprised by the bright lights. I didn't know the small town; although we'd spent a lot of time here during the past few days we'd had no time for a walk. Now I chose a narrow street which ran steeply downhill. Somewhere in the neighbourhood there was obviously a fair: the wind carried snatches of round-about music to me and I was meeting children with coloured balloons, hooters and large puffs of candy-floss.

I used to love fairs, the sideshows of conjurers, fire-eaters and tightrope walkers, but I couldn't recall when I'd last been to one. Over the last few years I'd neglected all my interests except one, all my friends, all my near and dear ones, everybody except one. Most of all I'd neglected my work.

I wasn't satisfied with the way I was spending my life, but I couldn't blame anyone for it except myself. I'd come to the end of the little street and below me lay a wide open space. Above the merry-go-round shone a wreath of deceptive but alluring lights and the circus tent was decorated with red and blue pennants. Gigantic white swans made a pretence of noble flight.

For a moment I stopped at my slightly elevated vantage point and watched the crowd milling below me. I longed to mix with it, not to have to worry about anybody, not to think of anything, of my guilt or my lies, even of my love, not to step into anyone else's life, not to belong to anyone, to move freely and unrecognised in the crowd, to catch snatches of conversation and human faces, to dream up incidents which I would shape according to my will, to have before me something other than perpetual escapes and guilty returns.

My wife maintains that I am unable to forget my wartime experiences. They, she says, are preventing me from getting close to another person: I know I would suffer when I lost that person too, but I cannot believe that I would not lose them. I remain alone, even though I am seemingly by her side. Clearly I would remain alone by anybody's side.

I ought to be getting back, I wouldn't like to spoil my lover's day of success with my moodiness. But I went on to a shooting gallery and asked the dolled-up beauty there for an air rifle. I scored enough to win a little bear on an elastic string and a parrot made of colourful rags and feathers. As I accepted my fairground trophies it struck me that they were more appropriate to me than those fantastic sculptures which I'd just left behind.

One of the rubbish searchers had just caught a red flag with his hook. With a great effort he extricated it from underneath the mass of ashes and other filth, rolled it round his pole, and when he'd got it out eventually waved his wife over and together they unrolled the rag. When they'd opened it out in the wind we could see that it was really a red flag which was now flying above the mountain of garbage.

The Khmer Rouge did not fill the void in their souls with objects or with the money they so despised. They understood that the void in the soul cannot be filled even by all the objects in the world, and that was why they tried to fill that void by human sacrifices. But the emptiness of the soul cannot be filled by anything, not even if the whole of mankind were driven to the sacrificial block: the emptiness would continue, terrifying and insatiable.

Everything on earth is gradually transformed into rubbish, into refuse, which must then, in one way or another, be removed from the earth – except that nothing can be removed from it. Some time ago our jerkish newspapers reported that some Czech inventor had invented a machine for the destruction of old – that is, useless – banknotes, securities and secret documents. Abroad, the article claimed, banknotes were destroyed in crushing mills the height of a two-storey building. The compressed waste mass, however, was so dense that each kilogram of it had to be doused with half a litre of petrol before it would burn; in contrast, the Czech invention did not exceed the dimensions of a medium-sized machine tool. This splendid machine, quite possibly the invention of none other than our captain, produced a shredded mass which could then be fed by pipes into the boiler of a central heating system: thus not only was petrol saved but also a lot of precious hard coal.

Methods and machines for the efficient and economical removal of uncomfortable people from this world have of course been known for a long time.

I watched the items on the carts piling up. Although I couldn't make out any details at that distance, I suspected that they were old boots and pots, bottles and dolls rather like the ones which had floated on the sea off the Irish coast, and certainly also sacks and old blankets. Where are the days when the poor from the hovels on the outskirts of our cities didn't even have a sack to call their own, to cover their nakedness? They are behind us and they are before us.

The light breeze rose again and this time it carried to us not only the stench of the garbage but also snatches of hoarse conversation and of delighted childish shrieks. If Brueghel or Hieronymus Bosch were alive now they would surely have sat here and drawn this scene. They might have added a few little figures at various points among that plastic mass, or they might have heightened the mountain so that its peak touched the heavens, and at its foot they might have placed a happy treasure seeker, a woman, a never satiated mad Margareta. What would they have called the picture? 'The Dance of Death' or, on the contrary, 'Earthly Paradise'? 'Armageddon' or just 'Dulle Griet'?

It struck me that any second now a new orange vehicle might arrive and tip out a load of skulls and bones. At just that moment those at the top of the heap were dragging out an old feather mattress and as they were trying to free it from the stranglehold of the rest of the rubbish its cover burst, and because a somewhat stronger gust of wind had just sprung up the feathers began to rise, and along with light scraps of paper and plastic and fine particles of ash began to circle in the air. The dancers underneath almost disappeared in the snowstorm, and I felt a sudden chill. Anxiously I looked at the sky to make sure the megaton cloud was not already sailing over from somewhere, but the sky still seemed clear and clean, though a chill was falling from it that made me shiver.

The Apocalypse can take different forms. The least dramatic, at first sight, is the one in which man perishes under an avalanche of useless objects, empty words, and excessive activity. Man becomes a volcano which imperceptibly sucks up the heat from below the ground until, in an instant, it trembles and buries itself.

The sweepers in their orange vests go on sweeping, sweeping silently and without interest, while their brothers the dustmen cart off what has been swept into piles and thrown away. They pile those useless objects into heaps which swell, spread and disintegrate, like yeast they rise skywards, like a cancerous tumour they invade their surroundings, human habitations, so that we find it difficult to distinguish between what are still objects of our life and what are objects of our death.

Of all the garbage that swamps us and threatens us by its breath of decay, the most dangerous are the masses of discarded ideas.

They tumble about us, they slide down the slopes of our lives. The souls they touch begin to wither and soon no one sees them alive again.

But those without souls do not vanish from the earth either. Their processions move through the world and subconsciously try to reshape it in their own image. They fill the streets, the squares, the stadiums and the department stores. When they burst into cheers over a winning goal, a successful pop song or a revolution it seems as if that roar would go on forever, but it is followed at once by the deathly silence of emptiness and oblivion.

They flee from that silence and seek something that would redeem it, a sacrifice they might cast on the altar of whatever demon they happen to be venerating. Now and then they'll fire a gun at random, or place a time bomb, or inject some narcotic into their veins and make love, they'll do anything to survive that dead period before the tremor of the volcano, before the lava fills the void. The void within them.

The images Kafka employs are often obscure, but they also seem to deliberately display a multitude of heterogeneous and disparate elements. We read his strictly logical narration, which often suggests a precise official memorandum, and suddenly we come across a detail or a statement which appears to have drifted in from another world, from another plot, and we are confused. In the story about the execution machine, for instance, why do some ladies' gloves suddenly appear and, without obvious reason, pass from the condemned man to the executioner and back? Why does the judge in *The Trial* hold a debt book instead of the trial papers? Why does the official in *The Castle* receive the surveyor K. in bed? What is the meaning of his absurd paean in praise of bureaucratic work? The author leads us through a savanna where, in addition to the antelopes and lions we would expect, polar bears and kangaroos are also roaming about as a matter of course.

Surely a writer as logical, as precise and as honest as Kafka must have meant something with his paradoxes, must have intended some hidden communication, must have wanted to create his own myth, his own legend about the world, some great, revolutionary message which perhaps he only surmised and was therefore unable to express clearly; he only adumbrated it, and it is up to us to decipher it and give it precise shape.

I don't know how many clever people were taken in by that mystery-cracking delusion, but they were numerous. I myself am convinced that no writer worthy of that name conceals anything deliberately, that he does not construe or invent any revolutionary messages. He doesn't even concern himself with them. Most authors, like most people, have their theme: their torments, and these impose themselves on anything they do, think or write.

Kafka with his shyness sought a way of communicating his torment and simultaneously concealing it. Yet it was so personal that it was not enough for him to express it only in hidden form, only in metaphor; time and again he was prompted to make an open confession of the experiences which touched on the essence of his being. As if he were relating an event twice. First he draws his fantastic image: a bizarre and mysterious trial, an execution machine, or a surveyor's desperate effort to get into an inaccessible castle, and second he assembles the fragments of real experiences and events. He writes everything on translucent sheets of paper or on glass and places them one over the other. Some things supplement each other, some things cover each other, some things find themselves in such surprising company that he must surely have been blissfully amazed himself. Behold, he no longer lies fatally exhausted and impotent in bed with his lover who offers him her redeeming and merciful proximity, but he finds himself, as a mortally weary surveyor, in bed with the castle official, and that man offers him his liberating bureaucratic mercy.

We didn't go to Switzerland, we didn't even go to Kutná Hora again. The exhibition was over, and all that was left to us was the attic studio, where the view of the window of the palace opposite was still blocked by the statue of Saint Stephen the Martyr. We'd meet, sit by the low table, drink wine and talk in that strange state of enchantment which stems from the knowledge that everything we do and experience takes on new meaning and importance the moment we impart it to the person we love. In the past we loved one another with longing and with an insatiability which seemed to me unchangeable, even though she was seized by impatience now and again. Something's got to change, surely we can't spend our entire lives in such immobility, in such hopeless repetition of the same actions, we don't want to end up as two clowns who are happy if in their old age they can be walk-ons in an amateur circus performance. A bitterness has crept into her conversation. She is angry about people who don't know how to live, she rails against artists who are betraying their mission, she curses all men who are treacherous and cowardly and unable to pursue anything in their lives to its conclusion. Most frequently she is angry with my wife.

We are lying by each other's side. It is evening, an autumnal rainy twilight, we are reluctant to tear ourselves away from one another, to get up and flee into discomfort. I kiss her, once more I embrace her. She presses herself to me: suppose we both stayed here until morning?

She's testing me, and I keep silent.

Anyway, she can't understand how I can live with that person. She'd heard some things about her, about what she does to her patients, that had made her quite sick.

I don't wish to end the day with a quarrel, but nevertheless I ask what she'd heard and from whom. But she refuses to give me any details. She'd spoken to somebody who knew my wife well. He'd said that it was criminal to treat people like that.

I try to discover if this is about some drugs my wife has prescribed.

We're still lying beside one another, but she is so angry she hardly seems to know where she is. Why bring up drugs? She knew nothing about drugs. Perhaps a perverted doctor would also prescribe perverted drugs, but had my wife never told me about that revolting, humiliating play-acting those poor wretches had to go in for? How she compelled them to vomit up their intimate

secrets, how she dug about in their beds? Did I really not
understand that that woman was a pervert? She's unable to live for
herself, unable to love, to look after a family, keep an eye on her
own husband, and so she's gone in for professional do-goodery. In
reality, and in this she was no different from all other do-gooders,
she merely got a kick out of the suffering of others, she merely
latched on to the lives of those who still managed to have real
emotions and were therefore suffering. And, like a leech, she
pretended to be helping them. Or did I think that a woman who
for ten years or whatever couldn't tell that her husband had
someone on the side, that he was living with her only out of pity,
could discover anything about the souls of others?

I tell her it isn't like that at all, but she starts shouting at me that
I shouldn't stand up for that person. She doesn't know why, on
top of everything that I'm doing to her, she should bother about
my wife's mission. She'd merely like to know if I was really so
blind that I couldn't see that everything those psychologists,
psychiatrists and similar psychopaths were doing was perverted,
the arrogance of miserable individuals and spiritual cripples
who're telling themselves that they are better than the rest?

Was she still talking about my wife?

We could leave my wife alone now, she didn't want to waste
another second of her time on her. But she begs me to think about
what she's told me, if only for the sake of my writing. I was
unlikely to produce anything while by the side of a person who
made a living out of dissecting the souls of others, as if they were
rats in a laboratory, ripping out all their secrets and then
trampling on them.

She has a fit of the shivers, she is transformed before my eyes.
Her face which a moment earlier had seemed gentle and loving is
now that of a stranger, and it frightens me.

I ought to silence her, somehow douse that flame of hate in her,
or flee from it before it singes me too, but how can I flee when that
flame is burning because of me?

At last I embrace her to soothe her and she curls up in my arms, she moans in ecstasy, everything drops away from her, the tenderness returns to her features: Do you at least understand that I love you, that I love you more than anything in the world, that I mean you well?

If I don't do something we'll both fall into the fire from which there will be no escape.

My darling, she insists, why won't you realise that we're made for each other? Tell me, are you happy with me?

I tell her that I am happy with her but I am aware of a tension within me, an unbearable tension pressing on my lungs so I can hardly breathe.

I walk home through the wet streets, as usual at a brisk pace. Always escaping – from whom and to whom? A place with an unmade bed and unswept floors, a place I spend so little time in that dust settles even on my desktop, my home is falling apart and I with it.

My wife enters. I feel I am in a different sphere, where no corrosive flames are flickering.

My wife is neither arrogant nor conceited, nor does she long to take possession of other people's secrets. If anything she is childishly trusting. She believes hopefully in the perfectibility of things and of people, and her belief has so much determined strength in it that it can perhaps encourage also those who are on the verge of despair.

I walk up to her and embrace her. At that moment my tension vanishes, I can breathe freely.

It's nice to have you home, she says. I've been looking forward to this.

The method of effectively and economically removing human garbage from this world, in a businesslike and precise manner, in the spirit of our revolutionary age, its ideas and aims, is most factually described in his autobiography by the commandant of Auschwitz, Hoess.

> The Jews earmarked for liquidation were led away to the crematoria as quietly as possible – the men in one group, the women in another ... When the Jews had undressed they

stepped into the gas chamber, which was equipped with showers
and water pipes, so that they assumed they were entering a
bath-house. First the women and children went in, and after
them the men . . . Now and again it would happen that the
women, while undressing, suddenly issued bone-chilling shrieks,
they would tear their hair and act like persons demented. In that
case they were led out quickly and killed by a bullet in the nape
of the neck . . .

The doors were swiftly screwed down and the waiting
disinfecters immediately injected cyclon through openings in the
roofs. It flowed down to the floor through special tubes, forming
the gas instantaneously. Through a little window in the door it
was possible to see how those standing nearest to these tubes fell
down dead immediately.

Hoess was a victim-maker with a burnt-out soul. He was
therefore exchangeable and replaceable, and has indeed been
exchanged and replaced a great many times.

The figure of the victim-maker with a burnt-out soul belongs to
the world in a revolutionary age. To a world in which the person
who in his actions perfectly embodies emptiness and vanity,
cruelty and a moral void, is granted the right to regard all those
who differ from him as garbage to be swept away, garbage of which
he cleanses the world. He is ready to cleanse it of anyone: of
Armenians, of kulaks, of gypsies, of counter-revolutionaries, of in-
tellectuals, of Jews, of Ibos, of Kampucheans, of priests, of blacks,
of lunatics, of Hindus, of factory owners, of Muslims, of the poor,
of prisoners-of-war. One day, perhaps not too far away, they will
cleanse it of people altogether. The brooms are becoming ever more
efficient. The Apocalypse – that is, the cleansing of the world of
human beings and of life altogether – is increasingly becoming a
mere technical problem.

Hoess factually describes the flames which licked up to the sky
twenty-four hours a day and roasted the corpses of his victims.
The flames were so high and so bright that the anti-aircraft
command lodged a complaint, and the smoke was so dense and
the stench so strong that the population in the whole neighbour-

hood began to panic. These reasons, he records, led to the rapid design and construction of crematoria. They built two, each with five huge furnaces, and together these were capable of incinerating two thousand murdered units, but that was not enough, so they set up another two incinerators, but even that was not enough. The largest number of persons gassed and incinerated ever achieved in one day, he records, was just under ten thousand.

That was how it was done, and looking at it purely from the technical point of view, it was a very primitive procedure. However, the human spirit has not been idle in this revolutionary age: the flames which the cleaners have at their disposal today are capable of simultaneously incinerating any number of people in their own homes.

Yet nothing has ever disappeared from this world or will disappear. The souls of the murdered, the souls of all those sacrificed, of all those burnt alive, gassed, frozen to death, shot dead, beaten to death with pickaxes, blown to smithereens, hanged or starved to death, of all the betrayed and of those torn from their mothers' wombs are rising above the land and the oceans and are filling space with their lamentations.

At first I was alarmed at my attempt to knock the great creator down from heaven to earth. But I don't believe that this can be done. Our heavens, after all, are linked to our earth. How can anyone unable to relate to the person he loves expect to relate to those he does not love? Kafka realised this, and to stand by the side of the woman he loved meant to him standing by the side of people, becoming one of them, participating in their order. He also realised what most of us are concealing from ourselves: that drawing close to another being, accepting another being as well as another order means the surrender of freedom. Man longs to get close to the person he loves, and in doing so hurts and betrays that person and himself, and thereby he commits a crime.

A lawyer by training, he wrote about one single case. He himself prepared the evidence for his own prosecution, he defended himself passionately, and mercilessly found himself guilty. He never abandoned his theme, but by living it through himself, completely and truthfully, he managed to embrace both the heights and the depths of life.

From below the mountain another flock of crows started up, darkening the sky and making the air vibrate with the beat of their wings. The birds alighted around the treasure-hunters who'd by then finished their work. But it didn't seem that the two groups took any notice of one another.

One of the men looked down towards us and called out something I couldn't make out. Immediately the others also started shouting at us. I could see my wife was beginning to be afraid. 'What are they shouting?'

I couldn't make it out. Most probably they were offering to start trading with us.

'Do you want to go over to them?'

She was prepared to go over to them with me, even though she was afraid of them. She'd been trying, at least over the past few years, to indulge my wishes and even my eccentric ideas. She raised no objections to my having been an orange-clad street-sweeper for several months now, although she must have wondered uneasily whether some ulterior motive, or at least a wish to escape from home, was not perhaps concealed behind my occupation. Sometimes when I got back home I felt a note of uncertainty in her question of how I was. Suppose she suspected me of doing something different from what I said I was doing? She had plenty of reasons to distrust me, but neither now nor in the past had she dared ask me straight out. She regarded distrust as something unworthy, something that soiled whoever let it enter their minds.

I realised how often I'd betrayed her confidence in the past. I felt a shaming sense of guilt as well as a need to compensate for it somehow. For a start I said that it was a lovely day, that we'd done well to get out into the country. It sounded a little paradoxical, standing as we were below the mountain of garbage.

Back home our daughter and little grand-daughter were waiting for us. Our son, too, sat down to dinner with us. He'd long been trying to find a place of his own and as always he had a multitude of carefully worked-out plans which, he hoped, would lead him to his objective, whereas our daughter, as always, was giving no thought to her future. There were times when she felt that everything, absolutely everything, still lay ahead of her, while at other times she felt that everything, absolutely everything, lay behind her, that there was nothing left to her but to live out her days – as tolerably as possible. For the most part, however, she gave herself joyfully to the moment. After dinner she wanted to draw me. She cut some large sheets out of wrapping paper, pinned one of them to a stiff folder, and made me sit in an armchair for a long time.

From the kitchen came the clatter of plates, there was the muted sound of my son's tape recorder, and my grand-daughter could be heard through the wall delightedly recounting some feeble-minded incident she'd seen on our jerkish television. I asked if I might close my eyes and my daughter, having warned me that this would make me look like my own deathmask, agreed. At least I wouldn't fidget.

From outside came the smell of the sea and a wave licked the sandy beach.

Hold on a little longer!

Her fingers were moving swiftly in the sand. How I love those beautiful fingers which so often touch me with tenderness and which, moreover, know how to turn shapelessness into shape.

I don't know if this is my likeness, I'm never sure of my own shape. I have an animal body and the wings of a swan, but I look happy.

Because you are happy, she explains. Or aren't you happy with me?

Aren't you afraid that the water will carry me away at night?

That's why I've given you wings, so you can fly away. You have wings so you can be free, so you can go wherever you please. By this she meant: so I could get to her at any time. But the water washed me away, complete with wings, and did not carry me to her, and I don't know if it ever will.

The charcoal swishes across the paper, the tape now sounds louder, my son's left the door of his room open. The year before we'd visited him in the provincial town where he was then doing his military service; we'd set out on Saturday morning, we'd decided to put up at a hotel and return on Sunday evening, but Lída had a headache and left early on her own, and I stayed on at the hotel alone. On Sunday morning the bus took me to the barracks where our son was waiting for us at the gates. I thought that he looked quite good in uniform, even though I'm not too fond of uniforms.

He asked me where I'd like to go, but I left it to him to decide: he knew his way around here better than me.

So he took me up some hill where Těsnohlídek was reported to have walked, along a cemetery wall with slender yews standing upright behind it, and down a farm track. The weather was cool and windy, around the birches by the track blew small leaves like flakes of coloured snow.

My son spoke about his experiences in the army, then he shyly mentioned that his girlfriend had visited him here too, and hastily returned to military matters. We were in no hurry with our conversation, we had the whole day before us. I couldn't recall when we had last spent a whole day together, if indeed I ever found that much time in the course of a single day. It seemed to me that my son was suddenly emerging from the dark or returning from a great distance. I'd spent time with so many people, I'd spent days and weeks with my lover, while my son was a fleeting figure in the evening or in the morning or at Sunday lunches. Of course he sat in the room sometimes, along with other guests, listening silently or perhaps coming over for a few words with me – most often about political events or about his classes, never about his personal worries or hopes, and as a rule I'd sit down at my desk after a while and thereby dismiss him. He'd also invite me to listen to protest songs which he'd recorded and which he was sure would interest me, and I'd either decline or else soon doze off while listening to them.

I knew that he had identified with my destiny to such an extent that, even though he'd studied engineering, he was closely – indeed more closely than I – following the fate of literature, at least in the part of the world we lived in, and he'd think up plans for making banned works known to the public, and took delight in any indication, however slight, of a turn for the better.

I regretted that for so long, for whole years on end, I'd never managed to find more time and interest for what made up his life. I now questioned him about his friends, about his girl, and about what he thought about the future. I could see that my interest pleased him, and it occurred to me that he might feel as lonely as I had at his age.

I decided to invite him out for a special meal, but when we got to the tavern all they had was cheap salami, bread and onions. At least I ordered some wine. Our conversation was leaping from one event to another, the most essential things we continued to carry locked up within us. It is difficult to voice the feelings a father and son have for each other. My father had also been unable to do it, we'd never talked about anything too personal. What we did talk about provided no opportunity for him to show any emotions whatever. I knew that he was childishly proud of what he regarded as my literary successes. But he never commented on what I had written, any more than on how I was living.

My bus was leaving in the evening. Peter was sorry I had to go so soon, he was off duty until midnight. I asked him what he would do with the rest of the evening. He said he'd go to the cinema or else return to the barracks and listen to the radio or read. I gave him a little spending money, and because it was getting chilly I got on the bus.

My son stood motionless outside, waiting. I noticed that the frosty wind was bending even the trunks of sturdy poplars, but my son was still waiting. He looked up at the little window behind which he saw my face, he stood there in a strange uniform, cast into a strange world, and waited faithfully for us to move off. Then, because the bus circled the square, he ran over to the other side so that I caught sight of him once more, standing on the stone surround of the fountain, close to the roadway, waving.

Then I was alone. The bus hurtled through the dark of the forest and I closed my eyes, but even in that double darkness I could see the figure of my son carved out of the stony greyness of strange houses, I could see him standing there, separated from me by impervious material, but at least waving to me. At that moment I was gripped with unease at my own doings, at my double life, from which loyalty had disappeared, to be replaced by pretence and betrayal.

My son was an adult now, and if I left home it shouldn't have any fatal effect on him. A child remains the child of his parents, even though their paths may divide. But is it conceivable that my departure for good would not strike a blow to his notions of loyalty, his faith in the fellow-feeling of his nearest and dearest, his concept of home?

'You may wriggle now,' my daughter said. She was looking quizzically at her production.

'Did it come out as a deathmask?' I wanted to know.

'Somehow it isn't you at all,' she complained, and held the sheet out to me.

'I don't know. How can I know what I look like when my eyes are closed?'

But for a deathmask there was still too much life in my features.

Dad had never been ill in his life. A year ago he started losing weight and stopped enjoying his food. Then they found a malignant tumour in his colon and decided to operate at once. I took him to hospital the day before his operation. I sought out the surgeon and tried to explain to him that although Dad was nearly eighty his mental faculties hadn't been affected by age, and his students still came to him for help when they were stumped by some complicated problem.

The surgeon was short and plump. In his white coat and cap he looked more like a chef than a medical man. He listened to me politely, as he must have listened to many similar persuasive speeches, he accepted my envelope with money, and assured me that he'd do anything in his power, I might get in touch with him the following day, about lunchtime.

Lída thought that I should stay at the hospital during the operation. Dad would feel that I was close by, and that would be reassuring for him and would perhaps make waiting easier for me.

I drove over to the hospital first thing in the morning. I was in time to see Dad on the trolley, as he was waiting in the corridor outside the theatre. From the distance it seemed to me that he was smiling and very slightly raising a hand to acknowledge he'd seen me.

Then I sat down a little way beyond reception, in a dim corridor where orderlies were ceaselessly wheeling trolleys to and fro, and new patients were walking past. There was so much bustle there that I couldn't concentrate on my father.

An hour later I was informed that the operation had not yet begun.

I phoned my wife at work to tell her I was staying on at the hospital, and she tried to reassure me, I shouldn't worry, the operation would be successful, Dad had a strong constitution – he'd even survived the death march just before the end of the war.

I also rang my lover, just to hear her voice, to tell her where I was, and that most probably there wouldn't be time for me to come and see her.

Only a short while later I caught sight of her, passing through reception with her rapid step. She kissed me. She brought me a gingerbread angel she'd baked for Saint Nicholas's, and a twig with yellow witch-hazel flowers. She'd managed to break it off from somewhere.

The waiting room had emptied after lunchtime and we sat down on a bench. She took my hand in hers and said: He'll be all right, I can feel it. His time hasn't come yet.

Then we were silent. I seemed to see a white corridor before me, I couldn't see all the way down to its end, and a trolley was moving along it. Dad was lying on it, white and unconscious and moving away from me. What does a man feel, what does a man think, when he is firmly convinced that there is no other life than the one that's just then threatening to slip away from him? What hopes does he have at his age? His own fear got a fierce hold on me. I got up and went to ask if the operation was finished but I was told that it wasn't, I had to be patient.

I returned to the waiting room. I could see Daria in the distance, but she was taking no notice of me, she sat there as if turned into stone, as if removed from her own body. When I walked over to her she looked up at last and it seemed to me that I could see pain in her features. It's all right now, she said. It looked bad, but it's all right now, I can feel it.

She took my hand and led me along the corridor to the exit. Outside large autumnal snowflakes were falling; they lay on the ground only briefly and then melted. We went into the little park behind the hospital, and she was talking to me softly. She said that man spent only an insignificant portion of time in this life, in the shape we know him. What is important is that he should spend it well, and fully develop his potential, because that would decide which way he went on. I was unable to concentrate properly on what she was saying, instead I just took in the timbre of her voice, her comforting, loving presence.

I had told her many times that I loved her. Now I didn't tell her anything, but that moment entered into me forever: the bedraggled park with a few rain-wet trees, her proximity, her voice, and her hand which was pressing mine. And if we are ever to be so far apart that we can no longer reach out to each other, that our voices are lost in the distance, she is now so firmly embedded in me that if ever she groans in pain or fear I shall hear her, no matter where I am. And if I'm alive I shall go to her to repay her for at least this pressure of her hand.

We returned to the hospital. The surgeon received me. The tumour had been a big one, and neglected, but it was out now. My father was sleeping.

I spotted the youngster the moment we entered the hall. He was standing below the stage and talking to one of the musicians. He was wearing jeans and a pullover with a Norwegian pattern. Perhaps it was the artificial light but he seemed to me even paler, more drawn, more sick than usual. I introduced him to Lída. She said she was glad to meet him, I'd told her a lot about him. She was also looking forward to the concert, it was good of him to have thought of us.

The youngster unexpectedly blushed and hurriedly rattled off the names of the composers and the compositions we were about to hear, he also told us the names of the clarinettist and the drummer, and we went off to look for our seats.

'Isn't he very sick?' my wife asked as we sat down.

I told her what I knew about his illness and also that there was possibly a drug available abroad that might help him, but that it was too expensive for it to be prescribed.

'And couldn't you get it for him?' she asked in surprise.

The music began. I am a bad listener, I can't concentrate even on the spoken word let alone on music. Lída, on the other hand, responds to tones with her whole being. I could see the music entering into her and arousing in her a pleasurable astonishment, taking her out of the not-too-hospitable tavern's dance hall.

I too could hear at least the echoes of primordial rhythms and glimpse the reflections of tribal fires around which half-naked dancers of both sexes were whirling.

When the first missionaries in Africa saw those painted and masked savages prancing round their fire they thought they had just glimpsed something akin to a ritual from hell. In reality, of course, what they saw were the last remnants of paradise. Those dancers may have been troubled by evil spirits, hunger or drought, but they were not weighed down by any sinful past or a retributory judgement in the future; the vision of the Apocalypse did not rise before them. They were still in the childhood of mankind.

I have never set foot on the Dark Continent, but when I had some time to spare in St Louis, where I'd been invited for the opening night of a play of mine, I got on a tourist excursion steamer down the Mississippi, and there was a black band playing on board. A colourful company was celebrating something, I don't know if it was a wedding, the birth of an heir or somebody's saint's day, or the fact that a manned spacecraft was then on the way to the moon which their not-too-distant ancestors may have revered as a deity, but I could feel that close to them, and under the influence of their music, I was slipping into another, more carefree and less knowing age.

This mood persisted even the following day when, at the home of the producer who, like me, was a native of Prague, we watched the television screen in the evening and I saw those strange bulky figures bouncing with light steps about the wasteland of the moon, while from the street came delighted cheers; I thought then that man, as he had always longed and as my father had promised me, had really got closer to heaven. It seemed to me that mankind was entering upon a new era full of promise.

During the interval the youngster came over to us, and because my wife knows more about music than I do I let them talk to each other while I went to the bar to get ourselves something to drink.

When I got back towards the end of the intermission the youngster was about to leave for his place just below the stage. My wife took a glass of juice, took a sip, and before the musicians started up again told me what she'd learned from the youngster about his life; needless to say, she'd learned more in those few minutes than I had in several weeks. His father, it appeared, had left his mother before he was even born, and because the mother was a little odd he grew up in children's homes. His mother was now dead and his only relative was a stepbrother with whom he didn't get on. She'd guess that the youngster was a sensitive boy but, because of his circumstances, had never completely grown up, almost certainly also because in his life he hadn't yet met a man with whom he wished to identify. I ought to bear this in mind, maybe he'd attach himself to me.

I couldn't think why the youngster should want to attach himself to me of all people, but I promised to watch out.

The master of ceremonies announced the next composition, a Gershwin medley. The musicians started up. At one point the clarinettist on the stage made use of a brief pause, held his instrument out towards the audience, motioned to someone, and a moment later we saw the youngster jumping up onto the stage and taking the clarinet.

'Surely that's him,' Lída said in surprise. She doesn't see too well at a distance and moreover she has a poor memory for faces.

From his borrowed instrument the youngster conjured up the glissando which opens the first part of 'Rhapsody in Blue'. I could see his pasty face turn red, either with excitement or with the effort.

Winter that year was severe. The sky remained blue and cold, the frozen snow crunched underfoot and the air stank so revoltingly that one regretted not being a fish. I went to see Dad nearly every day, he was picking up rapidly. He was once more working on his calculator. Don't you go thinking that I'm written off, he said to me, and immersed himself in his world of numbers, where he felt most at home. He no longer designed new motors, he'd come to the conclusion that there were too many in the world already, but he was searching for some new solution, for better machines for that better world which he was perhaps seeing in his mind's eye. Sometimes he'd put on his fur-lined coat and go out with me to walk down the chilly ugly street. The fate of the world had not ceased to interest him. He confided his fears and disappointments to me. It grieved him that socialism had not brought freedom to the people and that technology had not lightened their drudgery but was instead threatening them with annihilation. We stopped at the dairy. Here Dad thawed out because the pretty girl behind the counter smiled at him pleasantly, asked him how he was getting on and assured him that he was looking wonderful. Dad at any rate still believes that women are good creatures. Sympathetic and worthy of attention and love. He'd have gone on chatting to the dairy girl, but I was in a hurry to get to my own good creature.

We'd had to abandon the attic studio with its view of the palace opposite, and we now met in her basement workshop, where –

long, long ago – I'd first set eyes on her. From outside the window came the continual footsteps of strangers passing by and from the corners came a smell of mildew and mould. On the stone floor stood a storage heater. It was only seven years younger than me and just as stubborn, sometimes it worked and at others, for unfathomable reasons, it didn't switch itself on at night at all. Fortunately the thick mediaeval walls stopped the place from freezing up completely.

She is waiting for me. She hasn't even taken off her coat but her lips are hot. Again she presses herself to the tepid metal shell of the heater and I hurry to make some tea while she tells me her news. Listening to her I feel that the incidents I look for in vain are all homing in on her, all her encounters seem to have a special and higher meaning, something essential to tell her, to open, at least in part, a view into the infinite spaces of other people's inner lives.

As she speaks I watch a little cloud of her living breath rising from her mouth. The room is in semi-darkness which obliterates even those little lines which I would probably not have seen anyway with my long-sighted eyes. She seems to me tenderly and soulfully beautiful. I know that I still love her and I suspect that she must love me too if she's staying with me in this inhospitable and cold basement.

She notices my glance and presses herself against me – together we slip into the icy bed. But her body is warm, we cling to each other, ecstasy blots out the outside world, at this moment it doesn't matter where we are, we are in the seclusion of our love and we know that there isn't a palace in the world whose solitude we would exchange for this place of joint occupation.

Her slight body ceaselessly rears against mine, she trembles with delight, her eyes grow misty. Devoutly she begs me not to leave her, again and again she wants me, she knows no respite in her love-making any more than in her work, any more than in anything she undertakes, she sweeps me along like a vortex, she rouses in me a strength I never suspected I had. My head spins, I am in ecstasy, I am on earth solely for this moment, for this action.

Yet even so the moment must come when we are exhausted, when the chill that's seeping from the floor and the walls gets between us, enters her eyes. I know that she's asking herself how long I intend to make love to her without giving her any hope, without finding a solution which would bring her out of her icy loneliness. But she only asks what I'm going to do tonight.

I say that I will work, even though I know that my answer will seem unsatisfactory to her if I don't decide to stay with her. I want to know what she'll be doing.

Why should I care? I wasn't going to stay with her anyway, after all, there was my wife waiting for me at home, I have to be with her, act the part of the faithful loving husband, create an atmosphere of home. Yes, of course, I also had to work, make money so I could keep the lady, my wife, in appropriate style. Also I mustn't forget to buy something for dinner so she needn't put herself out, and bring her a little present so she should know what a fine model husband she has. All she wants to know now is why she should plunge with me into this sacchariney sticky filthy mess of ours? She curses the moment when I crossed her path. Why didn't I say something, why didn't I at least speak up in my defence?

I reached out for my cold shirt and she screamed that I should push off, that I should get back as fast as possible to that sacred cow of mine who has ruined her life. She'll still try to save herself, to dig herself out of the shit I have dragged her into.

Outside, darkness had fallen, and its icy maw swallowed us up instantly. The snow had turned grey and seemed to collapse under our feet. We got to the metro station and she asked: When shall I see you?

As always, Hope was looking down on us from her stone plinth with her invariably gentle, even warm smile.

Tomorrow I have to take Dad to the doctor. How about the day after?

She took hold of both my hands: I really won't see you all day tomorrow?

The youngster finished his part and handed the clarinet back to its owner. Somebody clapped, my wife clapped too, the youngster bowed awkwardly; when he jumped down from the stage his face was back to its usual pallor.

The concert was over. The people around us were pushing towards the exit. It had got cold outside, and a brilliant full moon stood in the cloudless sky.

To us, who'd stayed behind on earth, the astronaut Aldrin said then:

I'd like to take this opportunity to ask every person listening in, whoever and wherever they may be, to pause for a moment and contemplate the events of the past few hours, and to give thanks in his or her way!

The producer in St Louis casually mentioned to me that eighteen years earlier, after he'd escaped, he'd been sentenced to death in his native country for some fictitious political crimes. Now they wanted to rehabilitate him. When on that memorable day we went to bed at three in the morning he said: A pity, back home they couldn't even watch this properly, by now they're at work. And he showed me his watch. To my amazement it was still showing Central European Time.

'That was a nice day,' said my wife, my guide through sunny and nocturnal landscapes. She pressed herself close to me because she was shivering with cold, and I felt comforted by her closeness.

IV

Autumn is well advanced, the streets are full of dry leaves which add to our work, from the houses fly tired unenthusiastic flags, public buildings are displaying streamers with jerkish slogans which would undoubtedly please any chimpanzees that might happen along. Luckily we don't have to pick up any of this colourful textile rubbish: flags and slogans are put up and taken down by special motorised squads.

A little way short of the beflagged Palace of Culture we met our now familiar uniformed pair. The foppish one looked a little wilted, he'd probably come on duty after a heavy night; his companion seemed unchanged.

'Bloody mess, isn't it?' the fop addressed us, pointing vaguely ahead.

'People are pigs,' the foreman agreed. 'Hey, what about the murderer?' he remembered. 'Got him yet?'

'Signed, sealed and delivered,' the fop said casually. 'The lads did a good job.'

'Name of George,' his companion explained.

'George who?' the foreman asked curiously.

'Would you believe it, he was a juvenile.' The fop yawned. 'Introduced himself to a girl he wanted to strangle as George from Kladno. But he made a mistake there; she got away from him.'

'Told her he was a mining apprentice,' the fair one added.

'Yeah. Our lads chased up all the Georges who were mining apprentices, though they realised it might have been a trick.'

'That's right.' Our youngster sounded pleased. 'And was it?'

'Course it wasn't. The man was simple! Know how many women he raped? Go on, you tell him,' he encouraged his companion.

'Sixteen!'

'And they identified him beyond any doubt.'

'And he was a mining apprentice?' The foreman voiced his astonishment.

'I'm telling you he was simple. Fellow like that commits one murder, and then has to go on. Things ain't what they used to be – mining being an honourable job!' The fop yawned broadly. 'Still no pantaloons?' He turned to the captain.

'After my death!' the captain snapped. But maybe I misheard him and he really said: 'Save your breath!'

The fop didn't even laugh this time. He nodded to his companion and the two continued down the road.

Mrs Venus pushed her shovel into my hand and grabbed the cart. With her free hand she immediately produced a cigarette and lit it. Her eyes were wet with tears. As we were tipping the rubbish into the cart I asked if anything had happened to her.

She looked at me as if deciding what lay hidden behind my inquiry. 'Happened? Why should anything've happened to me? Only the old gent died.'

It took me a while to work out whom she was talking about. 'The one on your passage?'

'Well, he was eighty, so he died!' She flicked her cigarette butt into the dustbin on the handcart and lit another. To change the subject away from death she pointed to the palace: 'They say they found a gypsy buried in the concrete there!'

'You're telling me,' the foreman was angry; 'I've got a chum working in the garages there. Last month they came along with pneumatic drills and started to knock down the wall. And d'you know who they were looking for? That woman singer from the National Theatre, the one who went missing eight years ago.'

'Did they find her?' I asked.

'They didn't find anything. Their drills all got screwed up!'

'It's a monstrosity.' The captain gave the palace its proper description. 'They can drive a million people inside, they switch the radiation on and they've turned them into a million sheep!' At the thought of it he spat mightily. 'One day someone will set fire to it,' he added prophetically, 'and good luck to him!'

At that moment a suspicion grew inside me about the direction of his latest dreams.

My wife went off to the mountains for a week's skiing with our daughter and grand-daughter, but I didn't want to leave Dad for so long and therefore stayed behind at home. Only on one day did I go out into the country with my lover. She led me to some sandstone rocks where an anonymous sculptor had over the decades carved out statues of saints, knights and the Czech kings, as well as a lion which towered massively on a rocky ledge. We climbed up narrow icy chimneys and descended on steeply-cut steps. Half-hidden by the fir trunks and raspberry thickets we discovered ever new sculptures. I could see that she was touched and also amazed by the intensity of the creative will of some unknown person who, either not caring for an audience or, on the contrary, full of confidence in his own work, had imposed his visions on these lonely rocks.

I was curious whether it would amuse her to create a similar gallery for herself.

She said she preferred gardens, parks, the sea, and wide open spaces. And she preferred ordinary people to saints.

And whom did she regard as ordinary people?

Everybody else. Saintliness had been invented by those who were afraid of life and real emotions. That's why they elevated ecstatic rapture to something we should look up to, to something we should regard as a model.

And if she was given the kind of space she wanted, a garden by the seashore, what would she adorn it with?

She was taken aback by my question. She hadn't thought about it. Certainly with nothing that might give a person a sense of his own poverty, inadequacy or sinfulness.

We found a room for the night in a small hotel; it was built before the war and its tall windows reached almost down to the floor.

Of course there's something sacred in everyone, she added. She wasn't thinking of that contrived ecstasy, that baroque gesture, but of something untouchable and unportrayable, the human soul. At moments of enlightenment a person could catch a glimpse of it within himself, he could see his own face as others couldn't see it. If she were given a garden she'd like to fill it with such shapes that those who came to look at them might see themselves, the way they saw themselves at such an illuminated instant.

What shapes would they be?

The most natural ones. As in that Prévert poem:

> And it may happen to a sweeper
> as he waves
> his dirty broom
> about without a hope
> among the dusty ruins
> of a wasteful colonial exhibition
> that he halts amazed
> before a remarkable statue
> of dried leaves and blooms
> representing we believe
> dreams
> crimes celebrations lightning
> and laughter and again longing
> trees and birds
> also the moon and love and sun and death . . .

We spent a long time looking for accommodation for the night. The hotels were closed, or full up, or else taken over by children from 'nature schools'. In the end we found an inn where, for a bribe, they took us in.

As we stepped into the cold and ill-lit room I tried to embrace her, the way I always embraced her when we found ourselves alone, but she stopped me. She didn't even let me put our bags in the wardrobe until she had looked into it herself. Then she drew back the discoloured curtains, half-opened the window and sat down in an armchair which groaned even under her slight weight. Can't you feel something strange here? she asked. I felt nothing but fatigue.

She became even more restless. I could see that she was listening to something, that she was concentrating on something that was evidently hidden from me. I sat down in the other armchair. Through the open window came alien sounds, someone was starting up a motorbike and a dog was howling in the distance. A silent, sharp-edged patch of light moved across the wall and I realised that I was being gripped by dejection.

At last she stood up. She embraced me and quickly kissed me. Then she asked if I'd mind very much if we left again.

I didn't think it wise to leave this refuge, knowing that we wouldn't find anything else in the neighbourhood.

She said that if it came to the worst we could always stay in the open, it would be better than this unhappy place.

I shrugged and picked up the cases again.

In the car she pressed herself against me and begged me not to be angry, surely I knew that she'd never done anything like this before, but there was something evil, something unclean, in that room. Somebody must have died there in terror, without having made his peace, or else have suffered some other great torment.

I told her she'd acted correctly, I wouldn't wish her to be with me in a place she didn't feel happy in.

Just before midnight they took pity on us at a mountaineering club hostel. The dormitory was big enough for ten people, but we had it to ourselves. The walls were covered with colour photographs of mountain peaks and outside the window a real mountain towered into the sky. We chose a bed immediately by the window. At last we could embrace.

All of a sudden she burst into tears.

I was used to her sudden fits of crying, but each time I wondered afresh if I was responsible for them.

She kissed me through her tears. No, this time it wasn't my fault at all, on the contrary, she was grateful to me for showing such understanding and not wishing to stay in that dreadful room. Death had touched her there, and she still couldn't shake it off. Surely I knew that she was not afraid of dying, she was not clinging to life, never did, but suddenly she'd realised that death would part us.

She attempted to smile. Even though a fortune-teller had told her she'd live to eighty-seven, and even though the lifeline on my palm was long, one day it was bound to happen and then we wouldn't be seeing each other again, no matter where our souls would go or what fate they'd meet. I embraced her as if trying to carry her in my arms over that river of oblivion which would inevitably divide us.

I'm fine now, she whispered. I feel good with you, here I feel good with you. And she added that she could feel strength and calm issuing from me, that at last I was opening up, listening to my own voice and not just to those around me.

You belong to me regardless, she whispered as she fell asleep; you wouldn't be here with me if you didn't belong to me.

And I said nothing, I didn't reassure her, even though that evening I wanted to be with her, to stay with her, to shield her from the icy waters whose roar I'd managed to hear myself at a moment of total silence. I gazed through the window at the black mass of the mountain and watched the snowflakes being driven in the light of a solitary street lamp.

It occurred to me that she had really helped to drag me out of a state in which I was not listening to myself, in which I actually longed to escape from my own voice which had once urged me to honesty. She believed that that voice would lead me to her. How could it be otherwise when we are so often and so completely together?

But I was being called back by that voice to ancient longings which were not linked to her, to a time when my life seemed to me cleaner than it did now.

I looked at her. She was asleep, she was here with me, I could still touch her, still hold her tight, again submit to her voice, to her power. Feel the ecstasy of her proximity. Instead I was in full flight, I was returning to my wife. For one more attempt to be completely with her as I had never managed before, as neither of us had managed before, but as we had both longed to be at one time.

Maybe it will be a vain journey with a hopelessly obstinate longing for a return, for a long-past innocence; I shall be wandering blindly through landscapes which will be ever more parched, where not a single human being will be seen, let alone a close and loved being; what I will find eventually will be that majestic inescapable river, but I shan't be able to stop. At that point I understood that it was not the river that would divide us, but myself.

She sighed softly in her sleep and I went rigid at the thought that she had been listening to me the whole time. How was I to tell her? If I were the person she wanted to see in me, the person I wanted to be, I'd wake her now and tell her that I was leaving: Farewell, my love, there is no other way, I can't decide differently even though I love you, you most loveable of all women I've ever met. But I didn't do it, that voice within me was not yet strong enough.

Shortly before nine – we were just getting ready to put our tools into the dustbin recess by the supermarket and to make for the tavern, as was appropriate at that time of day – a garbage truck pulled up alongside us and out jumped Franta, the little idiot. His forage cap at a rakish angle, a red kerchief round his neck, he treated us all to a smile. The foreman walked up towards him but Franta, before saying anything, produced a packet of Benson & Hedges from his pocket, holding it out first to Mrs Venus, then to the foreman and then, one by one, to the rest of us. Only then did he take the foreman aside and talk to him for a while. I could clearly hear him uttering some barely articulated screeches in his castrato's falsetto.

'God, he stank like a perfume counter,' Mrs Venus said the moment Franta had driven off in the direction of the Pankrác prison. 'Must have done a chemist's somewhere. And a tobacconist's too,' she added, remembering the golden pack.

'I don't like it!' The foreman was staring after the vanished garbage truck as if expecting some message from that direction.

I wanted to know what he didn't like, but he didn't like anything: neither the cigarette, nor the kerchief, nor the unexpected visit.

'Did he say anything to you?' I wanted to know.

'What can he say? D'you think he can talk?' The foreman retrieved his shovel from the recess. 'That shit's getting ready for some hanky-panky. We'd better not go anywhere, we'll have our beer on the hoof!'

The youngster set out to get some beer from the supermarket and I joined him, I said I'd get a snack for myself. Mrs Venus asked us to get her her favourite cigarettes, while the captain wanted a box of matches.

'I'm somehow half-croaked.' The youngster was all hunched up as if shaken by the shivers. 'But last night, have you heard?'

There'd been a real New Orleans band performing in Prague, hardly anyone knew about it, it wasn't a public performance, but he'd managed to get in. 'You should have heard them! The pianist they had, a real second Scott Joplin, and the stuff they played! At the end they asked us if we'd like to jam with them. Think of it, them and us!' The youngster's cheeks were flushed with excitement. He stopped at the entrance to the supermarket and demonstrated how one of his friends had strummed on a washboard. 'I couldn't stop myself and tried to blow a little, but I had a sick turn. Surely this must stop sometime, don't you think?'

I said I was sure it would, he just had to be patient.

'I can join the boys whenever I like,' he said. 'We were a happy crew. You saw for yourself how they let me play the solo in the Gershwin.'

'You played superbly.'

'You really can't play it otherwise. I imagine that when he composed it he was thinking of something noble, something . . .'

He was vainly searching for a word which would describe the blissful state of a spirit creating.

Our daughter told my wife and me about a dream she'd had. She was walking in the forest with her husband when they heard strange soft music. They stepped out into a clearing and there they saw a tall naked Negro blowing a golden trumpet. The trumpet was so bright it illuminated the whole clearing, filled it with so much light that objects were losing their shadows. Suddenly from all sides brilliantly coloured birds came flying in, perhaps they were hummingbirds, also parrots and birds of paradise, she'd never seen such birds in the flesh. But her husband noticed that there was a swing hanging between some branches. He sat her on it and then disappeared somewhere. But the swing began to swing of its own accord, the music was still there, a kind of music she'd never heard before. She looked about, trying to discover where it came from, but couldn't see a single musician. It was then that she realised that the music was coming straight out of the ground, that the stones were humming and the trees singing like some gigantic violin. In the clearing stood some naked people, among whom she also recognised us, and on the shoulders, the heads and the extended fingers of everyone those magnificent brightly coloured birds were perching. She was naked too, but she didn't feel ashamed because she was still quite small. At that moment one of the coloured birds approached and sat on her hand. Its plumage had colours she'd never seen before. She was also aware of a delicious perfume she'd never smelled before, and it was then she understood that she was in paradise.

'And what seemed to you most beautiful in that dream?' my wife wanted to know.

Our daughter thought for a moment and then said: 'That I was a little girl again.'

Daria attributed my loneliness and reluctance to attach myself to anyone to the stars. I am a Saturnian person, my Saturn is in fact retrograde and Capricornian, there was a smell of bones coming straight out of it. Love alone could liberate me from my loneliness:

real love, embracing my whole being. That was the kind of love she was offering me, to save me. She offered me her proximity, such sharing that I became alarmed. Man is afraid to attain what he longs for, just as subconsciously he longs for what he is afraid of. We are afraid we might lose the person we love. To avoid losing that person we drive him or her away.

She wanted us, at least once in a while, to be together for a few days. At least some movement, some change to that immobility, she lamented. But I resisted so I shouldn't have to invent more lies at home – surely we'd been together recently.

That I had the nerve to hold that against her! That single night? And you're with her – she meant my wife – all the time! You're acting the model husband! The hypocrisy of it! What kind of life are you leading? It's all so miserable and vile!

I couldn't think of an excuse. I tried to placate her with presents.

I don't want you to buy me. I want you to love me!

I do love her, but I can't go on like this. I'd like to find some conciliation – with her and with all those I am fond of, but I can't muster the courage to reveal the truth to all of them. And she keeps urging me more and more often: When will you finally make up your mind? Have you no pity at all?

For whom?

For yourself. For me! How can you treat me like this? she cries.

Her husband has gone away. She has remained behind for a week, entirely on her own. One day she'll be entirely alone with only her stones, they are more merciful than me. What kind of life had I made for her? she cries. Well then, so lie for my sake if you can't speak the truth for my sake!

At home I say that I'm off to visit a friend whose daughter is getting married.

A good idea, my wife says, you're always at home on your own, at least it'll make a change for you. And she begins to wonder what present I should take along for my friend's daughter. And she'll bake me a Kugelhopf for the journey.

But there'll be plenty of food at the wedding! And we kiss goodbye. It's shameful. How can I treat her like this!

We arrived at a chalet in the foothills. In the small wood-panelled hall tropical plants are growing and lianas climbing, even though spring has not yet come outside, a black terrier is lying lazily and devotedly by the feet of the woman guarding the door. I stiffen as I show her my identity card, which proves me guilty, but the receptionist cares little about other people's infidelities, she has her own worries and my lover inspires confidence in her. Indeed the two women chat together as if they'd known one another for years, while the terrier on the floor regards me without interest as I wait in this strange hall like a faithful unfaithful dog.

Our room looks out on the lake. For a while we gaze at the deserted water, then we embrace. She wants to know if I like it here, if I'm glad to be here with her. I assure her that I do and that I am. At our moments of ecstasy we whisper to each other, as we have done for years, that we love one another.

Before supper we set out for a walk. We stroll round the lake and continue through the woods until we find ourselves on a wide piece of flat ground in the midst of which, as in a dream, stands an extensive wooden construction: a pattern of roofs, turrets, silos and metal hoppers. Probably a stone-crushing mill or a building for the shredding of old banknotes, securities and secret documents, all brought here by the lorries which are now parked in the deserted yard. We don't see a living soul anywhere, only a few rooks cawing from beneath a tall wooden tower. For a while we stand waiting, in case a face appears in one of the windows, or somebody yells at us to get out of here. She is also anxiously looking about in case some vision appears from somewhere in the darkness, but nothing happens, except for the wind making a half-open door creak now and then. We step through that door. In the vestibule, where everything is covered with a layer of grey dust, towers the metallic bulk of some machinery. The huge motionless wheels glisten greasily in the twilight. We climb some rusting iron stairs, up to a boarded platform above the machinery. Through a narrow window we can see the woods and beyond them part of the lake, now darkening in the fading light. Across the sky float drink-sodden faces with reddish noses. Through the cracks in the walls or in the roof rustles the wind. Do you still love me at all? she asks. She picks up some old sacks and rags. She takes off her coat and her soft leather skirt and lays them down on the blackened boards, we make love on the platform of the abandoned mill.

The dusk is obliterating her features. I see her now as I saw her when we first met. I feel as though I were returning to those days, or rather as though I were outside any definite time. With her I am outside anything, and that emptiness bewitches me. I am tossed by the waves, I rise up in my net so high that I can see absolutely nothing from it.

The floorboards are creaking, the wind is rattling some loose corrugated iron, grains of dust are swirling in the air, but these sounds merely heighten the silence in here, the absolute isolation. I say tender words to her and she replies to me. Then we just lie by each other in the darkness. I am conscious of the familiar scent of her body and the smell of stone and timber, and suddenly it hits me that I know this enclosure, that I've been here before. I feel the icy touch of fear, even though I have probably only been reminded of the wooden huts in the fortress ghetto of my childhood, or perhaps of the wooden floors of the barracks to which I was forcibly confined, and where death reigned. At just this moment I have to think of death!

My uneasiness won't go, we make love again, I clutch her to myself in the darkness of this seclusion, in my own ecstasy, I press myself to her, grateful that she is here with me, that she has climbed up with me to this spot which is more suggestive of some elevated hell, where the bones of sinners are ground to dust, than a place intended for love-making.

Out of the blue she asks: Do you also make love with your wife?

Her question snatches me back into the present.

I don't want you to sleep with another woman, I want you to be with me alone! She draws away from me. Do you hear what I'm saying?

I hear her. What am I to say? How can I chase away her question, how can I chase her away, she who's lying next to me, when she wants nothing but that I accept the consequences of the fact that I am embracing her, that I've been embracing her for quite a few years now, that I call her to me and that I hasten to her whenever she calls. The meanness of my situation and my behaviour overwhelms me and stifles all the words within me.

She pushes me away, gets up hurriedly, dusts down her skirt and dresses. For a while she rummages in her bag, then strikes a match and runs down the creaking stairs. Tell me, who do you think you are? she asks when we are back in our room. You think I have to take everything from you, you think I couldn't find another man like you? Maybe she really couldn't find another man who'd treat her the way I do, she adds, who'd treat her like a slut from the streets.

I never ask her how she lives with her husband, but now I say that, after all, she isn't living on her own either.

What did I mean by that? The fact that she had a husband suited me very well. If she were on her own I'd have dumped her long ago, I'd be afraid for my splendid marriage.

A few weeks ago we were at the cinema together. In the interval she noticed that in the row in front of us sat her husband with a strange woman. From that moment onwards I could see that she couldn't keep her eyes on the screen. When the film was over she kissed me hurriedly, I mustn't mind her leaving me now, and she ran off after those two. The following day we met as usual. Her eyes were swollen from crying and from lack of sleep. Her husband, she explained to me, had consistently denied the existence of that woman, now at last she'd caught him. They'd been awake all night, she said things to him he'd probably never forget, she'd reminded him of what he'd be without her. In the end she'd given him a choice: either he stayed with her alone, or else he could pack his things and leave. He had to promise to stay with her.

I was afraid she might have had to make a similar promise. But she had not accepted any talk about herself and me: that was totally different. After all, she'd never denied or concealed my existence.

I am disgusting, she now screams at me, first I get her into such a humiliating and shaming situation, she'd never thought this kind of thing could happen to her, and now I have the effrontery to reproach her with it.

She starts to sob.

How long have I now been listening to her passionate accusations which seem to her flawless? I am the only guilty party and I have no hope of defending myself.

She changes her clothes and attends to her eyes. She'll have a drink somewhere but she doesn't want me to come with her.

She wants me to persuade her to stay with me or to let me go with her. She loves me, she merely demands that I should decide for her, she is afraid that otherwise she might lose me. In order not to lose me she's going out. She slams the door behind her.

On the other bed, near enough for me to touch it, lies her open suitcase. Immediately next to it lies her leather skirt, the stone dust is still clinging to it.

The Garden of Eden, as a learned rabbi described it two thousand years ago, has two gates adorned with rubies. At each of them stand sixty thousand comforters. The joyful features of each one of them shines like the light in the firmament. When a just and faithful person approaches they will take off his clothes, in which he'd risen from the grave, and clothe him in eight robes of clouds of glory, on his head they will place two crowns, one of precious stones and pearls, the other of gold from Parvaim, into his hands they will place eight twigs of myrtle, and they will say to him: Go forth and eat your nourishment in joy!

Each person, according to the honour he deserves, has his chamber, from which flow four springs: one of milk, one of wine, one of balsam, and one of honey. Sixty angels hover over each just and faithful person. They repeat to him: Go forth and eat honey in joy, for thou hast devoted thyself to the Torah, which is like unto honey, and drink wine, for thou hast devoted thyself to the Torah, which is like unto wine.

For the just there is no more night, night-time is transformed for them into three periods of wakefulness. During the first the just becomes a child and enters among children and delights with them in childish games. In the second he becomes a young man, he enters among young men and delights in their games. In the third he becomes an old man, he enters among old men and delights in their games. In the midst of the Garden of Eden grows the Tree of Life, its branches reach out over the whole garden and provide five hundred thousand kinds of fruit – all different in appearance and taste.

The just and faithful are divided into seven classes and in their midst the Holy Everlasting, blessed be his name, explains to them the Writ, where it is said: I shall choose from all the land the faithful, so they can dwell with me.

When I awoke in the morning I realised that I was alone in the room. Her skirt and suitcase had disappeared. It was odd I didn't wake up when she packed her things, I am a rather light sleeper.

I went down to the hall where the talkative receptionist was watering the plants.

The lady had been in a hurry to catch the morning train, she told me. She asked how long I intended to stay. But I had no reason to stay on at all. I went back up to my room and began to pack my things. I realised that my predominating sensation was relief.

We have been expelled from paradise, but paradise was not destroyed, Kafka wrote. And he added: In a sense, the expulsion from paradise was a blessing, because if we hadn't been driven out paradise itself would have had to be destroyed.

The vision of paradise persists within us, and with it also the vision of togetherness. For in paradise there is no such thing as isolation, man lives there in the company of angels and in the proximity of God. In paradise we shall be ranged in a higher and eternal order, which eludes us on earth, where we are cast, where we are outcast.

We long for paradise and we long to escape from loneliness.

We attempt to do so by seeking a great love, or else we blunder from one person to another in the hope that someone will at last take notice of us, will long to meet us or at least to talk to us. Some write poetry for this reason, or go on protest marches, cheer some figure, make friends with the heroes of television serials, believe in gods or in revolutionary comradeship, turn into informers to ensure they are sympathetically received at least at some police department, or they strangle someone. Even murder is an encounter between one man and another.

Out of his isolation man can be liberated not only by love but also by hate. Hate is mistakenly regarded as the opposite of love, whereas in reality it stands alongside love and the opposite of both of them is loneliness. We often believe that we are tied to someone by love, and meanwhile we're only tied to them by hate, which we prefer to loneliness.

Hate will remain with us so long as we do not accept that loneliness is our only possible, or indeed necessary, fate.

When we got back the others had gone on a little way with their equipment, up to the seats on which, while it was improper to sit down on duty, one could comfortably put down the bottles of beer.

The foreman smoked and talked a lot. He promised better jobs to all of us, provided of course he managed to gain influence in the organisation. He'd send us to clean at the building sites, where, admittedly, you may get a damn tough job but you can earn more. I could move up into his place, he'd fix that. He'd make some significant changes without delay. He'd try to introduce some light mechanisation, he'd also make sure they drove us straight to our workplace. This would save a lot of time, we'd make more money, our earnings would really go up. That's what he'd do, whereas those in charge of street cleaning now didn't give a monkey's, all they were interested in were their own bonuses, and they relied on perverts walking about all ponged up like hard-currency tarts.

The foreman was getting more and more agitated, and less assured. He stopped talking only when he took a swig from his bottle or when he looked in the direction of the prison, from where, it seemed, he was expecting the insidious attack.

He wouldn't like us to think he was afraid of anything, he knew what was what, and he'd been in a few tight spots in his life. Had he ever told us how, years ago, when they first introduced the supersonic MIG-19s, it happened that a machine, almost as soon as it had taken off, sucked in a pigeon or some other bird, and instantly plunged down again. It was piloted by his chum, Lojza Havrda. He should have ejected straight away, stands to reason, but because it was a brand-new plane he didn't want to abandon it. Naturally he was way off the runway, and as he tried to brake his MIG he took along with him anything that stood in his way: bushes, empty drums, and the mock planes outside the hangar. Worst of all, he was headed straight for the new quarters. They were just having their midday break when someone yelled: Get the hell out! He'd looked out of the window and saw the eight-ton giant, fully tanked up, tearing straight towards them. No one quite knew what was happening, they leapt out of the back windows. He alone stayed behind and watched Lojza wrestling with that kite. It was like a dream, but a few yards from the men's quarters he braked it to a halt. Now of course he should have got out of the crate as quickly as possible, but not Lojza! And he, the foreman, had wasted no time then, jumped out of the window and raced up to the plane. Found Lojza in the cockpit, all bloody, unable to move by himself. He got him out of the harness and carried him down on his back. Not till he'd dragged his mate to the crew quarters did it occur to him that the whole caboodle could have blown up, and them with it.

'And did it?' I asked.

The foreman hesitated, as if he couldn't remember, then he shook his head. 'The fire crew drove up and sprayed it with foam.'

'D'you know that he gave me a picture?' Mrs Venus said to me.

'Who?' I didn't understand.

'My old gent, of course. About a month ago. A big picture he had over his bed.'

'Oil?'

'Virgin with the infant Jesus. Said to me: "You take this picture, dear lady, I can't see it any longer anyway."'

The beer was finished. The youngster picked up the empties and put them into his big bag; he'd take them back to the supermarket. He was walking slowly, as if the uphill journey exhausted him.

I too found it difficult to breathe. A blanket was spreading over the city, and smoke and fog were billowing right down into the streets.

I thought we wouldn't see each other in a hurry, that she'd also made a decision for me. She hadn't just left the chalet in the foothills, but she'd left me as well, she'd been wise to withdraw from me. Even though the dawning day would now and again greet me with dead eyes, I still felt a sense of relief.

For nearly a month we both remained silent, then I phoned her to ask how she was.

She'd been in bed for the best part of a week, she informed me, she couldn't even move, she felt so sick. Her voice was full of pain, reproach, but also tenderness. I suddenly realised that I'd been waiting for that voice all that time. I was still close to her, so close she could move me with a few words.

Why did you wait so long before you rang? she asked. You were offended? I was able to offend you after all you've done to me?

This is a way of telling me she still loves me, she's waiting for me. An hour later I give her a purple gerbera and kiss her. Her lips are dry.

She'd gone to the country when she didn't hear from me, she'd planted some trees, she'd obviously injured her back, for three days she'd lain motionless in her cottage, alone.

She limps over to the bed and I fill a vase with water.

A neighbour had found her and called for an ambulance, at the hospital they'd given her a jab so she could at least manage the bus ride. And I hadn't even phoned her. You could really forget me so soon? she asks.

I know I won't forget her as long as I live, but for her the inevitable question is: What good does it do to lie somewhere all alone?

You've never considered staying with me altogether?

She's testing my resolution, my devotion, she forgets that I couldn't very well stay with her even if I wanted to. After all, she's got her husband. Maybe she's prepared to drop him, but I've never asked her to do that, I've never wanted that kind of arrangement.

How could I possibly not consider it?

But what good is that to her? she asks.

What good is it to her that I have spent nights reflecting on how I would, how we would, live – what use is it to her when nothing has actually changed, when I'm not really with her, when I see her only in secret?

I go out to the supermarket and then cook lunch for us.

You're so good to me, she says. When you have time! When you can fit me in.

I want to wash up, but she asks me to leave everything and come to her. She's lying down. I hold her hand. She looks at me, her eyes, as always, draw me into depths where there isn't room for anything else, for anything except her.

She asks what I've been doing all this time.

I tell her about Dad, about my son, I try to explain what I've been writing about, but she wants to know if I've thought of her, if I thought of her every day.

She'd left me in the middle of the night and she'd left me on my own in a strange hotel, and then for a few more weeks, so I should feel the hopelessness of living without her. I'm beginning to understand that she left me in order to push me, at long last, into making a decision.

She asks: How can you live like this? How can you believe that you'll write anything when all the time you're living a lie?

She regards me with anxious love. She's hoping I will at last find the strength to live truthfully. That is, to stay with her according to the command of my heart. She believes that she understands me. She's been appealing to me for so long to abandon my unworthy life of lies, and it hasn't occurred to her that by doing so she is appealing to me to leave her. She is right, I must make up my mind to do it.

On the little table by the bed lie a few books. I pick up the one on top – short stories by Borges. I read her one of them. It is about a young man who is crucified for an illicit love affair.

The plot sounds outrageous to our ears, we've got used to the notion that there is no such thing as illicit love, or, more accurately, that all's fair in love.

She listens to me attentively. I ask her if she wants me to read another story.

Better still, come to me!

She isn't thinking about her painful back, she presses herself to me and moans with pleasure: My darling, I love you so much, and you torture me! Why do you keep hurting me when you know that you'll never feel so good with anyone else, that no one will ever love you as I do?

I embrace her once more and then I have to hurry, her husband will be home shortly.

Will you come again tomorrow?

Her gentle fingers, her lips, her eyes: No one will ever love you as I do! No one will make love to you as I do! Why won't you admit to yourself that you belong to me? Let's go away somewhere together. We'll make love till we die! Why do you resist when you know it's bound to happen? Surely it couldn't be so perfect if there was anything bad about it.

She looks at me, I look at her face. She's changed over the years, there is less tenderness and enchantment in her now, and there is more tiredness, or even bitterness. She has aged. Over the last few years she has aged at my side, in my arms, in her vain waiting, in bad dreams and in fits of crying. In sleepless nights more little lines have appeared in her face, and I have only been able to kiss them away temporarily.

I was aware of a surge of regret or even pity, and promised to come the next day without fail.

We were approaching the metro station. We watched the crowds of people who, out of a need to be transported as quickly as possible from one place to another, were voluntarily descending into an inhospitable underworld. Around the stations there is always an increase in litter, the grass is almost invisible under a multitude of bits of paper and rubbish, of course we don't sweep the grass, even if it is totally covered with rubbish. I noticed the youngster falling behind, then stopping completely, leaning against a street lamp and remaining motionless.

I walked back to him. His pallid face had turned even whiter, and there were droplets of sweat on his forehead.

'Are you all right?' I asked.

He looked at me without answering. In his right hand he was still holding the scraper, his left hand was pressing below his stomach.

'Does it hurt there?'

'It's nothing. It catches me there now and then.'

'Shouldn't you see your doctor?'

He said that mostly it passes by itself.

But it didn't look to me as if his pain was passing. I offered to accompany him to the doctor. The foreman let us go without objections. 'If you finish in time, you know where to find us!'

It didn't take us more than twenty minutes to get to the hospital, but even so it seemed a long time to me. On the bus I made the youngster sit in the seat for disabled passengers. He was silent. From his postman's bag he produced a dirty, army-khaki handerchief and wiped his forehead with it. Who does his laundry? I knew nothing about him, I could not picture the place where he slept.

We got off in front of the hospital. I suggested he lean on me but he shook his head. He gritted his teeth but didn't complain.

The young nurse with whom we checked in was angry that we had no kind of personal papers with us, but in the end accepted the information the youngster gave her and sent us to the waiting room with its depressing atmosphere of silence and greyness. We sat down on a peeling bench. The sweat was trickling down his cheeks.

'Probably got over-excited last night. At that concert.'

'Not at all, that was quite fantastic.' After a while he added:

'I've always wanted to play in a decent band, but at the children's home we had a director ... well, he didn't think music was a proper career, we each had to learn something proper, like working a pneumatic grinder or cutting out soles – he was a qualified shoemaker.'

He took off his orange vest and put it on the seat beside him. 'I never told the boys what I'm doing now. I mean this business.'

'Do you have to do it?'

'They've cut back my pension – it's not enough to keep body and soul together!' He turned white as the pain gripped him.

I am sure that at his age I'd have felt humiliated by having to be a street-sweeper. It would humiliate me even now if I had no other choice and if I had to be a regular sweeper like him.

All of a sudden it came to me how little in fact I had in common with what I pretended to be. What does my fate really have in common with the fate of those with whom I work? What was a desperate choice to the youngster was to me, at best, a rather grim game, which tested my perseverence, of which I was actually proud, and which moreover afforded entertaining and unexpected insights. I felt ashamed. I too took off my sweeper's vest, rolled it up beside me and decided never again to put it on.

He mopped his face once more.

'Aren't you thirsty?' it occurred to me to ask.

'I wouldn't mind a drink, that's a fact.'

I went off in search of a glass.

Ten years ago I'd worked in the next block. I'd come in three times a week, and put on white trousers and a white jacket, on which as a rule at least one button was missing, but I never became a genuine hospital orderly.

When does a person genuinely become what he otherwise only pretends to be? Most probably when he finds himself in a spot from which he cannot or doesn't want to escape, the place of his torture. Genuineness is always associated with torture because it closes all doors of escape, because it leads a person to the edge of the precipice into which he can crash at any moment.

The nurse in reception lent me a jam jar and herself filled it with water. But when I returned to the waiting room the youngster was already in the consulting room.

I sat down and put the glass of water on the chair next to me.

Even a person who manages to lie his way through his whole life cannot escape that one moment of truth, the moment from which there is no escape, from which he cannot lie or buy his way out.

I recalled the day when I was sitting in another, similar hospital waiting room. If I phoned you now, would you come again?

You're waiting at the hospital again? Has anything happened to your dad?'

He's not well, but now I'm here with someone else. We were sweeping together and he was taken ill in the street.

And you've taken him to hospital. You see what a good person you are? You haven't changed at all over the years.

He was really in need of help. His liver's all gone. I've written abroad for some drug but so far it hasn't arrived.

I've often been ill. So ill I thought it was the end.

I didn't know.

How could you have known? You'd have had to phone me, at least. But of course you had no time left for that while you were comforting the sick. Must be a great feeling to help others. Especially the poor and needy. That was your wife's idea, about that drug?

I'm sorry you were ill.

No need for you to grieve. I was very ill, but you're probably worse if you've taken up good deeds. What are you trying to make yourself believe about yourself? Doesn't it seem a little cheap to lie your way out of everything?

I'm not lying my way out of anything. You can't simply judge me from your own viewpoint.

So how am I to judge you? Do you remember sometimes what you used to say to me when we were together? I thought it also meant something to you, something real, something one can't just walk away from. And now you're trying to exchange me for a few good deeds! Why don't you say something? Hasn't it occurred to you at all that you've betrayed me?

Kafka endeavoured to be honest in his writing, in his profession and in his love. At the same time he realised, or at least suspected, that a person who wants to live honestly chooses torture and renunciation, a monastic life devoted to a single god, and sacrifices everything for it. He could not, at the same time, be an honest writer and an honest lover, let alone husband, even though he longed to be both. For a very brief instant he was deluded into believing that he could manage both, and that was when he wrote most of his works. Every time, however, he saw through the illusion, he froze up, and stopped motionless in torment. He'd then either lay his manuscript aside and never return to it, or sever all his ties and ask his lovers to leave him.

Only fools – with whom our revolutionary and non-monastic age abounds – believe they can combine anything with anything else, have a little of everything, take a small step back and still create something, experience something complete. These fools reassure each other, they even reward each other with decorations which are just as dishonest as they are themselves.

I too have behaved foolishly in my life in order to relieve my own torture. I have been unable either to love honestly or to walk away or to devote myself entirely to my work. Perhaps I have wasted everything I've ever longed for in life, and on top of it I have betrayed the people I wanted to love.

At last the youngster appeared in the door. 'Have you been waiting for me with that water all this time?' He'd had an injection and the doctor had ordered two days' rest. I offered to see him home, but he declined. If I didn't mind, he'd like to sit down for a little while, after which we might rejoin the others.

'When I was a little boy,' he reminisced, 'my grannie would sometimes wait for me at the school. She'd always take me to the fast-food buffet, the Dukla in Libeň, a little way beyond the Sokol gym if you know the neighbourhood. She'd have a beer and I'd get an ice-cream. And if she had another one, I got another one too, she was fair all right. And how she could play the accordion!' The youngster sighed. I preferred not to ask what had happened to her, it seemed to me that everything connected with him would be touched by tragedy.

Outside, a fine rain had begun to fall. The youngster put on his orange vest but I, faithful to the vow I'd just taken, carried mine rolled up under my arm.

Everything in life tends towards an end, and anyone rebelling against that end merely acts foolishly. The only question is what the end actually means, what change it makes in a world from which nothing can disappear, not a speck of dust, not a single surge of compassion or tenderness, not a single act of hatred or betrayal.

I had to leave for the mountains, on doctor's orders, and my lover also needed a break. Her work was tiring her out, she complained of being permanently exhausted. To work her material, often hammering into stone for hours on end, was enough to wear out even a strong man, but I knew that she had a different kind of weariness in mind. She reproaches me for her having to remain in the border region between love and betrayal, between meeting and parting, in a space which, she claims, I have set out for her and where strength is quickly consumed, exhausted by hopeless yearnings and pointless rebellion.

We could go somewhere together. I know that she wants to be with me completely just once in a while. I mention the possibility to her. She agrees, and a moment later I wonder if I really want that joint trip, if I wouldn't have preferred to remain on my own. And suppose my wife offers to come with me? I am alarmed at the mere thought. What excuses, what lies would I invent? I am terrified like a habitual criminal who knows that he's bound to be caught in the end.

But my wife suggests nothing of the kind, she doesn't suspect me. She says a stay in the mountains will do me good. Everybody needs a change of scene from time to time. She'll visit Dad for me, I'm not to worry about him, he's doing well now anyway.

I know that my wife is immersed in her own world, which, as happens in work that brings one face to face with the sorrow and suffering produced by sick minds, is unlike the real world. In it no one wishes to hurt anyone else, evil appears in it only as suppressed, unawakened or misdirected good, and betrayal is as incomprehensible as murder.

Who does she see in me when she lies down by my side, when she nestles up against me and whispers that she feels good with me? What justifies her reasserted and ever newly betrayed trust? Or does she believe that one day I will, after all, prove myself worthy of that trust?

My lover observes my embarrassment: Do you actually want me to come with you?

I don't answer quickly enough, I don't say yes convincingly enough, my uncertainty can be read in my eyes, and she cries. She suspected that I'd be scared at the last moment, she knows me now, I've lost the notion of freedom, I no longer have any self-respect, I've become a slave to the mirage of my despicable marriage, I can no longer manage without my yoke and now I'm trying to impose it on her. What am I trying to do to her, how dare I treat her like this, humiliate her like this.

I try to placate her, but she's crying more and more, she's shaken by sobs, she can't be comforted. This is the end, the absolute end, she'll never go anywhere with me again, she never wants to see me again!

I am conscious of relief and, simultaneously, of regret.

Once more she looks up at me, her beautiful eyes, which always lured me into the depths, have turned bloodshot, as though the sun had just set in them. I kiss her swollen, now ugly, eyes, also her hands which have so often embraced me, which have so tenderly touched me: I don't understand why she is crying, I do want her to come along with me, I'm begging her to.

She'll think it over, I should phone her from there.

And here I am, alone, in the Lower Tatra. I walk through meadows fragrant with warmth. Above me, on the mountainsides, snow is still lying. At dinner I talk to an elderly doctor about yoga, he tells me about the remarkable properties of medicinal herbs. I walk along forest paths and enjoy the silence all round me, I recover in that solitude, even though I know it is short-lived, as is the relief I am feeling; the rack to which I have tied myself is waiting, it is within me.

I gaze at the distant peaks. Mist rises above the lowlands. I look back to where the waves roll, where the surf roars, washing away my likeness moulded in sand, she bathes in abandoned rock-pools, the soil is black, the path is barred by an ever thicker tangle of roots, carrion crows fly darkly over the tree-tops. I walk with her among the rocks until we find ourselves in the middle of a snow-covered expanse of flat ground, I embrace her: is it possible we love each other so much?

Nights descend, prison nights, nights as long as life, her face is above me, my wife is beside me, I am alone with my love, with my betrayal. She bends down to me at night, she calls me to herself, she calls me to herself forever: We'll go away together, darling, we'll be happy. And I actually set out towards her, I run through cold streets, streets deserted and devoid of people, empty in a way not even the deepest night could make them, I drag myself through the streets of the dead ice-bound city and an uneasiness rises up in me, suddenly I hear a voice within me, from the very bottom of my being, asking: What have you done? Halfway I stop in my flight and return to where I've come from, to the side of my wife. I act this way night after night, until suddenly I realise that I don't want to leave, that I no longer want to walk through this dead city, at least not for the moment. I say: For the moment, and eventually I am overcome by the relief of sleep.

She too is reconciled, for the moment, to having waited in vain, but after a while she starts asking again why I haven't come, what has been happening to me? Didn't I love her, weren't we blissfully happy when we're together, so why couldn't I make up my mind? She seeks an explanation, she puts forward factual and plausible reasons for my behaviour and instantly rejects them, she's angry with me, she cries, she's in despair at my immobility, my obstinacy, my insensitivity and my philistinism. She assures me that there was no decision to make: I wouldn't be leaving my wife now, I'd left her long ago, and I was only a burden to her. And the children were grown-up now, they'd remain my children wherever I was. I listen to her in silence, I do not argue with her. The voice which holds me back time and again isn't, after all, a reason; it can't even be broken down into reasons, it is above reasoning. Is it possible, I wonder, that she does not hear a similar voice within her, a voice of doubt if not of warning?

Not even now, here amidst the mountains with no one urging me to do anything, can I break that voice down into separate reasons: into love for my wife or my children, or regret, or a sense of duty. But I know that if I hadn't obeyed it I'd feel even worse than I do anyway.

Perhaps there is within us still, above everything else, some ancient law, a law beyond logic, that forbids us to abandon those near and dear to us. We are dimly aware of it but we pretend not to know about it, that it has long ceased to be valid and that we may therefore disregard it. And we dismiss the voice within us as foolish and reactionary, preventing us from tasting something of the bliss of paradise while we are still in this life.

We break the ancient laws which echo within us and we believe that we may do so with impunity. Surely man, on his road to greater freedom, on his road to his dreamed-of heaven, should be permitted everything. We are all, each for himself and all together, pursuing the notion of earthly bliss and, in doing so, are piling guilt upon ourselves, even though we refuse to admit it. But what bliss can a man attain with a soul weighed down by guilt? His only way out is to kill the soul within him, and join the crowd of those who roam the world in search of something to fill the void which yawns within them after their soul is dead. Man is no longer conscious of the connection between the way he lives his own life and the fate of the world, which he laments, of which he is afraid, because he suspects that together with the world he is entering the age of the Apocalypse.

The mist from the valley below me is rising and has almost reached me. I know that I must change my way of life, which piles guilt upon me, but I'm not leading it on my own. I feel fettered from all sides, I've let myself be chained to the rockface without having brought fire to anyone.

What was there left in my favour? What could I claim in my defence? What order, what honesty, what loyalty?

Suddenly from the mists a familiar figure emerges. I stiffen. From the mists her heavenly eyes look on me: You could give me up?

There is no reason that could stand up in her eyes. I might at best make some excuses, beg her to understand, beg for forgiveness or for punishment, but there's no point in any of this, none of it will bring her relief.

I phoned her as I'd promised. She said she'd join me for ten days, she was looking forward to it. She added: We'll have a lovely farewell holiday. But I didn't believe that she meant it.

We found our companions in place – that is, in the tavern. The first to catch sight of us was the captain. He touched two fingers to his cap.

I joined him and noticed that the table before him already bore four empty glasses.

'I'm celebrating!' he explained.

He didn't look to me like a man celebrating, more like a man drowning his sorrows. Nevertheless I asked: 'Has one of your inventions been accepted?'

'Haven't I told you? They've found the *Titanic*!' He gave a short laugh and spat on the floor.

'The *Titanic*?'

'With everything she had on board. Only the people have gone.'

'That a fact? So what happened to them?' The youngster was no longer in pain and was therefore able to show interest in the pain or death of others.

'Probably jumped overboard,' the captain explained casually. 'No one stays on a ship that's going down. Everybody thinks he'll save himself somehow.'

The foreman, evidently still preoccupied with the morning visit, decided to find out how things really stood; he'd ring the office. For a while he searched in his pockets, then he borrowed two one-crown pieces from Mr Rada and with a demonstratively self-assured gait made for the telephone.

'That really must have been terrible, finding yourself in the water like that,' the youngster reflected, 'and nothing solid anywhere.'

'That's life,' said the captain. 'One moment you're sailing, everyone saying "Sir" to you, and in your head maybe a whole academy of science, and suddenly you're in the water. You go down – finish!'

The waiter brought more beer, and before the captain he also placed a tot of rum.

The captain took a sip: 'And all your ideas, windmills, encyclopaedias, end of the Ice Age – everything goes down with you.' He got up and unsteadily walked over to the battered billiard table. From the sleeve of his black leather jacket projected his even blacker metal hook. With this he adroitly picked up a cue and played a shot.

I watched the ball moving precisely in the desired direction.

'Do you know that I've written to her?' he said to me when he got back to the table.

'To whom?'

'To Mary. Asking if she wanted to come back.'

'And did you get a reply?'

'Came back yesterday. Addressee unknown. So she's unknown now!'

'Probably moved away.'

'Person's here one moment, gone the next. All going to the bottom!' The captain turned away from his glass; he muttered something to himself and softly uttered some figures. Perhaps some new and revolutionary invention, or the number of days he'd spent on his own. Or the number of tricks he'd scored in the round of cards he'd just finished. There was sadness in his features, maybe in his poetic mind some clear vision, perhaps his last one, was just then fading and disintegrating. Again I experienced a sense of shame at sitting there studying him. High time for me to get up and get away from all that street-sweeping. I looked around at the others, as if expecting that they'd read my thoughts, but they were all engrossed in their own troubles.

From the billiard table they were calling the captain again. For a moment he pretended not to hear them, then he rose, firmly gripped his chair, then the back of my chair, then he held on to the table and, moving along the wall, made it to the billiards. He picked up a cue with his hook and concentrated for a moment before imparting the right speed to his ball. I watched the red ball move over the green baize, passing the other balls without coming anywhere near them.

'You'd better not drink any more,' I said to him when he got back.

He turned his clouded eyes on me. 'And why not?' His question reminded me of my daughter's classmate who'd put an end to his own life at the northern tip of Žofín island years ago.

By then the foreman was returning from the telephone, his face purple, as if he were near a stroke. He sat down heavily, picked up his glass, raised it to his lips and put it down again. 'Well folks, we've got a new dispatcher!'

'Would it be you?' Mrs Venus guessed.

'Don't try to be funny with me, Zoulová, I'm not in the mood!' He fell silent to give us time to go on guessing, then he announced: 'It's that fucking bastard!'

'Franta? But he's an idiot,' Mrs Venus said, surprised.

'That's just why,' Mr Rada explained while the captain began to laugh, laughing softly and contentedly, as if something about that piece of news gave him particular pleasure. Maybe at that moment he gained a clearer understanding of that radiation which turns us all into sheep.

The foreman finally swallowed his first gulp of beer, then drained his glass, and finally announced: 'If they think I'll let that

shit make out my work schedule for me they've got another think coming! This is the end of my work for his organisation!'

'Don't take on so,' Mrs Venus tried to comfort him. 'He isn't
going to stink up his office for long! He'll grass on them too, and
he'll be kicked upstairs again!'

They were calling the captain again from the billiards, but he
had difficulty getting up, he turned towards the corner of the
room, waved his hand and sat down again.

'No,' said the foreman, 'I've had it!'

'It's getting cold now anyway,' the youngster piped up. 'I think
that's what was behind my funny turn.' This was evidently his way
of announcing that he too intended to leave. I ought to join them
as well, but I was still too much of a stranger to think it
appropriate to emphasise my departure. As I got up a moment
later I merely said to the foreman; 'All the best, I'm sure we'll meet
again.' But he got to his feet, ceremoniously shook hands with me,
addressed me by my name, and said: 'Thank you for your work!'

It was a long time since any superior of mine had thanked me
for my work.

Mr Rada joined me as usual. 'You see, the things they'll fight
over!'

He seemed dejected today. To cheer him up I enquired about his
brother, whether he was about to go off to any foreign parts again.

'Don't talk to me about him,' he said. 'It's all I can think about
anyway. Just imagine, he's joined the Party! So they can make him
a chief surgeon. Would you believe it? A man who speaks twelve
languages, and after all he's seen in the world, after what he
himself told me not so long ago!'

I suggested that perhaps it was a good thing that just such men
should be chief surgeons. It wasn't his fault that the post required
a Party card.

'A man isn't responsible for the situation into which he is born,'
he proclaimed, 'but he is responsible for his decisions and actions.
When my mother heard about it she nearly had a stroke. Have you
any idea what she's already been through in her life because of

those people? And I . . . I used to be proud of him, I thought that the Lord had endowed him with special grace . . . even if he didn't acknowledge it, even if he acted as if he didn't acknowledge Him . . . I believed that one day he'd see the truth.'

In his depression he began to reminisce about the years he'd spent in the forced labour camp. Among the prisoners there'd been so many unforgettable characters, who, even in those conditions, were aiming at higher things. Some of them had there, in the camp, received the sacrament of baptism, he himself had secretly baptised a few of them. Thinking back to those days it was clear to him that, in spite of all he'd been through, God's love had not abandoned mankind. He believed, for just that reason, that he'd spent the best or at least the most meaningful years of his life there.

We'd reached the little street where our unknown artist lived and exhibited. I looked up curiously to his window, but this time it contained no artefact; instead a live person, presumably the artist himself, was standing in the window-frame, clad only in a narrow strip of sack-cloth. On his head was a fool's cap with little bells, on top of this cap he'd placed a laurel wreath, and in his right hand he held a large bell-shaped blossom, I'd say of deadly nightshade.

Thus he stood, motionless, his forehead almost pressed to the glass, as if awaiting our arrival. I was surprised to find that he was still young, his hair, where it peeped out from beneath his fool's cap, was dark and his skin was swarthy. We looked at him and he looked at us without giving any sign of seeing us, of taking any notice of us.

'Well really!' Mr Rada was outraged. 'That's a bit much!'

But I was aware of sympathy for the unknown young man who offered himself up to our gaze, who had no hesitation in exhibiting his misery, longings and hope. Hope of what? Of fame, of being understood, or at least of getting somebody to stop, look, and see. Standing there with my orange fool's vest – in what way did I differ from him? In my misery, my longings, or perhaps in my hope?

So I waited for my lover at the small railway station in the foothills. All round me half-drunk gypsies were noisily conversing.

A total stranger, smelling of dirt and liquor, invited me to have a drink with him.

I escaped to the very end of the platform and stood waiting there for the train.

Was I waiting for it with hope or with fear, out of longing or out of a sense of duty? What was there left for me to wait for, what to hope for?

At the most for some conditional postponement that would briefly prolong our torment and our bliss.

The train pulled in, I caught sight of her getting off the last carriage, a bulging rucksack on her back. She saw me, waved to me, and even at that distance I could see that she'd come in love.

I was suddenly flooded with gratitude; undeservedly rewarded, I embraced her.

It was getting dark. The station had emptied, and the lights of some train were approaching in the distance.

I wished it would be a special train, a train just for the two of us. We'd board it, we'd draw the curtains across the windows, we'd lock the door, the train would move off, speed along through the day and the night, over bridges and through valleys, it would carry us beyond seven frontiers, away from our past lives, it would take us into the ancient garden where one might live without sin.

Along the track clanked a tanker train, filling the air with the stench of crude oil. I picked up her pack and we walked out of the station.

That evening I phoned my wife from the hotel where we'd taken a room. In her voice too I was aware of love and of her pleasure at hearing me. She told me she'd been invited to an ethological conference somewhere near where I was staying. No, not just yet, in a week's time, but we might meet then, that would be nice, I must be feeling rather blue being on my own for so long, besides, we'd been to the place she was going to before, surely I remembered, on our honeymoon . . .

I was in a panic. I wasn't sure. How could I tell, a week from now. And she too seemed taken aback; of course, she said, if it didn't suit me I needn't come to see her. She just thought that I might like to, but she didn't want to push me or make things difficult for me.

I promised to phone her to let her know, and hung up.

I was finally trapped. My mind, trained on those lines, was still concocting excuses, but I suspected that I wouldn't escape this time, nor did I wish to.

Why hadn't she asked straight out? Why hadn't she objected? The strange humility of her voice still rang in my ears. I was seized by a sense of sadness and regret, I also felt tenderness towards my wife who wanted to comfort me in my pretended solitude, who promised me from afar that we'd walk up among the rocks, where so long ago we'd felt happy, where we'd started our life together. If I were here on my own I'd go to her at once and tell her that, in spite of everything I'd done, I'd never stopped being fond of her and that I didn't want to leave her. If I were here on my own I wouldn't have had to put her off, I'd be glad to have her come.

I couldn't bear to stay indoors. The moon was shining on the flank of the mountain and a hostile wind blew down its slopes. Daria wanted to know what I was doing. But I felt ambushed by my own emotions – I felt unable to assure her that I longed to remain with her.

She faced me on the narrow footpath: But you invited me here! I beg you, maybe this is the last time I'll beg you for anything, that you should at least behave like . . . at least like a decent host!

The wind was blowing her hair into her face. Now she really looked like a witch, like a sorceress who'd emerged from some depth of the mountains.

But I'll pack my things and leave this instant if that's what you want!

There was no need for her to leave immediately. We could stay here a whole week, just three days less than we'd intended.

You want to bargain with me? Amidst the silent noctural landscape she screamed at me: I was a coward, a liar and a hypocrite. A trader in emotions. A dealer with no feelings. At least not for her. How could I be so cruel to her, so shameless?

She was right.

I took her by the hand and led her further along the path below the mountain. In the dusk we stumbled over projecting roots and stones. I tried to talk as if nothing had happened. We're here together, after all those months we're together at last.

The following day we left for another place in the mountains.

I felt humiliated by the knowledge that I was fleeing, fleeing belatedly, at a moment when I no longer wished to flee from anywhere or from anybody. Except from myself.

Spring was exceptionally beautiful that year. The meadows turned purple with wild crocus and clumps of coltsfoot sprang up along the paths. But we climbed to higher altitudes, we were climbing side by side for the last time, we waded through drifts of hardened snow, clambered over great rocks, watched the flight of the eagle and the leaps of the chamois, and when we returned to the twilight of the mountain chalet we made love just as we'd been making love over the years whenever we met.

Then she fell asleep, exhausted, while I lay motionless on the bed, listening to the soft drip of water outside and gazing through the window at the mountain glistening in the moonlight, wondering what I'd do when I got back home, how I would live, even if I could live, but my thoughts stumbled at the first step over the huge boulder that lay in my path.

Then I listened to her quiet breath, and remorse overcame me: What have I brought you to, my pet, where have you followed me, where have we set out together, we stride across snowy wastes, the night is deep and frosty, the silence of the universe is engulfing us. You wanted to save me, I wanted to be with you at all your difficult moments, I probably didn't love you as I should have, I was unable, I was unwilling, to love you more. I am still very fond of you, you've grown painfully into me. If I were stronger, if I were wiser, wise enough to know everything essential about myself, I would have driven you away as soon as you'd come close to me because I would have known that I would not remain with you the way you wanted me to, how happy I would have been if I'd remained alone, because I wouldn't then have met a woman I longed for so much. I didn't decide to drive you away. I wasn't wise enough, and I was moreover afraid of your pain and of my own, I was afraid of a life in which you weren't present; I believed that with you my life would be full of hope, that I'd found another safety net to spread out between myself and nothingness.

The mountain tops were beginning to emerge from the darkness and the sky above them was turning pale. The mountain rose straight up, it towered, virtually eternal, into a sky that was even more eternal, while we mortals , here only for a single winking of the divine eye, have, in our longing to fill our lives, in our longing for ecstasy, filled our brief moment with suffering.

On the tenth day we returned home, each to our own home. We said goodbye, we kissed once more, and she hoped I'd be strong and not do anything against her.

But I am not strong, at least not in the way she meant. I don't wish to demonstrate my strength towards the woman who had for so many years shared both good and bad with me. I go back, in my mind I turn over some sentences attempting an explanation.

What a fool I am, my wife laments, to have trusted you again.

She is standing there facing me, dropping her eyes. She doesn't know what to do, what to say. She says she's decided to move out, she's looking for somewhere to live.

I ask her not to do anything silly.

The silliest thing I ever did was to trust you again.

She wants me at least to explain how I could do what I did, while I assured her that I never stopped loving her.

I loved the other woman too!

You see how embarrassing it is! There's no sense in it any more. How could you deceive me so?

I keep silent. I have no answer other than that it just happened like that. But I won't deceive you again!

Supposing you do mean what you say, how will you prove it to me?

I don't know how I can prove anything – I'll stay with you.

That's what you tell me now, but what will you tell her?

I'll tell her the same thing.

Very well. We'll go and see her and you can tell her straight away. I want to be present.

No, I can't do that.

Why not? Why can't you tell her in front of me, if you really want to tell her?

I am silent. I am trapped.

You see, you wanted to deceive me again.

I didn't want to deceive you.

You expect me to believe you?

There's nothing I can say. I can't promise or swear.

I'm an idiot, how could I have been such an idiot! Even if I wanted to believe you I can't any longer.

Again she asks to go and see the other woman. I can say whatever I like to her, but maybe at such a moment I would be speaking the truth.

At the moment, however, it isn't the truth I'm afraid of. I simply know that I cannot part from the woman I've been in love with for so long, with whom I'd made love without witnesses and with whom I'd forgotten my loneliness – I cannot part from her in a theatrical scene.

I'll tell her on my own. Or I'll write her a letter.

And why should I believe that you'll do that?

I shrug.

Night. My wife is sobbing in the next room. She's waiting for me to come to her. I'll tell her I'm sorry for everything that's happened, that I've realised that I can only be happy with her. And I'll tell the other woman to her face so that she too will hear it, so that everyone who knows about us should know that we love one another.

But I can't do anything of the kind, I can't even say any more than I've said already. I can see myself, I see myself from a great height. Not yet stooping but greying at the temples, I'm standing at the corner, in the familiar spot with a single tree against which I can lean. The clock at the corner has stopped. I wait and wait, no one comes, I wait for her, at least, to show up, but she is not coming.

I kneel down on the ground and press my forehead against the tree-trunk. I can't manage to cry. I embrace the trunk, I hold it frantically as though someone might wish to tear me away from it. I'd whisper her name, but I can't. I notice that the clock has moved, but I know that this is the only movement – no one will ever come again.

So what are you waiting for? What do you want? What do you feel? What are you longing for?

The following day I wrote her a letter. I won't return to a life of lies. I won't leave my wife, and I can't live by her side and torment her by informing her that I also love another woman, even if she herself were able to live like that. I also wrote that what we had together will be with me all my life. I would have liked to add something tender, such as that there might be a time when I would come to her at some difficult moment, though differently from the way she'd imagined, also that what we had together couldn't have been devoid of some meaning, that some part of it might cast a light into our future lives, that I would never hide that light in myself – but I felt that all words were pointless and in vain, that I was perhaps improperly comforting myself and her.

After two days I posted the letter. As the flap of the postbox dropped back I was conscious of the familiar old vertigo getting hold of me.

I knew that I'd never see her or hear her voice again. But from time to time, in the middle of the night I would start up from my sleep and with my fingertips touch her high forehead, and feel a strange distant pain enter into me, and then a soft snapping sound. My net was tearing, I had no idea how many threads were still left, but there couldn't be many.

I should have liked to know if the man in the window experienced anything similar, whether he felt a sudden sense of relief from this unexpected meeting. I thought that he might step out of his frame, open the window and perhaps ask us in, or at least wave to us with his flower, but this would probably have disturbed something delicate and mysterious that was extending between us, between me and him, he would have crossed that invisible, barely perceptible boundary that divides art from mere tomfoolery, so that I was actually glad to see him remain motionless.

'They don't know what to think of next,' was Mr Rada's judgement on what he'd just seen.

His remark seemed unfair to me. Before beginning to judge and condemn one another, people should do more to understand one another.

We got back to the office. I thought that perhaps that little idiot Franta might already be inside, but it was the same woman as always. She accepted my vest from me, returned my ID card, and handed out my final pay to me.

'You're right,' Mr Rada said to me in parting, 'we're not here to judge others.' But I was sure he was thinking of his brother rather than of the strange artist.

I followed him with my eyes. He stopped at the bus stop. He was a tall, well-built man, with just a slight stoop, as if he were carrying a load on his back. Even if he took on his burden for others he possibly took it on needlessly. Who can see into the soul of another person, even the one closest to him, even his own son or his brother who was like a son?

I might still have caught up with him, but just then the bus came along and he got on. I probably wouldn't see him again, nor would I meet his brother, unless I found myself in his care.

It occurred to me that I might spend the banknote I'd just earned, my last swept-up fifty crowns, in some festive way, and so I walked down into Nusle, where there are lots of shops.

In a little market they were selling flowers. My daily wage was just sufficient for five chrysanthemums. I chose three butter-yellow ones and two amber ones, colours my wife was fond of. At home I put the bunch in a vase and placed it on her table. I picked up the shopping bag with my lunch, which she had prepared for me in the morning, and set out to visit Dad at the hospital.

He opened his eyes, saw me, slightly moved his lips in an attempted smile, and closed his eyes again. He'd hardly spoken these past few days, either it tired him out too much or else he didn't think anything was sufficiently important for him to utter aloud. The last time he spoke to me he recalled that my mother used to reproach him for devoting too little attention to me, for not looking after my upbringing enough. But surely you didn't expect any sermons? he asked. And I said hurriedly that he'd always been a model to me, the way he lived and, above all, the way he worked. After all, I stayed with you lot, Dad said. His eyes misted up with tears. I understood that hidden behind these few words was some long-past difficult decision, perhaps even a sacrifice.

I unscrewed the stopper of the thermos flask and put a little custard on a spoon. Without opening his eyes Dad swallowed a few mouthfuls. Then he said: I had a fall today and couldn't get up. And the sister, the pretty one, shouted at me to get up at once, she wasn't going to lift me up. Tell me, how can a woman be so wicked? Dad fell silent for a long time. Suddenly he opened his eyes: D'you remember that hat of mine flying off on that bridge? What a laugh that was! He again closed his eyes. I said I remembered, but he no longer heard me.

As I tidied his things in his bedside table I noticed his little notebook. Day after day he'd entered in it, in an increasingly shaky hand, his temperature and the medication he took. The last entry was three days old and I couldn't make out the numbers. My throat was constricted by pity. I stroked Dad's forehead and left the ward. Outside I didn't make for the main gate but walked down a narrow path to the back entrance. The path wound between overgrown lawns, past the morgue. Immediately behind the morgue was a huge heap of broken bricks, rusty cans and shattered infusion bottles, also a rusting old electric motor, maybe one of those for which Dad had calculated the design. He'd spent whole days and evenings calculating motors. When I visited him

I'd be afraid to disturb him in his work. And so we hurriedly covered what news there was in the world, and in our lives, but about the most important thing, about our sojourn here, we talked very little.

Round the bend in the path appeared an orderly, pushing the metal cart into which the dead were placed. I used to push that cart too. I gave him a wide berth, but I couldn't get rid of the thought that he was making for that refuse heap in order to tip out his load there.

I returned to the wooden footbridge.

The train roared past beneath us, the hat flew off and jerkily sailed down in clouds of smoke.

Dad laughed and I felt happy. It was a moment of total proximity, a touch of something linking our lives, and nothing has effaced it or soiled it over all these years.

Dad was bending down low and fished out his hat, all black with soot and grime. He was not afraid to put it on his head, he gave me one more wave of his hand and walked away still laughing.

V

◆

The alarm went off at six o'clock, my wife and my son had to get up to go to work. I ought to get up too. Dad died two days ago and I should go and see his pupils at the Academy and get one of those he was fond of to speak at his funeral. And yesterday afternoon I received a package with the drug I'd written off for some time ago for that youngster Štycha, I ought to give it to him as soon as possible. I hadn't written off for any drug for Dad, there was probably no such thing.

By now it was too late to catch my mates in the changing room anyway. If I had any time left, I'd find them at the tavern during their mid-morning break.

On the final day of Dad's life Peter and I left for the hospital first thing in the morning. It was a Sunday and there were only two nurses on duty in the department. One of them told me that 'it could happen' at any moment.

Dad was lying in his bed, his lips slightly open, breathing heavily. The pauses between breaths seemed to me incredibly long. His eyes were firmly shut. He hadn't eaten or drunk anything for two days, his veins were so torn with punctures that they couldn't feed him artificially any more. I tried to give him a spoonful of sweetened tea but at first he was unable to swallow it. When he finally managed it I could see that it had taken all his strength, and that another drop might make him choke. The last drop of hope had dried up, vanished in the dust. All I could do was to mop Dad's lips and tongue with a piece of moistened cotton-wool.

Then I sat down by his bed and took his hand, as he used to take mine when I was a little boy and he was taking me for a walk to the airfield. My grown-up son was standing in the door, crying.

Then suddenly Dad breathed out, but he didn't breathe in again. I could see the terrible effort of his lungs, as they strained to catch another breath, his faced closed up in a grimace of such pain that it went right through me. What kind of son was I if I couldn't even give him a tiny puff of breath?

I got up and in my mind begged: Lord, receive his soul, you know how good it was! Then I walked out in the corridor, deserted on a Sunday, and all around there were walls, and one more wall, quite thin, transparent but nonetheless impermeable, was slipping between that moment and everything that preceded it.

In the room next door my son was listening to the news. In Colombia, on the very day my father died, a volcano erupted. The red-hot lava melted the snow and ice in the neighbourhood of the crater. The water together with the ash produced a flow of mud which rushed downhill into the valley, where it engulfed human habitations. It was estimated that twenty thousand people remained buried under the mudslide.

My wife bent over me and kissed me goodbye. She whispered that I should sleep on, she'd get home early.

I couldn't fall asleep again. When I closed my eyes Dad's face returned to me in its final pain-distorted shape, and his chopped breath came to me from all corners.

A bell rang again, this time the front door.

Early morning visits fill me with foreboding. But standing at the door was only the fair-haired young man from Svatá Hora, and in his features there was even more painful anxiety than usual. It was obvious that something serious had happened, or else he wouldn't have called at this hour.

He asked me to come with him, he wanted to talk to me outside. In the street he informed me that he and his friends had been pulled in for questioning. In his case the interrogation had gone on for half a day and had touched on my reading two years before, my stories, my opinions, as well as the opinions of other authors who'd refused to write in jerkish language in the society that was accomplishing 'the greatest freedom of man and the human race'. They also asked him why and how often he visited me, and several times in this context they mentioned the destroyed monument.

Life – and hence also death – went on.

I tried to calm him. Surely they wouldn't accuse either him or me of blowing up a monument. They merely liked bracketing these two offences – the reading of short stories written in a language comprehensible only to humans, and the destruction of a statue of an officially-proclaimed giant. Even they must realise that the latter was more criminal than the former.

But the young man was in the depths of despair. This was the first time he'd been interrogated and had experienced the stubbornly uncompromising and suspicious jerkish spirit. I've been aware of it for years, recording how under its influence living voices were falling silent and language was being lost. It pervades everything, it gets into the water and into the air, it mingles with our blood. Mothers give birth to shrunken cripples and the landscape to dead trees, birds drop in mid-flight and children's bodies are afflicted by malignant tumours.

He was walking beside me, afraid. He'd already handed in his notice at work, he'd found a job as projectionist in a cinema, and he was hoping to be accepted as a correspondence student of jerkish literature. True, he'd learn there that Charlie Chaplin left the United States, that bastion of unfreedom, but he'd have a little time left over to read books and reflect. But suppose they didn't accept him now. He wanted to know where he'd find a safety net for himself when the one they'd assigned to him as well as the one offered to him at the department store were so large-meshed that a person fell through at once. Of course, everybody should weave his own net, he knew that. But if they burst in, if they stole into his home and tore it up for him? Fight them or begin to weave a finer mesh from scratch? How often could a person start from scratch?

Only nine o'clock. If I hurried I might be able to catch the youngster in the Božena tavern, hand over the drug, and then go and find a funeral speaker.

The tavern was still half-empty at this early hour, and I didn't have to search through a crowd: my former companions, apart from the youngster and the captain, were sitting at the table next to the bar. Enthroned at the head of the table, to my surprise, was our foreman, moreover in new overalls.

I entered unobserved and managed to overhear the foreman earnestly recounting how someone was a real show-off, always nose-dived right to the ground and pulled out only when all those who were merely standing and staring had plastered their trousers.

'And what are you doing here?' Mrs Venus had spotted me. 'Come to help us?'

The foreman turned his head irritably, he didn't like anyone spoiling his heroic episodes. I produced the medicine from my pocket and asked about the youngster; did anyone know where I might find him.

'This is no kindergarten,' the foreman informed me. 'If he comes, he's here, if he don't, he ain't. We haven't seen him' – he turned to Mrs Venus as his witness – 'for at least a week.'

'This isn't the weather for him, you remember that sick turn he had. Maybe they'll give you his address at the office,' Mrs Venus said. 'Bound to have it there. Why don't you sit down?'

I ordered tea with rum.

'Maybe you don't know yet,' Mrs Venus continued, 'that they've locked our Mr Pinz up in the loony bin?'

Obviously I hadn't heard about what had happened to the captain.

'Wanted to set fire to the place he was living in. Scraped off the heads of matches, tried to make a bomb from them. Had it all ready, God knows what he'd intended it for. But then that Mary of his turned up, just looked in after all those years, and when he asked her if she'd stay with him she told him he was a nut and she'd sooner string herself up. So he decided to set that bomb off outside his own door.'

'The stupidity of it,' the foreman said in disgust, 'scraping off two hundred thousand match-heads, stuffing them into a metal soda siphon, and then using it on a building like that! But if I was you I wouldn't put my nose in that office, there's another idiot sitting there!' And he returned to his airfield, where his friend didn't manage to pull out of a spin that time and rammed himself with his MIG so deep into the ground that when they'd put out the fire and cut the wreckage up with a blow-torch they were left with a hole big enough for twenty blokes to hide in.

When the rescue teams arrived in the area of the volcanic disaster they found, in addition to the thousands of dead, a few who'd survived on the roofs of houses or in tree-tops, and also some who were stuck in the mud and couldn't get out by themselves. Of one little girl only the head was showing. Below the surface her legs were firmly clutched by her drowned aunt. The rescuers spent many hours trying to free the girl, and themselves got stuck in the mud in the attempt. All that time a reporter with a television camera was filming them, so he could bring the fate of the little girl closer to those who were contentedly or perhaps sympathetically bored in their own nets and wanted to be witnesses. After sixty hours the little girl's sufferings were over and the tired reporter was able to return to his television net. By the time they'd cut the clip they needed from the recorded shots, the little girl's soul had already risen and was lamenting above the dark waters and the mud, above the red-hot crater of the volcano, and also above a million TV screens which were flickering all over the world in order to show the vain struggle of the rescuers and the touching death of the little girl, who'd never rise from the ashes but who became famous for those few exciting seconds. And who heard the calling of her soul, who was shaken by her sobs? Who at least pictured her features at the moment when her lungs were vainly trying to catch that last breath of air?

'In case you don't get his address there' – Mrs Venus returned to the youngster – 'you could try that Dana of his. He might be there.' And she described for me the house where the woman Dana lived. I've no idea how she knew. The house was in the Little Quarter.

The tea with rum had warmed me through nicely and I was now able to set out for the office. My way led me through the familiar little street of family homes, and when I got to the artist's window I gazed in amazement on a vest which, suspended from a cord, shone brilliantly with its orange colour. Set out behind it into the depths of the room were the stems and stalks of exotic plants. They had been arranged by the artist's hand to suggest human figures. As I stared into the window I could make out individual likenesses, familiar facial features. A woman with a jockey cap on her head undoubtedly represented Mrs Venus, still without her Red-Indian wrinkles, but already with a sorrowful expression around her mouth. At the same time, however, there was something joyous in her attitude, in the gestures of her hands. Perhaps the artist had caught her just at the moment when she was about to mount the filly she'd nursed back to health. A moment later I identified a sculptural likeness of the foreman, carrying a wounded airman out of an imaginary aircraft and, in doing so, very nearly soaring up himself on the wings of his bravery. I also recognised the captain, his stocky, as yet unbowed figure looked good in a naval uniform. Perhaps, after all, there was in him both the eccentric inventor and a great prankster. But at the beginning of his actions probably stood a childlike dream, a mirage of distant voyages. Mr Rada, on the other hand, stood there in ugly brown convict's garb and was pouring water from a billy-can onto the head of another convict. His face was frozen at the instant of sudden inner illumination, at the touch of bliss. At that moment I heard the notes of Gershwin's rhapsody. In the youngster's expression there was so much concentration on his own playing and so much happiness that he seemed transformed. His clarinet was intended to suggest not so much a musical instrument as a conjurer's wand which caused rocks to part and transported humans into the realm of their own dreams.

I realised then that all these faces were, in their likeness, both real and unreal. They seemed younger and more attractive, as though nothing of the working of time or life had marked them. At the same time I understood that this exhibition had been prepared by a different artist, by a woman artist. The sculptor here had only let her use his exhibition window and she, surmising the direction of my walking, had set out for me her park, a garden where a person might see his own likeness as he himself wished it to appear at moments of grace. Maybe she had done this to remind me of her, or to demonstrate to me her loving and generous vision of what art should represent of life.

I was still looking for myself among the sculptures, but I didn't see my own face: there was only a tall pillar, as if hewn from stone, but I couldn't see its top through the window. I remembered, and I wondered if it might have a smile at the top. But I knew that I wouldn't find a smile – I'd have to be at peace with myself first.

The figures were now slowly beginning to dissolve before my eyes, and I was surprised to find myself in the grip of nostalgia. A person may think that the fate of people who are sufficiently remote does not touch him. Yet all of a sudden he will catch sight of them in an unexpected situation, will recognise their unsuspected likeness to him, whether it be beautiful or terrible, and he realises that not only have they touched him, but they have actually entered into him. This is what happens so long as life isn't totally extinct in a person. My father, in a dying flash of consciousness, suffered from the thought that a strange woman could be more wicked than he'd thought possible.

Long ago, in my childhood, he had convinced me that paradise was a human invention. And yet he yearned for it, he yearned for human contact and he yearned for eternity. He wanted to cut himself adrift from the earth and to rise to the sky, to get to the edge of the mystery. Did he realise what he was turning down?

Coming along the opposite pavement was the uniformed patrol. The foppish one, however, was accompanied this time by a policeman I hadn't seen before. I was prepared to pass them without acknowledging them when the fop suddenly changed direction and made straight for me.

I stiffened, as always. Why had my presence in the world

annoyed them this time?

The fop carelessly raised his hand to his cap. 'Day off today?' he asked.

'Sort of,' I answered evasively.

'What about the one in the high-water trousers then?'

I said I'd heard the captain had been taken to an asylum.

'What else could we do, we didn't really want to,' the fop explained. 'We said to him, stop this nonsense, grandad, in the middle of the night. But instead of pissing off he lit that bottle of his. Would have killed him if we hadn't nabbed him, his fuse was only one metre!' he added with professional outrage. 'Anyway, they'll let him go, everybody'll testify that he's screwy, that he walked about in those ridiculous trousers even in the snow – I ask you!' He turned to his companion, but he had walked on out of earshot. 'But d'you know that he put on long trousers that evening, real baggy ones, perfect pantaloons, and a tie as well!' The fop shrugged his shoulders in amazement and raised two fingers to his cap. 'He was touched all right,' he said, tapping his forehead, and walked away.

Sitting behind the desk at the office really was the little idiot, and he didn't know the youngster's address, or more correctly refused to know it – he might have had to get up from his chair and look up some file. A smile spread over his fleshy lips – the self-assured smile of a man who had been given power. Power over those who swept up garbage, and hence also over the garbage itself, and hence over the world of things. He explained something to me in his jerkish language but I didn't understand, we lacked an interpreter.

No matter, I thought to myself in an upsurge of spite, I'll find the youngster without him! I got on a tram which took me to the Little Quarter.

The spot which Mrs Venus had described was well known to me. It was on the other side of the place at the windows of which I used to look from the little attic I'd visited so often.

I'd frequently had to walk round the building but I'd never

taken any notice of it. The walls were thick and the staircase dark. I thought I sniffed the familiar smell of gas.

I was lucky at least that the youngster's lady friend had a split shift and was therefore at home at this hour. She asked me into the hall. I didn't know if she was on her own, all other sounds were drowned by a noisy military band, and from somewhere came the rattle of a washing machine.

'But he's not here,' she informed me when I'd explained who I was looking for. She was a bulky, powerful woman of mature years. I couldn't picture her in the youngster's embrace. 'And he won't come again,' she declared.

I said I'd got him the drug he'd been waiting for. Perhaps I could leave it with her for when he dropped in.

'But he won't be dropping in,' she said with the finality one uses in talking about the dead. 'I told him not to come again.'

I asked her where I could find him.

'I've no idea where he could be, he never said where he came from.' Suddenly she remembered: 'Didn't he play somewhere? Maybe those musicians of his could tell you.'

I thanked her. I'd got to the door when she added: 'He was such a poor little thing, if you ever met him. He'd sit down and just look. Couldn't even eat anything proper, and as for drink only juice. Once he came in from somewhere, all wet through, I made him a grog, he didn't tell me he wasn't allowed to, and he nearly died on me.'

The youngster had gone and the waters had closed over him. I didn't know what to do with his medicine. Maybe the woman who used to sit in the office might help, might at least remember the name of the street or the town he'd come from. But I was in no mood to search for her. I began to suspect that by the time I tracked down the youngster the medicine might have become superfluous.

I left the house. It was midday, the low sun lit up the side of the palace, on the window ledge the pigeons were warming themselves as in the past. They were probably different pigeons, but who can tell them apart?

It suddenly occurred to me that I had nowhere to go, no one to see. Except that I had to arrange for a funeral oration. They'd be having their midday break at the Academy, and what then, what afterwards? Here I was with a medicine I had no use for, all round me people were hurrying whom I had no use for either. My net was suddenly swinging, a few threads snapped, and below me I saw darkness.

My daughter told me about her dream of the end of the world. She was walking through a landscape with her husband, it seemed a vast expanse, bordered only by the horizon. It was a clear day. Suddenly the light began to turn yellow, until it was sulphurous, and at that moment the left part of the horizon began to move towards the right part, and as the two parts approached one another the light faded, it was getting dark, and the earth started trembling. The two of them lay down side by side, closed their eyes and began to pray: Shema Yisrael Adonai elohenu Adonai ekhad. When they opened their eyes again she saw above her the entire universe and in it our sun with its planets, including our earth and the moon. Whoever had seen this, she realised, could no longer be alive. She also realised that no life was left on earth. The horizons collided, the land masses burst and the waters flooded everything. Just then she noticed that among the planets a large fiery-red sharp-edged gambler's die was orbiting, and also revolving, so she could watch the white dots on its sides, and she wondered who had cast the die, whether it had been the humans themselves or the Eternal Holy One, blessed be his name!

I walked round the palace and entered the little square. I walked over the familiar uneven pavement and pushed the heavy door open. In the hallway I was surrounded by a familiar smell. I climbed the wooden stairs. Waving on a line were nappies, the nappies of some new child. Anyway, I never even saw the child, I had no eyes for her. But the roof of the monastery rose up as before, insofar as it is possible to say that anything can be the same at two different moments in time, and I climbed on towards the attic. The door was adorned on the outside by a poster which used to be there, but the smell of oil and gas still came through all the cracks. The name by the bell-push meant nothing to me.

I didn't ring. There was no point in it. Even if I'd been able to ring a bell into the past, and she really appeared at the door, what would I say to her? I didn't have a single sentence prepared, not a single new sentence.

In front of the building stood a small group of tourists, gazing with appropriate interest at the wall of the palace. What can they see there, what can they feel? These walls do not speak to them, they don't remind them of a single breath, of a single cry or a shed tear. After all, I had something that they didn't.

Slowly I drifted along the little streets, roughly by the same route that the author I am writing about at the moment would take to the Castle.

What used to fascinate me most about literature at one time was that fantasy knows no frontiers, that it is as infinite as the universe into which we may fall. I used to think that this was what fascinated and attracted me in Kafka. For him a human would be transformed into an animal and an animal into a human, dream seemed to be reality for him and, simultaneously, reality was a dream. From his books there spoke a mystery which excited me.

Later I was to understand that there is nothing more mysterious, nothing more fantastic, than life itself. Whoever exalts himself above it, whoever isn't content with horrors already reached and passions already experienced, must sooner or later reveal himself as a false diver who, out of fear of what he might discover in the depths, descends no further than into a solidly built basement.

Kafka, too, did not portray anything but the reality of his own life. He presented himself as an animal, or he lay down on his bed in his cleverly constructed murdering machine to punish himself for his guilt. He felt guilty about his inability to love, or at least to love the way he wanted to. He was unable to get close to his father or to come together with a woman. He knew that in his longing for honesty he resembled a flier and his life a flight under an infinite sky, where a flier is always lonely and longs in vain for human contact. The longer he flies the more his soul is weighed down by guilt and forced down towards the ground. The flier can jettison his soul and continue his flight without it – or crash. He crashed, but for a moment at least he managed to rise from the ashes in order, second by second, movement by movement, to describe his fall.

Like everyone who hangs on for a moment above the abyss, or who has risen from the ashes and realises how tenuous his net is, Kafka was purged of anger and hate just as his language was of superfluous words. The author is already standing on the edge of the black hole, yet he still longs to look into another's eyes in truth and in love, to speak to him in a language which his fall has cleansed of all hatreds and of all vanity.

Anyone longing to become a writer, for even a few moments of his life, will vainly weave fantastic events unless he has experienced that fall during which he doesn't know where or whether it will come to an end, and unless his longing for human contact awakens in him the strength to rise, purged, from the ashes.

A tension was growing in me, tearing up my thoughts. I needed to do something – to talk, to shout, to cry, to write something, at least to chalk up on the wall the names of those I shall never see again.

I was passing a baker's shop from which the smell of sweet rolls wafted out. These rolls were baked only at this bakery, a little way from the stone bridge, a little way from our palace. The last time I was in there to buy some was the day before I started street-sweeping. Then, as I entered the bakery, I was racked by longing, I was afraid that the time when I was granted the grace of human contact was coming to an end, and I saw only the edge of the precipice before me. My greatest fear was that I had dragged her to that abyss with me.

At the news stand I bought a jerkish evening paper to see if they'd noticed Dad's death. I pushed the paper into my pocket and leaned against the stone parapet. Below me, above a little ornamental balcony, was the picture of the Virgin Mary which was said to have been carried here on the waves of a great flood. By my side stood Brokoff's Turk, with his many-buttoned doublet and with a dog guarding his Christian prisoners, above him the three founders of the Order of the Holy Trinity. Observe, darling, how most of the life is in the dog and in the Turk; animals and heathens have no prescribed gestures, they're alive, they aren't saints. Saintliness doesn't belong to life, it was invented by various cripples who were unable, or afraid, to live and therefore wanted to torture those who knew how to live.

The sun was bright on the roofs of the houses and the almost bare branches of the horse-chestnuts cast a filigree of shadows on the ground. From the bridge came the discontinuous click of footfalls. I thought I could even hear the hum of the weir.

I tore myself away from the parapet. Time was moving on and I had to find a funeral speaker. I cast one last glance down into the neighbourhood where we had sometimes walked together to the nearby park, and just then I saw her. I couldn't, from my height, make out her face clearly, but I recognised her hurried, life-hungry way of walking. I looked after her, I followed her with my eyes as she passed under the arch of the bridge. I could have let her lose herself again in the distance from which she'd appeared, but I ran down the stairs, caught up with her and uttered her name.

She stopped. For a while she stared at me as if I were an apparition. 'Where have you sprung from?' she asked, the blood rushing into her face.

I tried to explain that I'd got a drug for someone but that that person had vanished from the surface of the earth, in fact not even his former woman friend knew where I might find him.

'Yes,' she agreed, 'one instant a person's here, and the next instant it's as if he'd never existed!' She looked at me. How many reproaches did she have prepared for this moment? Or was she, on the contrary, about to persuade me that I'd made a mistake, that I'd betrayed myself?

'What about your Dad?' she asked instead. 'I prayed for him,' she said when I told her, and simultaneously her eyes embraced and gently kissed me.

Suddenly I felt the touch of time, the time on the far side of the thin wall. She was sitting with me in the hospital waiting room, then we walked out, snow was falling.

I quickly asked about her daughter and about her work.

Just like me, she said, I was more interested in her work than in her. But she wasn't doing anything at the moment. She'd discovered the joys of laziness. Sometimes she'd read the cards for friends or she'd botch up some figure from her dreams. Some of them still bore my likeness.

We walked along the little streets where we used to walk so often, and as always she talked to me as we walked. In the summer she'd made the acquaintance of an old woman herbalist and had got a lot of recipes from her. For days on end she'd collected and dried herbs – besides, what was she to do with her time when I hadn't been in touch even once? If I was ever in pain or if my soul felt heavy I might phone her: she could mix me a tisane – I obviously wasn't interested in anything else.

We stopped at the edge of the park. I still had to find a funeral speaker. 'You've never ceased to exist for me!'

She could have asked, as she'd done before, what good that was to her, or what use, or she could have complained about the sorrow I'd caused her, about how I'd hurt her. But she didn't wish to torment me at that moment. She only said: 'That's good!' And she added: 'Maybe our souls will meet somewhere. We'll meet in some future life. Provided you don't find an excuse at the last moment.' We briefly embraced and kissed goodbye, and she walked away at her hurried pace.

I couldn't move. I didn't even tell her that I'd never intended to hurt her, nor did I ask her if she understood that I hadn't done anything against her, that it was just that I was unable to return to her in this halfway manner, to be a little and to not be a little, I can only honestly be or honestly not be – like herself.

She stopped at the corner. She looked back, and when she saw me at the spot where she'd left me her hand rose up like the wing of a featherless little bird and from the distance touched my forehead.

At last I moved.

On the path that went to the bank of the Čertovka stream a few figures were busying themselves in their familiar orange vests. With slow, seemingly weary movements, the movements I knew so well, they were sweeping the withered leaves into small heaps.

Down there we stood and kissed in a long embrace.

A fine thing! A fine thing!

It occurred to me that I put on that orange vest for a time because I was longing for a cleansing. Man longs for a cleansing but instead he starts cleaning up his surroundings. But until man cleanses himself he's wasting his time cleaning up the world around him.

In the middle of the swept path lay the brownish lobed leaf of a horse-chestnut. Perhaps they'd overlooked it or perhaps it had just sailed down from above. I picked it up and for a while studied its wrinkled veins. The leaf trembled in my fingers as if it were alive.

I was still full of that unexpected meeting.

People search for images of paradise and cannot find anything other than objects from this world.

But paradise cannot be fixed in an image, for paradise is the state of meeting. With God, and also with humans. What matters, of course, is that the meeting should take place in cleanliness.

Paradise is, above all else, the state in which the soul feels clean.

I sat down on a bench and took the evening paper from my pocket. I scanned the big headlines, which repeated hundred-year-old untruths, and the lesser headlines, which dealt with yesterday. Needless to say, there was no mention of Dad.

Gently I took the pages apart, and with precise movements, which seemed to come to me automatically, I pleated them into an elaborate aeroplane.

I walked to the river, spread my legs, and aimed the nose of my paper flying machine obliquely at the sky. It rose up, perhaps assisted by the updraught from the water or perhaps just because, thanks to Dad's instruction, I had made it particularly well, but it was quite a while before it abandoned its upward course, and I, following it with my eyes, saw the blue of the sky and a few seagulls and above them a white cloud gilded by the sun. Then my glider began to lose height and circling down it settled on the water. I watched it slowly and irretrievably floating away into the distance.

Remember that a man never cries, unexpectedly came my father's voice in the silence around me.

I'm not crying, I said, and from somewhere deep down within me came a sound of laughter like that which, in my childhood, used to make me happy.

1983–1986

A NOTE ON THE TYPE

The text of this book was set in Sabon, a typeface designed by
Jan Tschichold (1902–1974), the well-known German typographer.
Because it was designed in Frankfurt, Sabon was named for the famous
Frankfurt type founder Jacques Sabon, who died in 1580 while manager
of the Egenolff foundry.
Based loosely on the original designs of Claude Garamond (c. 1480–
1561), Sabon is unique in that it was explicitly designed for
hot-metal composition on both the Monotype and Linotype
machines as well as for film composition.

Printed and bound by
Fairfield Graphics, Fairfield, Pennsylvania

Title page and binding design by
George J. McKeon

language + abuse of cosmic depth - 87